Viking Shadow

Viking Shadow

Book 20 in the Dragon Heart Series

By

Griff Hosker

Viking Shadow

Published by Sword Books Ltd 2018
Copyright © Griff Hosker First Edition

The author has asserted their moral right under the Copyright, Designs and Patents Act, 1988, to be identified as the author of this work.

All Rights reserved. No part of this publication may be reproduced, copied, stored in a retrieval system, or transmitted, in any form or by any means, without the prior written consent of the copyright holder, nor be otherwise circulated in any form of binding or cover other than that in which it is published and without a similar condition being imposed on the subsequent purchaser.

Cover by Design for Writers

Dedication:
For Matthew you have followed Dragonheart through your teenage years, long may the journey continue

Table of Contents

Viking Shadow i
Table of Contents iii
Prologue 1
Chapter 1 8
Chapter 2 21
Chapter 3 33
Chapter 4 44
Chapter 5 57
Chapter 6 68
Chapter 7 81
Chapter 8 90
Chapter 9 99
Chapter 10 110
Chapter 11 120
Chapter 12 130
Chapter 13 143
Chapter 14 161
Chapter 15 171
Chapter 16 185
Chapter 17 200
Chapter 18 215
Epilogue 233
Glossary 237
Maps and drawings 244
Historical note 246
Other books by Griff Hosker 249

Part One

Dragonheart and the Shadow of Death

Prologue

I dreamed. That was not unusual. I often dreamed and those dreams meant something was going to happen. They were a way to see into the future. There were many times when I understood the dreams but there were other dreams whose meanings were hidden from me. Then I would seek an interpretation from Kara, my daughter, or Aiden, her husband. She was a witch and he a galdramenn. This dream was different from any I had before.

I was standing in the river. I was fishing and I was young. I was with the other boys by the bank of the Dunum, hauling in the nets filled with the salmon caught overnight. It was hard to see anything with the low mist which we called a sea fret hanging over the river. The cold chilled you to your very bones. I had taken off my rabbit fur boots before I entered the water as I did not want them to be wet and soggy all day. It was better to have cold feet for a short time. I waded to the furthest point from the shore. Suddenly a dragon ship loomed up out of the early morning mist. I could not move. It was as though I was stuck to the river bed. A one-eyed warrior reached down and plucked me from the water.

The warrior changed to Haaken One Eye and Aiden was fitting a metal plate into his skull. I saw Prince Butar being slain but it was on the island of Mann for my son Arturus was also slain. I tried to run away from the death and pain but I found myself sinking into the river bed. It was the sucking me down. A witch appeared above me and she began to push me down into the cloying life devouring mud. I could not get out. I was choking. I was dying and then all went black. I reached up and found fur. Úlfarr the wolf who had saved my grandson pulled me

from the darkness and the ooze. The wolf lifted me up and I stood on the top of Úlfarrberg and I sat with the wolf. Even as I looked into his eyes he began to disappear.
It was then I noticed that I was bleeding. The blood came from my stomach. I lifted my kyrtle and it would not stop. Erika, my dead wife, flew down from above and tried to staunch it but she could not. Brigid, my recently deceased wife came and laid her cross on the wound but it did nothing. I was dying and faces flashed before me. They were all the warriors who had died and gone to Valhalla. Cnut, Snorri, Olaf the Toothless and then old Ragnar. All flashed before my eyes and then I saw Josephus. The Greek slave beckoned me towards him. I had not thought of him these many years. Then I saw a horseman. I looked closely. It was a boy. He was smaller than Ulla War Cry and he galloped towards me. Was it Hrolf? Had the slave I rescued come back for me? As I reached out for his hand he was swept away and I was alone once more. I was alone in a dark place with no light. I heard nothing. I felt nothing. Was I dead?

Then I woke and found that I was damp and I was wet. I wondered if I had succumbed to the old man's illness and could no longer control my bladder. I put my hand to the damp and it came away bloody. The blood in my dream was not a dream. It was a reality. The bleeding had begun some while ago. It had become worse over the past moon.

When we had returned from the catastrophic Danish raid on Lundenwic we knew that we had been lucky to escape with our lives. A handful of us only had returned. I had only taken the threttanessa, **'Red Snake'** but she had been fully crewed and now half of the crew were in Valhalla. She was in the graveyard of all drekar at the bottom of the ocean. The riches we had gained in no way compensated for the men who had died. They never did. I had returned to my home in Cyninges-tūn. It was an empty home now. Old Uhtric, my servant and former slave was the only one who lived there now. Yet I was comfortable within my walls. I walked the Water and visited the graves of my two wives. I stared at old Olaf and, now, after my dream, I waited for death. None had lived as long as I. I had seen well over sixty summers. Old Ragnar had been the oldest Viking I had known and I had outlived him. I believed that the sword which was touched by the gods had kept me alive but I could not see a purpose in that life now. Ragnar, my grandson, led the clan. He would do a better job than I for he was not burdened by the pressure of legend. My son, Gruffyd also prospered. The two of them were more than capable of seeing that the clan lived on. They raided and they traded. They had children and the clan was happy. They were my legacy for the future. Yet I was still alive and I could see no purpose in my life. Why was the Allfather keeping me alive?

After the dream and a walk around the Water, I went into the steam hut. I had asked Uhtric to light it early. It was hot and it cleansed me. I had just emerged from the steam hut when I spied Aiden, Kara and Ylva walking towards me. The steam hut helped my aching bones and joints. I used it most days now. As I headed towards my hall they waited for me. Even though we lived in the same Stad I had not seen them since I had returned from the raid more than a month since. I had, I think, been avoiding them and I knew not why. One reason may have been the disconcerting trick they had of reading my mind. I wished my dark and melancholy thoughts to remain with me. They were not fit for others. I slowed for they rarely came together. One might visit me or perhaps two but three of them did not bode well. Had they dreamed?

They smiled as I approached. My granddaughter, Ylva, came and took one arm while Kara, my daughter took the other. "You look well, Dragonheart. Did you enjoy the steam hut?"

I could play this game of questions and answers which meant nothing. "I always enjoy the steam hut."

"We have not seen you since your return from the raid, father. You keep to yourself." My daughter was now the image of her mother, Erika.

"You do not want an old man hanging around. I am a relic from the past. I am almost the last of the Ulfheonar."

"Father, you have left behind the days of being a warrior. You are the stuff of legend. Why are you not at Whale Island? There you have a crew of grandchildren. You should be there with them."

"My action almost resulted in my grandson, Sámr, being killed. Astrid is a kind woman but her eyes showed fear that I might have lost him. I think it is safer for everyone if I stay away from my family. I bring only death to those around me."

We had reached my hall. I wondered if they would enter. Aiden did not wait for an invite. He pushed open the door and shouted, "Uhtric, fetch that cheese we brought and the ale. Put a log on the fire. This hall is as gloomy as Dragonheart's face."

Uhtric shuffled out. He was beaming, "Aye galdramenn. It is good to hear cheerful voices here once more."

I flashed him a look which, in the past, would have withered him. Now he just smiled. I had truly lost all the power and influence I once had. Ylva moved my favourite chair closer to the fire and Kara laid my wolf skin upon it. I sat. I just wanted to be left alone. I still had the pain in my gut. The steam hut had made my muscles and joints easier but it did nothing for the pain which ached inside me. I just hoped that I would not bleed while they were there for Kara would notice. They fussed around and cut me a hunk of bread and some fresh cheese. Deidra and Macha made good cheese and they brewed fine beer. The bread was smothered in butter and, I confess, I felt hungry. Ylva put some wild berry pickle on the cheese. She knew I loved it. Aiden handed me the horn of ale and I swallowed some. They were patient. They waited for me to finish the bread and cheese and the beer before they spoke.

Kara's voice was quiet but I detected a little anger beneath her words. "When were you going to tell us about the bleeding?"

I flashed a look of pure hatred towards Uhtric. Only he could have known. He washed my clothes. I should have made him swear an oath.

"Grandfather, how long has this been going on?"

"I am old. Old men are afflicted by such things."

Aiden asked, "You have pain?" He came over to me and touched my side, "Here?"

I nodded, "Sometimes."

"And the bleeding which was infrequent but is now more regular?"

"Perhaps."

Ylva and Kara exchanged a look I had never seen before. They were frightened. Aiden knelt next to me, "Old friend, Dragonheart, you need our help. You are ill." He looked at his wife and then back at me. "You may even be dying. Let us help you."

I smiled at Aiden. He too had been a slave. We had much in common. "All men die!"

"But not yet!" Kara's voice was normally calm. "Your time is not come. We have not dreamed it and this would be the wrong way for the Dragonheart to die!" Now she sounded like Brigid, my late wife.

Aiden's voice was calm and reassuring but his eyes told me that he worried that he could do nothing for me. "There are potions we can give you. They will ease the pain and they will slow the bleeding. There are foods you can eat which will ease your discomfort."

"But I will still die." They said nothing. "Perhaps if I throw the sword that was touched by the gods into the Water of Cyninges-tūn then I can use another sword, go into battle and enjoy a warrior's death. I am ready!"

For the first time in a long time, Kara began to weep. "But we are not." Ylva suddenly ran from the room. That was unlike her.

Aiden said, gently, "Let us give you the potions to ease the pain and to lessen the bleeding."

I was suspicious. "They will not make me reliant upon others? I will not be an invalid and lie in bed waiting for death. I will face death as I have faced all my enemies with a sword in hand and defiance in my heart!"

Aiden said, "No, they will not and do not speak of death. We said you may be dying. There might be ways to heal you."

Ylva had returned with a fresh horn of ale. "Grandfather, I have put the potion in this ale. I beg you to drink it and then my mother can examine you. She can determine what causes the pain and the bleeding."

I saw the concern on their faces and I did wish the pain to diminish. Most of all I wanted the bleeding to stop. I did not like waking up in the morning in a bed which was damp and sticky. I nodded. They led me to my bed. Uhtric had put fresh bedding there. He stood nearby in case he was needed. I drank the horn of ale and lay down. As soon as the liquid slipped down I felt warmth.

Kara said softly, "You may close your eyes if you wish. We added something to make you sleep."

I was about to tell her off when I found that I was slipping into a dark hole. I slept. It was a dreamless sleep. When I woke there was just Aiden seated by my bed. He had one of the candles we had taken from a church on a raid. He was reading by its light. I sat up. There was no blood.

Aiden laid down the parchment he was reading. He smiled. He was getting old too but he still looked like the young slave we had taken from Hibernia. He had youthful eyes and a mouth upon which a smile ever played. "You feel better?"

I nodded, "I do. Am I healed or do I take this potion every day?"

"You are not healed. The potion merely confuses the disease you have." He leaned forward, "Dragonheart, lord, we can do no more here. You will be dead within a year if we just continue with this treatment."

I now knew when my death would come. Aiden had often spoken of dreaming about my death. Now, it seemed, he could do better. He could predict it. "Thank you, it is good to know. Then I will go on the next raid with my son and I will enjoy a glorious death and join my oar brothers in Valhalla."

Aiden became animated and he took my hands in his, "No, lord, you misunderstand me!" He took the parchment he had been reading. "You took this in a raid, three years since. I read it when you took it and thought no more of it. Now I know that you were meant to bring it. This was *wyrd*. It is the Norns once more. This speaks of healers in Miklagård. They know how to cut open men and heal that which is hidden beneath their flesh."

I remembered the dream. Josephus! "As you did when you put the plate in Haaken One Eye's skull?"

"Aye but that was as nothing compared with what they can do."

"Then what are you saying?"

"That we sail to Miklagård and pay these healers to make you whole once more. The Allfather has sent you more coin than you can spend in a lifetime."

I laughed, "Especially if that lifetime is just one year."

He nodded, "Use it for this."

I thought about it. I had been to Miklagård before. The Blue Sea was a different world. It would be one last adventure. Even if they could not heal me there would be opportunities on the voyage for a glorious death. Then I realised I could not go alone. "It is a long voyage. Is it fair for me to ask others to risk their lives with me?"

It was Aiden who laughed. He laughed so loudly that Uhtric raced in. Aiden waved him away. "Dragonheart, there are many men in the clan who would follow you across the western seas to the edge of the world if you asked and they would deem it an honour to do so. The problem will be limiting those who wish to come with us."

"Us?"

"You do not think that I would miss the opportunity to return to Miklagård with you, did you? I would wish to see these healers at work myself. I will go with you!"

Chapter 1

When the four of us headed to Whale Island I asked about my illness. They had examined me and they knew what I did not. Kara said, "There is something in you which needs to be removed. I can feel it. I know not why it causes the bleeding. To be truthful, father, we were not even certain that the potion would work."

Ylva said, "We dreamed and used the steam hut. Your wife, my grandmother, came to us and told us what we needed for the potion. It was the spirits who have given you relief."

"But," added Kara, "the bleeding will return. The potion slows down the damage that is all. The gods need to give wings to your drekar and carry you to Miklagård as quickly as possible."

I smiled, "Do not forget the Norns. They will not allow me to make the voyage without a web hindering us. Since I took Ylva back from them and killed their witches then I am their enemy."

We had just entered the forest north of Úlfarrston and Ylva put her hand on mine. "I read your thoughts, grandfather. You hope that they do bar your way so that you can die with a sword in your hand!"

"And would that be so bad?"

"For us, it would. We are selfish. The gods will have you for eternity. Let us enjoy your company a while longer!"

The gloomy forest ended our conversation for a while, for it seemed to depress us all in equal measure. We were lost in our own thoughts. Ylva was correct. She knew what was in my mind. A long voyage meant I would rarely wear my mail. I was no longer young. If I fought at sea, without mail then the odds were that I would die. I would go to Valhalla. If I died on a ship, or at sea, then it would be far from the Land of the Wolf and my family, my people and my clan would be safe. That was the main reason I was leaving. Word would soon get out that the Dragonheart was dying. There were men who wished to own my sword. A dying Dragonheart was a less daunting prospect than a fit one. I needed to be away from my land. I would draw the danger to me. That posed me a problem. In a perfect world, I would travel alone but a man cannot sail a drekar by himself. The ones who came with me would be risking their lives too. It was a heavy weight to bear.

As we neared Whale Island I saw that **'Heart of the Dragon'** had her mast and yard ready with sail furled. She was at the quay and ready for the sea. I turned to Aiden. He smiled, "You did not think that while we prepared to come south that we were idle? We sent word, two days since. Your crew have chosen themselves. All is ready. We will sail on the afternoon tide for it will take two months for the voyage. Your time is now precious. We no longer count your life in years but in moons."

When we reached Ragnar's Stad I was overwhelmed by the reception. My grandson, son, their wives and all their children save Sámr were gathered. I saw the concern carved upon their faces. I smiled, "I am not dead yet. Come, smile. Ulla War Cry, why so gloomy?"

Astrid put her arms around me and hugged me, "We are sad for we do not wish you to leave the Land of the Wolf yet. You have kept yourself too long in your gloomy hall. When you return we would have you live here so that we can see you when we will. Your grandchildren and great-grandchildren need to hear the stories from your own lips!"

"You are kind. Let me get this voyage over and then we will see." I stepped back. "If I do not return then you will see me when you dream for I will be with Erika in the spirit world and I promise that I will be there to watch over you from the Otherworld."

I saw tears spring in the eyes of the women. Ragnar and Gruffyd came over. Ragnar was now as tall as me and broader. He put his arm around me. "Do not talk like that grandfather. We all wished to come but Kara chose the ones who would go with you. She is wise. Know that you could have crewed your ship many times over. The only married men who will be with you are Erik Short Toe and Haaken One Eye." Ragnar smiled. "There was no way we could dissuade Haaken from accompanying you and Erik hopes to see the grandchildren of Josephus."

I looked around, "And Sámr?"

"We knew that one of the family had to be with you and Sámr would not be dissuaded. After the last voyage to Lundenwic, we knew that it was *wyrd*. He is on the drekar with the others."

Aiden said, "We need to go or we shall miss the tide and we do not have days to waste in tears which are not needed for the Dragonheart will return!" He hurried me from the hall to the quay. I think he did this to make the parting less tearful.

The crew waited patiently. I recognised all of them. They smiled. The oars were only single-manned. I wondered at that. My chest had been brought aboard already. I climbed aboard and wrapped my wolf cloak tightly about me. Once we left the coast then the cold winds of Einmánuður would strike us. My eyes did not leave my family as we headed up the channel which would take us to the sea. The crew had to row for the first half mile until we could turn and use the sail. The steering board was turned and Erik shouted, "Oars in!" I heard them sliding through the holes and then the covers were placed over them. There was the sound of rattling as the oars were placed on the mast fish. When the last face disappeared from view I turned.

Sámr was walking down the centre board with his own wolf cloak wrapped around him and Haaken One Eye rose to greet me. "Well old friend, another adventure. You did not think to leave me behind, did you? Who else would tell the tale?"

I laughed, "And the tale, I have no doubt, will tell of the great deeds of Haaken One Eye."

"The world needs such tales."

I saw then that Olaf Leather Neck was there too. I had two of my Ulfheonar with me. That was good. I spied others who had been on the recent raid: Ráðgeir Ráðgeirson, Lars Long Nose, Siggi Eainarson, Siggi Long Face and Galmr Hrolfsson. I was touched. We had all bonded when our drekar had sunk and we had had to fight our way home. It was a good sign.

I saw them watching me. The sun was setting in the west and I said, "Friends, if this is to be the last time that I see the Land of the Wolf I would take it in alone so that I can recall the view in the Otherworld." They nodded and moved away. I stood next to Erik and looked at Old Olaf. I could still see his rocky outline to the north. I swear that I could see Úlfarrberg in the distance. I had so many memories. Would I recall them in the Otherworld?

That would be a new adventure too. The only sounds I could hear were the sea birds and the slap of canvas and rigging as my drekar slipped south. I stood there until the sky was black and I could see nothing else. When I turned I saw that Sámr, Haaken and Aiden were watching me.

Haaken said, "Now tell me, Dragonheart, that you will not be so maudlin and melancholy all the way to Miklagård and back!"

"You are convinced that we will get back?"

"I know so, for Aiden has told me and he is galdramenn, that you will be healed. As for the rest? What cannot the last of the Ulfheonar do?" He put his arm around Sámr. "And here we have the embodiment of Dragonheart and Wolf Killer! I look forward to watching this young cub make his name. Sámr is too short a name! We need something more and this voyage will bring it!"

There was something infectious about Haaken One Eye's confidence. It seemed reflected in the drekar which flew across the ocean as though she was a bird.

I sat on my chest and took the ale skin Sámr proffered. "You organized this quickly, galdramenn."

He sat on his own chest which was next to mine. The rest of the men's chests would be used as seats when they rowed. "Kara and I have been needing a ship to go to Miklagård for some time. There are ingredients we can only buy there. It is too dangerous a journey for a knarr and your drekar have been used for war and raids. We have seal skins and seal oil to trade as well as many animal skins and tanned hides. Our miners had a surplus of iron and we have that and some copper. Whatever the ingredients and your healing cost we should have enough."

"I have gold with me."

"Then that can be for emergencies. On a two-month voyage, I think there may be expenses we have not foreseen. It is a long voyage and fraught with problems we cannot see." He tapped his chest. "I am glad that I have the maps and charts old Josephus left for me and the ones which Aiden has made. They are more valuable than gold!"

Erik Short Toe said, "Aye, I can guarantee that. It is sixteen years since Raven Wing Island was lost as a safe haven for us. I am not certain where Hrolf the Horseman set up his new home. Had we known we could have used that as one overnight stop.

As it is we will have to risk bare beaches and inlets. We will need to hope we can find water nearby."

Olaf Leather Neck snorted, "Or we could be Vikings and take it from ships we find."

I smiled, "Aye we could."

Aiden rubbed his grey-flecked beard, "I think I heard that Hrolf the Horseman has a stronghold at somewhere called the Haugr. His ships traded in Dyflin."

Erik shook his head, "If we are to take the Dragonheart to Miklagård as soon as possible then we cannot afford to waste time seeking a harbour which may or may not be there."

Haaken rubbed his hand, "Excellent. Then we are alone!"

I asked, "Why are the oars only singly manned?"

Haaken nodded, "That was what I said! Ask Aiden. He is the one who gave the orders." There was a hint of resentment in Haaken One Eye's words.

"We go not to fight. We go to trade and to get you healed. With fewer men and fewer chests we will be lighter and faster." I was not convinced but I nodded. We needed unity on the voyage. "And besides Erika came to Kara in a dream and told us to single crew the oars." That satisfied me. Erika was in the spirit world and she knew what we needed.

We made good time and sailed through the Angle Sea by Ynys Môn. We sped by the island with the small monastery and the puffins. The Allfather had sent a good wind to begin our journey and we would not need to stop until Erik Short Toe tired. Even then any one of us could have steered. We took advantage of the wind.

Aiden reminded me to take my potion. For the rest, especially Sámr, this was a reminder of the real purpose of our voyage. They were trying to save the life of the Dragonheart. As I drank it there was a hushed silence. Kara had told me that they had put in a sleeping draught too. It seemed to help the potion work. I was happy to take it for it took away most of the pain. I am a warrior. I can endure the pain of battle but a nagging pain deep in my gut was something else. It was as though there was a worm inside eating me from within. Erik's ship's boys: Lars and Petr Svensson had rigged apiece of old sail at the stern. It afforded shelter from spray and from rain. I wrapped myself in my cloak and was soon asleep. The motion of the ship and the potion helped. It was a dreamless sleep and for that I was grateful. Since the strange dream, I had dreamed of the dead. Every friend and member of my family who had died seemed to visit me. They appeared as though alive and I found it disconcerting. The night without a dream was more than welcome.

When I woke it was daylight. I had been sailing long enough to know which way the wind blew. It had veered since I had slept. I rose and went to the leeward side to make water. Sometimes there was blood in my water. This time there was not and I intoned my thanks to the Allfather. I turned and saw that Olaf Leather Neck was steering. He pointed ahead, "Om Walum. Erik Short Toe has been asleep for a while. He wishes me to wake him when we near the coast called An Lysardh for then we will have to turn and the men will need to row." He nodded to the rocky coast to the east of us. "If memory serves we are almost there. That is where we fought with Egbert."

I remembered. We had won but the Danes who had been with us had not taken advantage of our success. They had pushed on towards Wessex and been destroyed by King Egbert and his army.

"The men all slept?"

"Aye jarl. They can row when we need them." He looked up at the sky. "And we still have half a day of daylight. Better that we row when we can see Syllingar and then risk Wessex!"

He was right. The witch who lived on Syllingar had almost taken Sámr and his brother. They had no love for me and I would not risk their wrath by sailing at night. I did not wake Sámr or the others. Although Sámr was not yet a warrior and therefore would not row yet there were no idle hands on this drekar. He would be serving as a ship's boy. He needed his sleep. Soon he would be racing up the rigging and either furling or unfurling the sail. I saw that Aiden was not asleep. He was mixing something in a clay pot. I took a piece of stale bread and some cheese and wandered over to him.

"What are you making?"

"Why your potion, of course. You do not think it makes itself, do you? We have to make a fresh potion every three days or it loses its efficacy." I watched him finish and carefully pour the liquid into an amphora. He placed a cork in the end. "And you, Dragonheart, does the potion help? Has there been blood?"

"A little but it is the lack of aching, nagging pain which is most beneficial."

He nodded. "Kara and I thought about giving you a diet which might help you but sailing for two months on a drekar would make that impossible. The potion will be less effective as time goes on. I just hope that we can make Miklagård before then."

Olaf said, quietly, "An Lysardh is coming up."

Erik's eyes were shut but I heard him say, "I am awake. I will rouse the crew."

He woke his ship's boys and they went around the oarsmen, gently shaking them. When they were all awake the boys, Sámr included, went to fetch the ale and the food. They would be rowing for most of the afternoon. They would eat well. They would need sustenance. When Sámr returned to us and the men were eating he asked, "Will they be rowing until dark?"

"They will but it will not be continuous. There will be rests for no man can row for that length of time. This is a skilled crew. We will not run an oar out at every bench. There will be two men at an oar. Once we are travelling at a speed that our captain likes then one man on each oar will stop rowing. They will turn and turn about. That is why they are called oar brothers. You row with a man you trust and you know." The men took their oars and went to their benches. "Olaf will start them with a chant but they will only sing that to get us up to speed."

"Who is Olaf's Oar brother?"

"Haaken One Eye. They work well together. When I rowed I was Haaken's oar brother. I miss those days."

Erik shouted, "Sámr, stop chattering and get on the forestay. We are about to raise the sail and make a turn. Now is when you earn your passage." I saw that my great-grandson was embarrassed for the rest of the crew were in position. He ran and scrambled up to the yard on which the sail hung. "Oars out. Prepare to come about!" The oars were held out, parallel with the sea. "Raise the sail!" The ship's boys hauled for all that they were worth and the sail was lowered as Erik turned us so that we were almost in the wind. He could have still used the wind but it would have taxed the boys and there was no need.

Olaf shouted, "Out oars!" The oars all slid further out and then dipped into the water.

Haaken began the chant. He had composed most of them. I knew which one it would be before he began. It was our saga.

From mountain high in the land of snow
Garth the slave began to grow
He changed with Ragnar when they lived alone
Warrior skills did Ragnar hone
The Dragonheart was born of cold
Fighting wolves, a warrior bold
The Dragonheart and Haaken Brave
A Viking warrior and a Saxon slave
When Vikings came he held the wall
He feared no foe however tall
Back to back both so brave
A Viking warrior and a Saxon slave
When the battle was done
They stood alone
With their vanquished foes
Lying at their toes
The Dragonheart and Haaken Brave
A Viking warrior and a Saxon slave
The Dragonheart and Haaken Brave
A Viking warrior and a Saxon slave

They soon had their speed up and Olaf shouted, "One man, rest!" Haaken let go of the oar. I knew that Olaf would keep rowing longer than any other. He was incredibly strong and took it as a sign of his strength that he would row longer than Haaken.

I stood with Erik watching the south. Erik was taking us as close to the coast of Om Walum as he could. We would be passing within sight of Karrek Loos yn Koos. That was preferable to risking the rocks of Syllingar and the witch who waited there. When we had passed the monastery at Karrek Loos yn Koos we knew we were safe; from the witches at least. The sun began to set and Erik shouted, "Lars, what can you see?"

"There is a bay coming up. I see no smoke."

No smoke meant that it was unoccupied. We wanted an empty and deserted beach. It had been a hard row during the afternoon. The ship's boys were also tired. I think, because I had had the most sleep, I was the one who was the least tired. Aiden had not rowed but he had watched me. Olaf had told me that. They were all worried about me. I wished that they weren't.

The bay was deserted. Lars swam ashore and Sámr went with him holding the rope. Having been to the bottom of the sea and back the sea held no fears for Sámr. They put a couple of turns around a large rock and then, using the mast as a pulley, we hauled the drekar into shallower water. With the dragon prow facing the sea we could leave quickly if we had to. The boys went to collect shellfish while Aiden lit a fire and we put on water to heat. With some dried meat, seaweed and shellfish, we would have a stew. Hot food was always welcome. We did not know when we would have some again.

The men who would keep watch later that night went for an hour or so of sleep while we cooked the food. We would wake them when it was ready. I sat on the beach with Erik and Aiden. We had the fire for light and we were looking at the map to plan our journey. "There are pirates in Brittany. The Bretons have ships that they fill with warriors. They have enough of them to be able to surround and take us. We need to be wary of them. I would stand out to sea if we could. Besides, there are many dangerous rocks around the coast. Vasconia is safer." Erik knew the waters well.

I was aware that we did not have a large crew. If we were too far from the coast and a storm came up we might not be able to resume our course easily. "Yet we need to stay close to the coast. Could we risk the Breton coast at night?" Their faces told me that they doubted it." Perhaps we could sail to the Land of the Horse. Hrolf the Horseman would make us welcome."

Aiden was dubious, "We know not how he fares. It has been some time since we had a message. I am inclined to think we lose time and sail east to Dorestad and the coast of Frisia. There are many inlets and islands; there are places we could anchor and it would be safer than risking the angry waters south of here. If we were to find the wrong wind then we would end up at Syllingar."

None of us wanted that. "Then it looks like we head for Frisia. Perhaps we are meant to go there for the wind is from the north and west at the moment."

Erik rubbed his salt-rimmed beard, "Frisia? But there are pirates there."

I laughed and shook my head. "There will be danger whatever we do. You cannot see the future, Erik Short Toe, not without dreaming first. You can predict and you can guess but that is all it is, guesswork. The Norns have spun their webs. If pirates do attack us or Bretons then I may get my wish; a glorious death, less painful than the one I envisage."

The two of them looked at each other. Aiden said, "Do not talk that way, Dragonheart."

"Then let us stop worrying about what might happen. We will anchor off Dorestad. That way we can put well out to see and avoid the Bretons. Now let us eat. I am ravenous. Kara's medicine is working." I was not hungry but I wished them to think I was. They were all worrying too much about me. A man with worries made mistakes. I wanted them to be the crew I had led for so many years. They had not worried then and we had been successful. The food was tasty. I did not eat as much as the oarsmen. I had done little. I was acutely aware that they were all surreptitiously watching me. I hoped this would not last all two months of the voyage.

When we had eaten, the majority of the crew returned to the drekar and slept. I sat with the two sentries and Aiden. We talked for a while and then Aiden yawned, "Come jarl, it is time we slept."

I shook my head. "I will need to make water again. It is easier to do so on a beach than on a drekar. When I have done then I will come to the ship."

He left us. Ráðulfr Magnusson was one of the sentries. He was young. The raid on Lundenwic had been only his second raid. He and Arne Petrsson had sharpened their swords and then looked at each other. Arne nodded. Ráðulfr spoke. "Jarl, forgive my impertinence but I thought that the sword which was touched by the gods meant you could never be killed."

"That is a rumour. It is part of the legend. It may be true but the sword cannot save me from what is eating me from within."

"If you die then what will happen to the sword?" He realised what he had said. "I am sorry, jarl, that did not come out right! I meant nothing by it."

"I am old, Ráðulfr, my death is close even without this sickness. It is a fair question and I have not thought about it. I suppose Ragnar or Gruffyd would have it."

I took it out and held it. In many ways, I was pleased that Ráðulfr had asked the question. Many great swords were killed when their owner died. I could not do that to such a weapon. Both Ragnar and Gruffyd would wish for the sword and I would not want the clan destroyed by jealousy and fighting over the weapon.

Still with the sword in my hand, I stood. I would go to make water. Before I could sheathe it, I saw a movement. I did not know what it was but my instincts took over, "There is danger; stand to!"

Ráðulfr and Arne stood and drew their swords. Ráðulfr pointed. We saw figures racing over the sand. He shouted, "To arms!"

"You two flank me and put the fire between us and them."

I saw as we moved closer to the sea that these were the men of Om Walum. I recognised their dress and their weapons. I had fought them. Ebrel and Bronnen came from this land. The men of Om Walum rarely wore mail and only a few had helmets but the three of us had neither mail nor helmets ourselves. There were more than fifty of them. Suddenly a handful of arrows flew over our heads and two men fell with the missiles in their bodies. Their leader had both a helmet and a shield. I heard him shout something but I did not understand the words. Behind me, I could hear my men jumping into the sea and coming to our aid. The men of Om Walum were closer. We would have to stem the tide and buy the others time.

They had to run around the fire to get to us and that broke up their line, "With me!" The two men with whom I fought were younger and fitter but I had done this for more years than I cared to contemplate. I stepped forward, drawing my seax as I did so. Using my sword, I blocked the spear which was rammed at me by the eager young warrior and, as I shifted the shaft away, I eviscerated him with my seax. I did not stop but stepped forward. The men who followed all had swords and one had a small shield. Ráðulfr Magnusson grabbed the shield with his left hand and pulled it forward. The man was not expecting that and he did not react quickly enough. Ráðulfr's sword took his head.

The man who faced me saw an old man. He was careless. He feinted with his sword but I watched his eyes. When the real strike came it was easy enough to use my seax to hold him at the hilt. I brought down the sword which was touched by the gods and hacked deep into his neck.

I heard a roar as Olaf Leather Neck and Haaken led my warriors to smash into the men of Om Walum. Arrows still plucked men from their feet. The leader suddenly seemed to realise that he had not managed to surprise us. Perhaps he had thought that we were drunk. It was a common misconception amongst the men we fought. I know not the reason but the sudden attack had failed and failed disastrously. He shouted something and his men tried to disengage and run back to the cliffs. That was easier said than done. The jarl had been attacked and the Clan of the Wolf had vengeance in their hearts. Olaf led my men to purse them.

Aiden and Sámr appeared. I saw that Sámr had his Saami bow. As I wiped the blood from my sword on the kyrtle of the last man I had slain I pointed to the body with an arrow sticking from its skull. "Was that you?" Sámr nodded. "A fine arrow!"

Aiden looked concerned, "And you, Dragonheart?"

I pointed to the skies, "The Allfather was watching over me. I rose to make water and I spied them. Had I not risen then they would have been upon us before I could give warning. We would be dead."

Aiden touched the red stone he wore about his neck. "I see the Norns' hands in this. We are still too close to Syllingar. The men of these parts would not attack Vikings without reason." He waved his hand. They have been slaughtered." I looked and saw in the flickering firelight that there were at least nine bodies close to the fire. Further away I saw shadows which could have been bodies.

I turned to Arne, "Go fetch a horn and sound it. There is little point in losing more sleep. Get the men back. I will make water and then I will sleep." I smiled at Aiden. "I will not need the sleeping draught this night."

Chapter 2

It took time to gather all of our men. When I awoke the sun was up and we were sailing along the coast. The men were rowing. The wind was not with us. Was this the work of the Norns? Aiden watched me as I rose. He pointed to a patch on the deck. "You might not have needed the sleeping draught but you needed Kara's potion. You bled."

I had felt the dampness. Perhaps that had awoken me. "It could have been worse. I will take it now. Let me make water first." As I stood at the leeward side I asked, "Erik, have we come far this day?"

I heard him say, "No, Jarl Dragonheart. It took time to collect all of the men. We left later than I would have wished."

That was my fault. I should have stayed awake and chivvied them. As Aiden had said, this was the work of the Norns. I wondered why they had delayed us. Was there some danger gathering ahead?

Aiden gave me the draught to drink. I did so. I looked at the crew. They were silent. Their faces were dark. They had almost lost the Dragonheart. If they returned home with the news that they had allowed me to fall in battle it would mark them for life. Some would be angry with me. The exception was Haaken One Eye. He was grinning.

"Even when he is unwell the Dragonheart is still a force to be reckoned with. Next time, Jarl, you and I will stand watch and then our foes will have to watch out!"

I laughed, "Aye for Haaken One Eye will talk them to death!"

After a short while rowing, and with the island of Wihtwara on the larboard side, Erik and I noticed the storm clouds looming large ahead of us. The wind was already freshening and shifting. At the moment it was blowing from the south and east. Which way would it turn? There was no point in lowering the sail yet for it swirled around. Erik shouted, "Ship's boys, be ready to lower the sail but await my command."

Four of them swarmed up the forestays and back stays to reach the yard. With feet dangling they looked in a precarious position. I was glad that Sámr was on the deck holding the forestay in preparation to tighten the sail when it was lowered. The oarsmen were struggling to make their strokes for the sea was becoming wilder.

Erik shouted, "In with the oars. We have a blow coming! May the Allfather smile kindly upon us."

I was wearing my wolf cloak but now I went to my chest and took out my sealskin cape. It would keep me drier. I put my boots and wolf cloak in the chest. The chest was also lined with seal skin. It would be dry. In the time it took to do that the wind increased and the first squall hit us.

Erik shook his head, "We will have to use the sail, jarl, and go where the wind takes us. We have no control at the moment. It is like fighting a sea monster!" I nodded, "Lower the sail!"

As soon as the sail was lowered he put the steering board over. We would be driven south rather than east. It could not be helped. At least we had sea room there. The only land was a group of islands many hundreds of leagues to the south. I had never seen them but Aiden said he had seen Roman maps where they were marked. When Sámr and Arne tightened their stays, the sail cracked and then tightened. The wind took us and we flew. The sky blackened as though it was night. This would be a test of the captain, the ship and the crew. *'Heart of the Dragon'* was not a young ship. She was, however, sound and she had the spirit of her maker, Bolli, in her. She would not die easily. Erik kept one eye on the masthead pennant which fluttered to show us the direction of the wind. We had sailed enough together in conditions like this to know that the wind could veer in a heartbeat. Erik had to watch the pennant and react. If we were caught beam on in full sail then it could be the end of us all. Now I saw the Norn's web. We had been delayed so that we would meet the storm at sea rather than being close to a beach or a port. What had the sisters in mind for us?

The wind shifted to take us south and west. We were sailing further from land. Each change meant work for the boys. I saw that Sámr's strength was a true asset. He was not yet ready to row but it would not be long for his chest was broad and, for his age, he was well muscled. He and Lars were the two strongest and they were the rocks upon which the others depended. We had no idea how long we sailed south and west. Erik and Aiden would have no idea where we were. The wind began to veer and we found ourselves sailing what appeared to be north and east. It was then that the Norns played one more trick. The ropes and the rigging had all been replaced before we left Whale Island but one of the forestays snapped.

Erik knew the danger. If we lost the mast and the sail then we were doomed. "Get another one rigged, loosen the back stays and the other forestay!"

This time old hands like Olaf Leather Neck helped the ship's boys. Their prompt action saved the mast but not the other forestay which also snapped. Our bows and our stern plunged into troughs as Erik fought to hold the drekar on course. It was not easy. Aiden went to help him. Once the two stays were replaced the ship stabilized and we resumed our course. We were just going where the sea determined. We were now heading for the coast of Wessex. There lay a country of my enemies. I made my way to the mast and peered up. There was a crack in the yard. It was not a large one but it was a warning.

I made my way back, "Erik there is a crack in the yard."

He handed the tiller to his son Arne and went to look for himself. When he returned his face told the story. "I thought there might be. I have a spare but that is not a task when we are on a stormy sea. We need a beach or a port."

Aiden said, "Then we are forced to head for Bruggas. It is safer than a Frankish port and, if my calculations are correct, then it is also the closest port."

Erik nodded as he helped his son to strain against the steering board, "And there are few beaches which we could use. Let us hope the storm abates soon."

Aiden nodded, "As the wind has veered in a circle then I think the wind will continue from our stern."

Erik shook his head in dismay and he looked at me. "We will be losing both time and distance. We sail north and we will have to spend a day, at least, in port. I am sorry, jarl."

"It cannot be helped. It is the Norns."

Our galdramenn was right although our torment lasted the rest of the day and into the early evening. As it began to abate we saw the estuary ahead. It was risky travelling along it at night but we had no choice. Our exhausted ship's boys were called into action again as they lined the prow to watch for danger. It was with some relief that we saw the dim lights of the houses of Bruggas. We had made a port. We had survived.

"It is too late to do anything about the yard this night. The crew are exhausted. They did well Erik Short Toe."

He nodded. He looked exhausted too. "I will go and pay the port dues."

"Aiden and I will see if we can buy some ale and some hot food."

Olaf Leather Neck struggled to his feet. He had worked as hard as any. "I will get my weapons and come with you."

"No, Olaf. I have my sword and I have a galdramenn. I will be safe."

We stepped on to the quay. Erik bad found the first berth that he could and that meant we were many paces from the nearest dwelling. I spied, ahead, a lively place. Hanging from a yard above the door was a saddle. I smiled at the memory. This was Freja's inn and she was a friend. "I think I know where we can get some food." As we approached the door Aiden was startled to see a Dane being hurled, bodily, into the water.

"Are you certain, jarl?"

I grinned, "I see, Sven, that you are affording your usual welcome to sailors."

He laughed, "Welcome Jarl Dragonheart! He tried to pay his bill with a lead coin coated in copper!" He shook his head, "As if that would fool Freja! Come inside, she will be pleased to see you!"

Inside it was busy, not to say rowdy, but I knew that there would be no trouble. Freja had eight horns pf ale in her hand and was serving a table of Saxons. She saw me and squealed, "Jarl Dragonheart! You are a sight for sore eyes. An honourable man at last." She turned and glared at two Frisians. "You two have been nursing those ales for long enough. Drink and leave or order more!" They immediately complied. After downing the ale, they scurried out of the room. You did not argue with Freja. I saw Aiden's eyes widen.

We sat and she pulled up another stool. She was a large woman and her buttocks hung over the side almost touching the ground. It did not seem to bother her.

"Olga, two ales! What brings you here, Jarl Dragonheart? More treasure for old Isaac the Jew?"

"No, we were caught in a storm. We have to repair the yard. I need a barrel of ale and hot food."

"The ale is ready now for I brewed a batch yesterday but the food will take a short time. You are at the end of the quay?" I nodded. "I will have the barrel sent down. We cannot have the Clan of the Wolf thirsty." She stood and glowered at the Saxons, "They are real men!" They recoiled at her words. She stood and went to the back room where they prepared and cooked the food.

Aiden said, "Is she volva? How did she know where we would be moored?"

"This is her town. She has the best ale and when ships arrive their captains and crew call in here. If she does not like them she sends them on their way but this way she keeps a close eye on how many ships have arrived."

I saw her men manhandle the barrel out of the door. Olga arrived with the ale. Aiden tasted the beer and nodded appreciatively. "This Jew, he is the one who sent us the money for Queen Osburga's crown?" I nodded as I quaffed half the horn. "Then we might visit him on the morrow. I have with me two holy books Gruffyd took in a raid on Wessex. I think they might fetch a higher price here than in Miklagård."

"I will take you then. I cannot see the yard being repaired in a hurry. Erik will want to replace the ropes too. The Norns have already delayed us."

"And I fear there will be more delays. We can expect such storms until we reach the Blue Sea."

Freja joined us a short while later. "So, jarl, I hear that you escaped the disaster of Aclea and the Danes perished?" I nodded. She shook her head, "I know not why you took up with them."

I finished my ale and Freja waved over Olga to refill it. "I gave my word. This is Aiden. He married my daughter and is a galdramenn."

"A witch?" Her hand involuntarily went to the charm around her neck.

Aiden smiled, "I prefer the term, wise man. I will have even more knowledge when we return from Miklagård."

Her eyes widened, "You sail the Blue Sea. Truly, Jarl Dragonheart, you are the stuff of legend. Others raid abbeys and you go to raid the Emperor."

I laughed, "I go to trade and… to seek advice."

She seemed disappointed, "Oh."

Olga brought my ale over and said, "The food is ready."

Freja nodded. "Have it taken to the Jarl's drekar." She had not asked for payment yet. I took two of the gold coins I had brought from my purse. It was more than enough for the food and the ale.

"That is too much."

"I need another barrel tomorrow before we sail. I would not leave you without your ale to sustain us."

"And you have such consideration! If I thought to take another husband then he would be just like you!"

By the time we returned to the ship the men had eaten. We had eaten in the *'Saddle'*. We were both full and ready for sleep. Olaf Leather Neck had placed two men at the quay. "Just to make certain that no one tries anything."

I laughed, "I saw one Saxon and two Danes tied up. The rest were little Frisians. I think we are safe."

The next morning, I was woken by the sound of men working. The old yard was being lowered. I was still replete from the meal the night before and so Aiden and I left, without eating, for the home of Isaac of Bruggas. Aiden carried the books in a leather satchel. Isaac did not live in the safe part of Bruggas but his home was like a fortress. No one bothered us for my sword marked me as a warrior.

We were greeted by Oddvakr, Isaac's Viking bodyguard. He recognised me, "We heard you had returned, Jarl. You are welcome." He glanced at Aiden. He did not know him.

"This is Aiden. He is married to my daughter. He is safe."

The Viking nodded.

Isaac appeared not to have moved since our last visit. He glanced up at me as though I had left the room but an hour before. "Ah, Jarl. How can I be of service? Do you have another crown you wish ransomed?"

Aiden took out the books. "We are sailing to Miklagård and thought you might pay more than they would for they are Orthodox."

For the first time that I could recall Isaac looked surprised. He did not even look at the books. "Can you read minds?"

"I do not understand."

He smiled, "I am sorry. Forgive an old man. How could you know?" He waved a hand at the books. "Yes, I will pay you for them and it will be a higher price than the Greeks might pay. There is something else." Like Oddvakr he glanced at Aiden.

"He is to be trusted."

Aiden shook his head, "Do I look like a brigand?" He was not used to this sort of treatment. At home, he was treated with respect and honour. Here in Bruggas, he was questioned.

Isaac spread his hands, "I apologize. There are many evil men in this town. It pays to be careful. If Jarl Dragonheart vouches for you then you are welcome." He waved over a servant who poured three large goblets of deep red wine. He raised his goblet, "Here is to the intervention of Mistress Fate." We drank and he wiped his mouth with a napkin. "I have a nephew, the son of my brother. He is staying with me. David brought me ... well let us say he had a perilous journey from Jerusalem to Bruggas and the journey was necessary. I have been trying to get a passage home for him but there are few captains willing to sail to the Blue Sea and the ones who have offered to take him I do not trust. You, I trust and I would make it worth your while for you to take him with you. If he is not safe with the Dragonheart then he is safe nowhere."

"Thank you for the compliment but we do not go to Jerusalem."

He flapped a hand, "If you can take him to Constantinopolis then he can easily make his way home from there. He knows the city well. He has a home there as well as in Jerusalem. It is in the west and the land of the Franks where Jews are in danger. We are the Christ-killers. What say you?"

"Of course, but I have to warn you that the journey will not be without risks."

"When David arrived here we knew that. His mission was vital. He is a good boy and can use a sword. He will not be a hindrance to you."

"Then we will take him."

He laughed, "Without agreeing on a price?"

"I trust you and if the price is not enough he will have to wave farewell to us from Bruggas' quay."

"Quite so. Oddvakr, fetch David ben Samuel."

When David ben Samuel came I saw that he was of an age with Gruffyd. He had the dark looks of his uncle but without the hook nose. His darker skin told of life under the hot sun.

I did not understand the words Isaac used. David ben Samuel answered and then, after smiling, gave a slight bow. "Thanks to Oddvakr, David speaks a few words of your language but I fear he will need patience."

Aiden nodded, "I have languages. I can read a little Greek and Latin."

"Good for David can speak Greek too."

"We sail as soon as the ship is repaired."

"Then David ben Samuel will follow. I will send your payment with Oddvakr." He clasped my right hand with both of his. "Thank you, Jarl. May Jehovah watch over you. I am in your debt. Do not hesitate to call in that debt."

"You pay us. That is enough."

"No, it is not, for you are helping a Jew and we Jews do not forget such kindness."

As we walked back Aiden could not help smiling. "Is it not *wyrd*, jarl that we go to a land where we cannot speak the language and someone who knows the city will be able to advise us."

"We know not how he might help us yet. Isaac may be friendlier than this David ben Samuel."

"He needs us, Jarl Dragonheart. I think this was meant to be. I can use him to help improve my Greek. Who knows he may even know of a healer in the city!"

By the time we reached the drekar, I could see them hauling the yard into place. Once that was secured then the sail would need to be attached. That was not a quick process. "Erik when can we leave?"

Erik looked at the yard, "On the evening tide."
"Is the ale and food loaded?"
Olaf nodded, "Aye, jarl."
"We will be taking a passenger with us. You had better rig some canvas near to the prow. He may need his privacy."
"A passenger?"
I nodded, "It may be useful and besides we are being paid. It cannot hurt."
Our passenger arrived shortly before we left. I had begun to worry that our departure might be delayed. It took three men to bring the chests of David ben Samuel the nephew of Isaac on board. I looked at Aiden and rolled my eyes. We would have to lift the deck for the smaller of them. The other two would not fit there. They were large solid ones and they each bore a lock. I hoped that they had something to keep out the wet. The passenger carried a large leather bag which he carried over his shoulder. At his waist hung a sword and a dagger. He had seal-skin boots. He was a traveller. It looked to contain that which he would need for the voyage.

Oddvakr was one of the men bringing the chests. He lifted them aboard and then said, "My master is sorry that the chests are so large." Oddvakr was a Viking and he knew the limitations of a dragon ship! "The smaller one contains your payment. My master thought it might help to make up for the inconvenience of the other two chests." He lowered his voice. "It is important that they travel with young David ben Samuel. The chests are lined with seal skin. They will come to no harm if left on the deck. I offered to come with you. I think I would like the adventure and it would be good to travel with the Dragonheart." He shrugged, "However, my master needs me." He clasped my arm. "May the Allfather be with you!" He turned and spoke to our passenger who answered him and embraced him. There was obvious affection there. I would have liked the big Viking to have travelled with us. He looked to be a handy man in a fight.

I waved over Ráðulfr Magnusson. "Put the two big chests near the prow, under the canvas we rigged." As he shouted for some of the crew to help him I said, "And, you, galdramenn, had better practise your Greek. Tell him where his berth is."

Aiden went and spoke some Greek. It was halting for he had not spoken it since Josephus had sailed with us. I went to the chest. It was filled with coins. We were being heavily overpaid and I wondered what danger our young passenger brought. Isaac could have bought two ships for the chest of coins he had paid us. The rest of the crew was busy and so I stored it close to the steerboard under the decking.

It was almost dark when the work was finished and Erik Short Toe wasted no time in leaving. We had a tricky estuary to negotiate and he wanted sea room. The wind was from the north east which meant we would not have to row and we could avoid Angia and the other Breton islands. I stood with Olaf and Haaken. "What is the story with our passenger, Jarl?"

"More than we were told, of that I am certain." Haaken cocked an eye. "We were paid too much to take him. He may bring danger but I am not certain."

Haaken laughed, "We are Vikings! We seek danger! It will make a good song!"

Olaf shook his head and said, quietly, "Have you forgotten that we go to heal the Dragonheart?"

"The god who touched the sword will not allow him to die of a worm in his gut! He is a legend. He will die a glorious death and I will be there with him!"

Olaf Leather Neck shook his head, "Jarl, you have been his friend for longer than me. How do you put up with him?"

I smiled, "That is easy, ignore half of what he says and laugh at the rest. He means no harm!"

Haaken was not put out. He sniffed, "When we are all in Valhalla it will be my tales of the Dragonheart and this clan that will be told. Then men will listen to all of my words."

Once we were buffeted by the larger waves of the open sea we felt happier. There would be no hidden sandbars and shoals. With lookouts straining to see deadly rocks we sought safety in the empty ocean. Few ships sailed at night. We were lucky to have such an experienced captain as Erik Short Toe. I stood with him at the stern. He gestured to the yard. "It was not the ship's fault the yard broke. That was a fierce storm. When we were in port I bought spare ropes."

"And have we a spare yard?"

He shook his head. "If we can find a stand of trees when we land then we can cut one down and fashion a spare one. It will have to be before we reach the Blue Sea. After that, I am not certain that we will find a suitable tree." Nodding towards the prow he asked, "And our passenger; what is his story?"

"Not that which we were told. Of that I am certain. We were paid too much just to carry a passenger. We were paid to protect him. And that means there will be men coming after him. We will be in danger."

"Perhaps but the sea is wide and we left shortly after he arrived."

A sudden thought struck me. "That may explain his late arrival. It was to put off pursuers."

Erik Short Toe was not convinced, "A drekar filled with Vikings is not the easiest of targets to take and we left late. I saw no other ships ready to sail."

"You may be right but I see a Norn's web and we will have to extricate ourselves from it sometime on this voyage."

"You have the best of crews. If they cannot do it then no one can."

Most of my men had already rolled into their furs and lay asleep when I took my wolf cloak from the chest. Aiden returned. "I had thought you were going to sleep with our passenger at the prow."

He smiled as he took his own cloak and blanket from the chest, "No Jarl but I had to explain to him many things. He has never sailed on a long ship before. Between his Norse and my Greek, we managed. I learned much. He is used to luxury. When he sailed the Blue Sea, he had a cabin and servants. This is his first voyage in such conditions. He must be desperate." I looked at him. He lowered his voice and nodded, "He is escaping something. He asked me where we would be putting in. I thought he was thinking of staying in inns to make himself more comfortable. I told him we would sleep on the deck or on beaches. He was more worried about whom we might meet. When I asked him who he meant, he said he was tired. He is the hunted."

"And who are the hunters?"

"I know not but we have more than fifty days to get into his mind. He knows not that he sails with a galdramenn and the Dragonheart." He took out his medicine flask, "Here, it is time for your potion."

I drank and then I slept but I could not get the young Jew from my thoughts. I came up with many explanations for his presence and the real reason for his flight but none made sense.

Chapter 3

When I woke we were out at sea. It was a grey day and there was no sign of land. We were, however, being followed by gulls. That meant that land was not far away. Looking at the pennant I saw that the wind still came from the north east and would help to take us south. When we had to turn south and east then we would slow but we were making good time. I made water and then went to speak with Erik's son, Arne. Arne had three fingers having lost the others when he was a ship's boy. He sailed with us despite having his own knarr. He had no wife. She had died of the coughing sickness two winters since.

"Well Arne, how goes it?"

He pointed east, "Frankia is just over the horizon. The lookout on the masthead keeps her in view. Father asked me to keep her well out to sea." He sniffed the air. "The wind will change but, for the present, the Allfather is with us." He gestured to a leather water-filled pail next to him and the lines which streamed from the upper sheerstrake. Siggi Knutson, his nephew, was hauling in another of the sparkling fish which were attracted by anything shiny. "The Allfather has sent us food this morning. Help yourself."

We called the fish the Magpie Fish for like that black and white bird it was attracted to all things shiny. Others called it the foolish fish for it was so easy to catch. I did not care what it was named for eaten raw it was delicious. Everything else we ate on the ship tasted of salt or vinegar. Both were pleasant tastes unless you ate them every day. I reached down and took one of the freshly caught fish which still showed signs of life. I smashed its head on to the sheerstrake to kill it and then, using my seax, slit open its belly to remove the guts. The screaming gulls swooped and fought for the treasure I threw over the side. Then I removed the head and tossed that too. Once more the morning was riven with their screams.

Aiden awoke, "Cannot a man sleep?"

I took out the backbone and split the fish in two. I handed one half to him. Here is the gift of Ran." I sheathed my seax and ate the raw fish. Kara had told me that it would help my condition. I guessed that the crew all knew that which was why Arne had his nephew fishing. It is doubtful that any would be left after all the crew had risen. This fish was very popular but did not keep well. Any that were left would be preserved in salt and vinegar. It would make Skreið.

The crew had all eaten and the pail was almost empty when our passenger emerged. There was just one dead fish remaining. He made his way down the centre of the drekar. The crew stared at him as though he had two heads. As he approached I was able to get a better look at him. His clothes were well-made. It explained the chests for there was no way to wash clothes at sea. When the voyage finished we would all stink. He was broader than I had thought when I had first seen him. A dagger hung from his belt.

Aiden smiled and spoke to him in halting Greek. David ben Samuel answered. I saw Aiden say, "Aah!"

"What is it?"

"The man's religion forbids him to eat the flesh of the pig. The salted meat we have will not do." He reached down and took out the last fish. He handed it to me. Aiden had many skills but gutting fish was not one of them. I gutted it and made it into two fillets. As the gulls fought over the remains I handed the fillets to Aiden. I saw him struggling for the words and then he handed over one of them. I saw the Jew nibble tentatively at the fish. Aiden said something and David closed his eyes and ate again. He was smiling when he opened them and he devoured both fillets.

I turned to Arne, "We had better have Siggi fishing each day."

"Further south they are different species of fish, Jarl Dragonheart. They may not be so easy to catch."

"Then our passenger will have a varied diet."

"When he has made water, I will try to teach him our words. We have little else to do and the weather is clement."

The weather held all day. I saw no more of either man. Erik came to take over the steering board at noon. After speaking with his son, he took the tiller. He pointed east. "I like not the coast there. The Franks have built towers at the mouth of the Liger and they have ships which hunt for the likes of us. We could defeat them but we might lose men and we do not have the luxury of a large crew. When the sun sets I will head closer to shore and we will anchor. The wind may well change on the morrow but I will not risk sailing this coast at night."

He was the captain and we were in his hands. There had been some blood on my kyrtle when I had awoken but there had not been as much as in the past. Perhaps the sea helped alleviate the conditions. I knew not.

Sámr came to join me. He was bare-chested and the sun had begun to redden his skin. "Your mother will blame me if you go home with peeled skin!"

He laughed, "I have put seal oil on. I will not shed my skin. It is easier this way for it means I have dry clothes to wear."

Erik laughed, "It is many years since the Dragonheart was a ship's boy. He has forgotten the soaking!"

"I spent little time as a ship's boy Erik. When I was Sámr's age I lived with Old Ragnar high in the mountains. All that I remember was having to leap ashore and tie us up. As that meant I was soon fighting then wet clothes were the least of my worries."

"When will I take an oar?" Sámr looked up at me expectantly. He knew that taking an oar was the first step to becoming a warrior.

I looked at Erik, "That depends upon our captain here?"

Erik ran his eye over Sámr. "You have the chest already. When we reach the Blue Sea, you can try." He grinned mischievously. "You can relieve Haaken One Eye then."

Sámr's face fell, "I will be Olaf Leather Neck's oar brother!"

"Then you have until the Blue Sea to reconsider your decision."

He smiled at me, "No, Jarl Dragonheart. This is *wyrd*. Rowing with Olaf will make me a better warrior. I can aspire to be the best."

For the next three days, the winds gradually changed direction but remained kind. We continued south sailing well off the coast during the day and closing at night. As we neared Al Andalus Erik said, "We will soon need water. We need to land during the day. If we can I would prefer to make it in Leon rather than Al Andalus. The Arabs of Córdoba are cruel and hate our people."

"Then put in now. This is Vasconia. We cannot sail without water and we have had no rain since Wessex."

He put the steering board over and we headed east. "Keep a watch for land. We seek a river! Any sail is a potential enemy!"

The shout roused my men. They knew what the change in direction meant. Blades were fetched and sharpened. Seal skin boots were taken from their chests. None had been idle on the voyage. Bone had been brought to carve for most while Haaken composed more chants for the rowers. The change in direction brought a different motion to the ship and I saw David and Aiden walk towards us. We had seen little of the two of them for the last few days. They had been camped by the prow beneath the canvas awning.

"We go to land?"

I nodded, "We need water."

Our passenger spoke, haltingly, "It is a village we find?"

I was surprised at his grasp of our language. Aiden shrugged, "He has a quick mind and he can speak many languages. By the time we reach the Blue Sea, it will be time for him to learn the curses of Olaf Leather Neck for he will have the rest of our words."

I shook my head, "We go to find water. We seek a river."

He looked relieved. The two of them stayed with us as we approached the coast. The thin grey line grew and became land. Erik turned us slightly and we headed obliquely towards the coast. I saw trees and occasional buildings. From Aiden's charts, we were close to the land of Vasconia. There was one mighty river but I hoped we were south of that.

Lars shouted, "I see a river. There is a small village with fishing boats!"

Erik looked at me. I nodded, "Who knows, we may get food too!"

As we headed inshore we had to use the oars. Erik shortened sail. It would make a safer approach although it would warn the villagers that the Vikings were coming. Lars shouted as he put another reef in the sail. "They are getting in the boats and heading upstream."

Erik laughed, "Then they are in for a shock for we will have to sail after them to get at the fresher water."

As we drew closer I saw others had fled across the sides of the valley. There would be a nearby citadel. I turned to Aiden, "when we get to the village take our passenger, Olaf and Haaken. See what you can find. I am certain that I can spy some sheep. It will take us time to get upstream, turn and then fill the barrels."

Erik nodded, "Good idea jarl. They may have fresh meat. Olaf Haaken, leave your oar. You get to go ashore."

"Excellent!"

Aiden turned to David and explained what they would be doing. It soon became apparent that this was a small village but not tiny. There were fourteen or so huts and they had built a quay to help them land their catch. Smoke came from the huts. They had been cooking. Erik timed it to perfection, "In oars." As the oars came in and the current struck us so we slowed and bumped gently next to the quay. Olaf and Haaken leapt quickly ashore. David was less confident. Olaf reached over and pulled him on to the quay. Aiden joined them.

"Oars out." The steerboard oars pushed us away from the quay and soon we were heading upstream. We had a current to fight and two fewer rowers. Erik shouted, "Lars, Sámr, Siggi, Arne, take two oars. You can row!"

I watched as they ran their oars out and then I began the chant to help them. It was the chant of the Ulfheonar and was used to get up to speed. The lines were short and rowing was faster. It would be a real test for my great-grandson.

Push your arms
Row the boat
Use your back
The Wolf will fly

Ulfheonar
Are real men
Teeth like iron
Arms like trees

Push your arms
Row the boat

Use your back
The Wolf will fly

Ragnar's Spirit
Guides us still
Dragon Heart
Wields it well

Push your arms
Row the boat
Use your back
The Wolf will fly

It was not a straight river and the twists and turns made it hard for Erik who had to keep us in the centre channel. Sven Svensson was at the prow watching for sandbars. I walked between the rowers. I saw that Lars and Sámr had an oar and they were both determined not to let down Erik. Sámr would need Aiden's salve for his hands would be red raw! I saw the fishing boats ahead of us. They would not escape us for we were faster. They did not know that we did not wish to harm them. We wanted water. They put ashore and landed on the bank to our steerboard. That told me that there was a citadel close by. I tied a piece of cord to a horn and I trailed it in the river. I pulled it up and tasted it. It was slightly brackish still. Another few lengths and we would be able to turn.

Sven was clinging to the dragon prow and he shouted, "Captain, the river narrows ten lengths upstream!"

I heard Erik shout, "Steerboard oars in! Larboard back water!"

We turned in our own length. I put the horn back in the water and this time, when I drew it, found it to be sweet. We could fill our barrels.

Tostig who was atop the mast shouted, "Jarl there is a citadel. It looks to be three miles or so away."

"Keep watch!"

With an anchor thrown out most of the crew began to help fill the barrels. "The rest of you get your bows. We may have company soon."

It was not an easy process to fill the barrels in a river. The large barrels we used for storage could not be dropped over the side and so we had to use smaller barrels and leather pails to haul up water and fill each barrel. When the six barrels were filled we would fill every other container. We could always catch food at sea but we were going to a sea where the rain was unpredictable and it was hot.

"Jarl, I can see horsemen. They are getting closer!"

"Archers, to the stern. Sámr, we will see just how good you are with a Saami bow. I hope the oar has not taken the strength from your back."

"It has not, Jarl Dragonheart."

The horsemen were Franks. They had banners and helmets. They had shields. I saw just one who was in mail and he rode at the head of the column. He was their lord. They were descending down a path which zig zagged down the valley side. I saw that five barrels had been filled. "Sámr, when the one with the mail gets close hit his horse. If that does not stop them then kill him."

Ráðulfr Magnusson rubbed his chin. "That would be a prodigious hit, jarl. It must be more than two hundred and fifty paces."

"Show him, Sámr!" My great grandson pulled back and, letting his breath out slowly, released the arrow. The arrow flew and hit the horse in the neck. It pitched the horseman from his saddle. He waved his arm and one of his men dismounted. The lord mounted the horse. He had just grabbed the reins when Sámr's arrow hit him in the shoulder. It was not a mortal wound but it worked. They began to back up the hill.

"That is a fine bow! Where did you get it?"

Sámr pointed to me, "Great grandfather gave it to me. It costs as much as a byrnie. I am honoured that he gave it to me."

"Secure the barrels. Pull in the anchor. Take the oars and let us keep her way."

It was a sedate cruise down the river. I saw Haaken. He was drinking something from a goblet and was seated on a chair on the quay. We tied up next to the quay and I said, "I see you are taking it easy!"

"With you away it meant I am the eldest warrior. I am just delegating. We found some sheep. Olaf butchered them and they are being cooked. They will be bringing down the little that we found. There was some food, pots and drinking vessels. There are also six fowl. We found cages. We may have eggs! There is a great quantity of freshly smoked fish. We have had a good raid… considering that we did not raid!"

Ráðulfr asked, "Will the horsemen not come?"

"They may do but it will take them longer and next time we use a shield wall backed by bows. I am not afraid of thirty horsemen!"

We loaded the ship with the pots, fowl, smoked fish, ale and wine. We found some coils of rope. They would always come in handy. Tostig shouted, "Jarl, the horsemen are returning."

I shouted, "Olaf, Aiden bring the pots with the food!" It did not matter if the food was not yet cooked. The boiling water would continue to cook it for a while. Beggars could not be choosers. Olaf carried one pot himself while David and Aiden struggled with the other. "Tostig, is it just the horsemen?"

"No, Jarl. I think they have the fishermen with them too."

That did not make any difference. They could have a thousand fishermen. If they had archers then we might be in trouble. "Load the ship. Archers, be ready to discourage them if they come close." I glanced at the sky. The sun was already at its height. We could make a few more leagues south but then we would need a beach. The real danger would begin when we sailed the coast of the Caliphate of Córdoba. Once the two steaming pots were aboard the ship's boys began to untie the ropes while Sámr and Lars started to lower the sail. The Franks chose that moment to attack. I picked up Sámr's bow and joined the eight or so archers. I nocked an arrow, pulled back and sent the missile into the midst of the horses charging down the path towards us. I saw a horseman tumble from his saddle. Two others were hit and one horse began bucking and biting as an arrow sank into its rump.

"Oars push off!"

There were just ten men on the larboard side and they used the oars to push us away from the quay. Sámr and Lars slid down the backstays and then ran to secure the forestays too. As the wind caught us we moved more swiftly and the Franks gave up. The wind had veered slightly and now came from the south and east. While we travelled west that was not a problem but we had to head south. Luckily the wind was not a strong one. Once we had turned Erik shouted, "We row until we find a beach. Haaken, get them moving along at pace eh?"

"Aye Erik!" He chose the song of the sword. Every warrior in the clan knew it. Haaken and I were about the last two who had witnessed it. The rest were dead. Partly for that reason it was still a powerful chant.

The storm was wild and the gods did roam
The enemy closed on the Prince's home
Two warriors stood on a lonely tower
Watching, waiting for hour on hour.
The storm came hard and Odin spoke
With a lightning bolt the sword he smote
Ragnar's Spirit burned hot that night
It glowed, a beacon shiny and bright
The two they stood against the foe
They were alone, nowhere to go
They fought in blood on a darkened hill
Dragon Heart and Cnut will save us still
Dragon Heart, Cnut and the Ulfheonar
Dragon Heart, Cnut and the Ulfheonar
The storm was wild and the Gods did roam
The enemy closed on the Prince's home
Two warriors stood on a lonely tower
Watching, waiting for hour on hour.
The storm came hard and Odin spoke
With a lightning bolt the sword he smote
Ragnar's Spirit burned hot that night
It glowed, a beacon shiny and bright
The two they stood against the foe
They were alone, nowhere to go
They fought in blood on a darkened hill
Dragon Heart and Cnut will save us still
Dragon Heart, Cnut and the Ulfheonar
Dragon Heart, Cnut and the Ulfheonar

We sailed swiftly south towards the hot lands of Al Andalus. First, we had to pass the mountains which divided Leon and the Asturias from Vasconia. We would seek a beach when the sun began to set. Aiden and David ben Samuel stood with me and we stirred the two pots. The meat was almost cooked. We had eaten mutton raw before now. I saw David ben Samuel observing me, surreptitiously. "What is it?"

He shook his head. "Sorry for staring. You are old. You older than Isaac." I nodded. "But you fight! You pull a bow!"

I spoke slowly so that he would understand me. "I am a warrior. I have spent all my life fighting. It is what I do." I looked at him. "Tell me, David ben Samuel, what do you do?"

He hesitated and then said, "I am a merchant."

I did not believe him but it made no difference to me. I had been well paid for my complicity.

"Aiden says you are ill. You bleed?"

I glared at Aiden, "He talks too much."

My galdramenn shrugged, "He needed to know, Jarl Dragonheart. How else will we find a doctor? He knows the city, I have discovered much since we first spoke. He is a clever man and he can help us."

David had picked up some of the words and he nodded, "I know doctors. I do not know if they can help you."

At least he was honest. "So long as they try then I will be satisfied."

Tostig's voice came down from the mast head, "Beach ahead, Captain, it looks deserted."

I turned to Erik, "This time we make certain! I am too old to be attacked with my breeks around my ankles."

When we landed I went with Olaf and four other men to climb the cliffs and check that there was no immediate danger. As the sun was setting it was easier to see the glow from any hut with an open door. By the time we reached the beach Aiden and David had organized the mutton stew. I saw that our passenger was pleased to be eating something other than fish. I was not certain if his diet would improve during the next fifty days. I had taken my blankets to the beach. I was embarrassed about the blood stains I left on the deck. The ship's boys cleaned them but it still disturbed me. I would stain the sand. Most of the crew also slept on the beach but David chose to sleep under his canvas. I lay next to Aiden.

"What have you learned?"

"That he keeps secrets well but I am used to that. I listen to that which is below the words. Being a merchant is how he earns money but it is not what he does. He knows the Regent of the Empire."

"Theodora isn't it?"

"Good, you have remembered. Sometimes I think you just nod when I say things and do not actually take in the words."

"I remembered because I thought it strange that such a large empire was ruled by a woman."

"It is not uncommon. The Empire, from what our passenger says, runs itself but there are people with power. The fact that he knows Theodora is more than interesting. What was he doing in Bruggas? He said he was staying with his uncle but Bruggas is tiny compared with the other trading centres. Lundenwic would have afforded him more trade and he would have been made more welcome there. No, he came to Bruggas from the Frankish Empire. Louis the Pious was a weak king, his son, Charles the Bald, is equally weak. I heard in Bruggas that the Clan of the Horse have taken land from him and he is helpless. He cannot take it back. Even the Bretons are beginning to take his land. King Charles is a descendant of Charlemagne, the Holy Roman Emperor. I think he is an emissary from Theodora to Charles the Bald."

"That may be but how does it help us?"

"Knowledge is power, jarl. You can never know too much! By the time we reach Sicily I will know more and by then my Greek will enable me to find out more when we are in Miklagård."

"Do not tempt the Norns. We have far to travel!"

Chapter 4

Over the next two days, we saw the landscape to larboard change dramatically. It was not just that the land looked drier, and rockier, with fewer trees it was the buildings. They were not Frankish. We had found the land of the Arab and the Moor. We were in the land of the dhow. They were very fast ships which could dart out from a bay and be upon an unsuspecting ship before they could run out oars. For that reason, we were standing well out to sea. The delays with the replacement of the yard and the water had added a day and a half to our voyage. It was the Norns. Had we not been delayed then we would not have come upon the Viking drekar being attacked by dhows!

Lars was the lookout and he was the most experienced of the ship's boys. "Jarl, there is a drekar inshore of us. She is being attacked by four ships. They are small and filled with dark-skinned men. The drekar is down by the bows and there is some wreckage there."

When you are a leader you need to lead. You have to make decisions quickly. Even as I took in the information I was running through the choices we could make in my head. We could continue on our journey as though nothing had happened and leave the Vikings there to the Arabs. We did not know the crew. They were not of our clan. The second choice was to risk all and try to save the crew. I made the obvious choice. The Norns had placed this drekar in our path and we ignored it at our peril.

"Erik, come about and let us shift these pirates! Clan of the Wolf, arm yourself. We go to war. Ship's boys you will need your bows."

None argued although, as Aiden explained it to him, our passenger looked mystified. This was our code. It bound us and every other Viking who sailed the seas. I strapped on Ragnar's Spirit and Wolf's Blood. I donned my seal-skin boots. Then I went to the bow to see the situation. The dhows were like little terriers attacking a bull. I saw, now, the wreckage of a ship as it floated away on the current. The drekar had rammed and sunk a dhow. The drekar had suffered damage and was clearly down by the bow. The Moors or Arabs, I could not differentiate, were swarming over the ship. The crew would not surrender. There was no point. They would be enslaved. This way they would fight to the end and die with a sword in their hand. They would reach Valhalla.

"Lay us next to the nearest dhow. We will use it like a bridge and it will keep the others from us." I watched as Sámr carefully laid his bow by the steering board and then joined Lars and Siggi to climb the mast. They would have to take in the sail quickly to take the way off us.

Olaf Leather Neck and Haaken joined me. They wore their helmets. Mine had a mask. On land I would have worn my helmet but, on a ship, I needed to be able to see and hear well. The dhow had a pitching deck and you did not shut off any sense willingly. Olaf pointed his war axe at the Vikings, "They are in two groups. One is by the steering board and one is by the prow."

"Then you lead half the men to the prow and I will lead the other half to the steering board. Go and divide the men."

Haaken stayed with me. Aiden and David ghosted up to my shoulder. Aiden said, "You do not need to go, Jarl."

"Of all those on board this drekar you, Aiden the galdramenn, know that I must. If I do not then the Sisters will put something even more dangerous in our way. I would rather use Ragnar's Spirit to fight some half-naked savages than risk losing the ship to some other danger on the voyage."

David ben Samuel said, "You fight these Arabs?" I nodded. "You are their leader! Why?"

"Because I am the leader." He shook his head in disbelief.

We were rapidly approaching and the Arabs had seen us. There was little that they could do about it for they were bound and tethered to the sinking drekar. I drew my sword and used the backstay to pull me up onto the sheerstrake.

Haaken laughed as he joined me, "This will make Odin laugh. Two old men with more white in their beards and hair than a mountain in Norway are going to leap across a sea and fight men with skin blacker than the night! This will be another song, jarl!"

"Then I hope I am here to hear it!" I said wryly.

Erik shouted, "Take in the sail! We come about!"

We all knew there would be a collision. Erik was using our side to absorb the blow. We had left the shields on the sheerstrake and if there was damage to us then the shields would take it. We could make new shields; a damaged drekar was harder to repair! Despite my age, my balance was still as good as it had ever been. As we collided I heard the crunch and crack as the dhow's hull was damaged. I went with the motion. Arrows flew from our yard and deck as the ship's boys sent arrows to clear the dhow's decks. There had been six men there. As Haaken and I jumped down there were none left alive.

I landed on something soft. I saw that it was a robe-covered Arab. He must have been the captain for the rest of the dead were dark skinned and half-naked. They had obligingly left the ropes they had used to scale the sides of the drekar. I sheathed my sword for I would need two hands to pull on the rope. The drekar was lower in the water now but the dhow was sinking. As I climbed I shouted, "Erik, pull us closer!" As I walked up the side of the drekar two ropes with hooks flew over us and secured the stern of the drekar. The dhow was crushed into splintered wood as Erik and his son pulled the two Norse ships together.

I was almost decapitated as I swung my leg over the gunwale. A half-naked warrior with gleaming black skin swung his curved sword towards my head. Suddenly a goose-fletched arrow appeared in his head and he fell back. As I drew my sword and glanced back I saw Sámr nocking another arrow. My great-grandson had saved my life. *Wyrd*. The press of warriors at the steering board was being attacked on all sides by a motley crew of warriors. Some wore leather mail while others were half-naked. Some had dark skin and some had skin the colour of David.

The Vikings could see little of us and we could see nothing of them. There were too many between us. I shouted, loudly and in Norse, "Clan of the Wolf! May the Allfather be with us!"

It was to rally my men and give the Vikings hope. If they knew that brothers in arms were close they could fight their way to us. As I brought my sword down to split open the back of the nearest warrior I drew Wolf's Blood. I lunged into the side of the warrior next to me. Our attack had taken them by surprise. They had thought their rear was safe. Even as they turned to face us I brought Ragnar's Spirit into the neck of the Moor who turned to face the new threat. As sticky warm blood gushed over my hand I felt Haaken One Eye join me to my right and Knut Snorrisson join me to my left. The three of us began to carve our way to the beleaguered crew at the steering board.

"Jarl! Hurry! The ship is sinking!"

I now knew who the attackers were. I was aware of water around the dead at my feet. Our sudden attack had killed more than ten of the men of the Caliphate of Córdoba. The pressure on those at the steering board had lessened. I could now see helmets. A Norse voice shouted, "Wedge! Let us join our friends! Clan of the Bear we fight for Jarl Beorn Beornsson!"

This was where we had to be strong for the crews of the dhow would try to escape the attack from the steering board. The bearded warrior who turned to face me wore a helmet and had a small round shield. His sword was straight and not curved. He wore leather armour studded with metal. He held his shield tightly to him. I swung Ragnar's Spirit from on high and he had to block it with his sword. Still holding Wolf's Blood, I grabbed the edge of the shield and pulled. It took him unawares and, as the sinking ship shifted, he lurched. Wolf's Blood darted forward and took him in the throat.

From our drekar came a cry from Sámr, "Jarl, the mast is going!"

The fore and back stays of the drekar had been severed and the hull damaged so much that the mast, yard and sail suddenly fell. It could have been the end of *'Heart of the Dragon'* if it had fallen towards my ship but the Norns spun complicated webs and it fell on to the two dhows on the other side of the stricken drekar. The yard and the top half of the mast broke free. One dhow lost its own mast and sail. I took advantage of the distraction of the cracking mast to sweep my sword in an arc. Two men were gutted by the edge of my sharp blade.

"Jarl, you must come back now." I heard Erik Short Toe's frantic plea.

The water was around my ankles. The attackers were fleeing and jumping into the remaining dhows. I saw as they parted, that there were just four men left at the steering board. One was wounded. "Back to my ship!"

We waded through body-littered water. The debris and wreckage were as dangerous as a sword. My ship's boys had thrown ropes and we hauled ourselves up. I looked to the bow and saw that Olaf had led my men there to safety. Even as we watched the three undamaged dhows headed east. There were men in the water. A few hands waved and then they sank beneath the waves. The dhow struck by the mast was also sinking. I looked to see if I had lost any men. They appeared to be aboard but some sported wounds.

I wondered why Erik did not order the sail to be raised when he shouted. "Lars and Sámr, go into the water. I would have that yard. The Allfather has sent it to us."

Sámr and Lars stripped off and dived into the water. The yard was still attached to the mast but the sinking dhow held it. I watched, with some trepidation as they cut the yard free and then began to haul it back to our ship. Arne Eriksson shouted, "Hurry! Sharks!" Attracted by the blood and the bodies, the fins of four sharks raced towards the debris. Siggi dived into the water to help the others. With eager hands, we plucked the three of them and the yard from the sea. Thwarted the sharks ignored the living and feasted upon the dead!

I smiled at Sámr, "Do not tell your mother what we just asked you to do or we shall never be able to take you to sea again." Aiden was tending the wounded warrior. "How is he?"

Aiden nodded, "He will live. I have to put in a few stitches. We cannot risk fire but the salt water will have kept it clean."

The wounded warrior raised his good arm, his left one, "I am Sven Stormbringer. My brother, Beorn, was the captain of our ship. He is in Valhalla now."

"Of that, I have no doubt."

"From your war cry, you are the Clan of the Wolf. Do you know Jarl Dragonheart?"

Haaken One Eye put his arm around my shoulders, "This is he and I am Haaken One Eye."

Sven said, "These are: Olaf Ulfsson, Sigiberht the Scar, Pridbjørn Ellesefsson, Leif Longshanks, Galmr Greybeard and Haldi Haldisson. This is *wyrd*. We had been raiding Wessex and sailed to the Land of the Horse. We met Jarl Hrolf the Horseman at his citadel, the Haugr. We raided with him and we heard of your exploits. We had known that there was a great warrior who lived south of the Picts and north of Mercia; we heard of his sword and we heard your name. We thought them legends. My brother believed they were stories told by a warrior who wished a name for himself."

I saw Olaf Leather Neck bristle with indignation, "Peace, Olaf, it is understandable."

The one called Leif Long Shanks took up the story, "We mean no offence. Sven Stormbringer is right, mighty one. Once we heard of your exploits we wanted to join you. Jarl Hrolf said that you had withdrawn into your home. You would not be raiding as much. He said the raid on Lundenwic had soured your appetite for battles."

I nodded, "Aye for we fought with Danes and they are a treacherous people."

Six of them nodded. Pridbjørn Ellesefsson cleaned his dagger on his kyrtle. He did not appear to agree with that statement.

"That I can understand. The jarl told us of your voyage to Miklagård and how you came back rich. We decided that we would venture there. We sailed too close to the coast and those Arabs and Moors sallied forth to attack us. We rammed one and sank it but they were like fleas on a dog. We slew many but they overwhelmed us. Had you not come then we would have all died and we would have been shark bait!"

"You are all welcome to join us for we go to Miklagård. If you wish me to put you ashore we can do so but it will be in Córdoba."

Most of them shook their heads. "No lord, we would not risk that land. We will sail with you." Sven, who was obviously the leader said, "We are the last six members of the Clan of the Bear. I speak for the others when I say we would join your crew if you would have us. We would swear an oath."

I looked at the seven of them, "Which one is not of the Clan of the Bear?"

As I had expected it was the sour-faced Pridbjørn Ellesefsson who raised his hand. "I was with six shield brothers. Our jarl was killed in the north of the land of the Angles. We had lost many brothers in the battle and in the journey to find a ship, Jarl Beorn took us on. I am the last. If you do not mind, Jarl Dragonheart, I will not swear an oath. I will row for you and I will fight for you but I cannot swear another oath until I have wreaked revenge on the man who slew my mother." He smiled, "You understand such an oath do you not?"

"I do. I will honour your wishes. It will be a long voyage. Choose your own oar brothers and put your goods where you will row." I pointed to the two chests of David ben Samuel. "You can use two of those if you wish and there is another spare with the war gear of the ship's boys." I looked at the pennant. "It seems to me that we will all be rowing sooner, rather than later."

Aiden said, "Sven Stormbringer will not be rowing for at least a moon."

The rescued man said, "Then I will stand a watch at the steering board. I am a navigator!"

"Good, then it is *wyrd* for we only have Erik and his son. This will make life easier for all." Even as I said it I could almost hear the webs being spun.

While they moved the chests Olaf Leather Neck came over, "That Pridbjørn Ellesefsson seems a little ungrateful!"

"We have both had oaths to keep. I understand him. Besides the alternative is to find a deserted place and land him. At least this way we have another sword should we be attacked!"

Aiden explained to David why we needed the chests. He nodded, "They will not need to try to open the chests, will they?"

Aiden shook his head, "Until they get some gear of their own they have nothing to place in the chests." He looked at the two chests. "Besides they are locked are they not?"

David ben Samuel smiled. "And the keys are around my neck. They can use the chests. I will have more room to sleep."

The rescued men had just eaten and drunk some of the ale we had taken from the village in Vasconia when Erik shouted, "Man the oars. The wind is shifting."

It seemed to me that the Allfather had stopped the wind from helping us just so that our new men could row with us. Haaken chose a chant to start the rowing which would help to do just that. We had passed Syllingar and the witch was far away. It was the song of Ylva and her rescue.

The Dragonheart sailed with warriors brave
To find the child he was meant to save

With Haaken and Ragnar's Spirit
They dared to delve with true warrior's grit
With Aðils Shape Shifter with scout skills honed
They found the island close by the rocky stones
The Jarl and Haaken will bravely roar
The Jarl and Haaken and the Ulfheonar
Beneath the earth the two they went
With the sword by Odin sent
In the dark the witch grew strong
Even though her deeds were wrong
A dragon's form she took to kill
Dragonheart faced her still
He drew the sword touched by the god
Made by Odin and staunched in blood
The Jarl and Haaken will bravely roar
The Jarl and Haaken and the Ulfheonar
With a mighty blow, he struck the beast
On Dragonheart's flesh he would not feast
The blade struck true and the witch she fled
Ylva lay as though she were dead
The witch's power could not match the blade
The Ulfheonar are not afraid
The Jarl and Haaken will bravely roar
The Jarl and Haaken and the Ulfheonar
And now the sword will strike once more
Using all the Allfather's power
Fear the wrath you Danish lost
You fight the wolf and pay the cost
The Jarl and Haaken will bravely roar
The Jarl and Haaken and the Ulfheonar

    I watched the new men listen to the words and smile. Haaken sang it four times but that was not enough for the new men to learn all of the words. They all sang the chorus. It was a start. When the command was given for one of each pair to stop rowing then they stopped singing too.
    With the wind against us, we could not row through the night and these waters were unfamiliar to all of the navigators. Only Erik had sailed them and that had been many years ago. We hove

to and dropped two sea anchors. We kept just a deck watch of two men. Aiden decided that as there were no chests at the prow he could share the awning with David. That allowed Sámr to join me at the steering board. Before we slept he went over the battle and the rescue of the yard. "Haaken says he will put that in a saga!"

I laughed, "Do not forget he still has to compose the tale of Sámr and Ulla War Cry. Do not be so greedy for fame. It will come."

He pulled his cloak a little tighter and mumbled, "By the time you were my age you had already slain a wolf and achieved fame."

"Do not be envious, Sámr, the Norns have influenced my life too much. I often wonder what might have happened had I not become the Dragonheart." I was not speaking that which was untrue. I often wondered about the life I might have led as just a warrior. Would I have even become a jarl? I doubted it. When the Norns had plucked me from that river they had ensured that my life would never be normal.

Over the next three days, we used to sail but the journey was interminable. The winds were not strong and they shifted. We could have used oars but that would have exhausted the men. With just over forty-five days left we had to conserve the strength of our rowers. The fact that we had six new ones pleased me. We could rest rowers more frequently. The coast of Córdoba was inhospitable. It was green enough and there were rivers but there were also galleys and citadels. We heeded the warning of the Clan of the Bears and stood well out to sea. When we passed through the patch of water David and Aiden called the Pillars of Hercules, we would have no choice. We would be close to our enemies on both sides. Córdoba and Africa!

Erik had decided to ration our water. We might not be able to find a river until we were in the Blue Sea. This is where David ben Samuel, our passenger, became invaluable. He knew the land and he knew the sea. He could now speak our language much better than he had and Aiden was convinced that he was more important than a merchant.

One night as we bobbed at anchor, Aiden, Erik and I sat with him and a chart. We had risked a candle to illuminate it. "Avoid

Africa. On both sides of the straits, the land is controlled by the Caliphate. I would head north. There are islands close to Frankia and there is Sicily. The Moors and the Empire fight over Sicily. It is possible to land there."

Aiden stared at the chart, "We would have many days sailing across the Blue Sea and we would have nowhere to land."

"Then you need to take what you can before you cross the sea."

I looked at him, "Then you are saying we raid the Caliphate."

His eyes were a door into his mind. He was telling the truth, "I would. On the other side of the straits, their vigilance is more relaxed. If you can get through the straits unharmed then there are rivers just north of the straits and there are villages." He smiled, "I confess I would like more mutton but I speak the truth."

I believed him. "Then we must row through the straits. Can we do so at night?"

"I would not recommend it. Try dawn. The Arabs and the Moors like to pray. When you hear their Mullahs calling them to prayers then that is a good time to risk the straits."

The new men fitted in well. The exception appeared to be Pridbjørn Ellesefsson. Even those from the Clan of the Bear appeared to find it hard to get on with him. It upset my crew. I spoke to Olaf and Haaken when they complained about him. "We cannot like every warrior. Perhaps we have been lucky and the Allfather has sent us warriors whom we get on with. Let us regard this as a test from the gods." I knew I had not convinced them but they did not argue. I suspect it was my illness. They were walking around me as though I was surrounded by cracked eggs. It was only Aiden and Haaken who ignored my ailment.

The weather and the air began to change after we had fought the dhows. The air became heavier and the weather warmer. The sea to the west was still grey and white flecked but, inshore it looked calmer. It would soon become too warm for wolf cloaks and seal skins. Aiden was already preparing potions and salves. We had sailed these waters and we knew the effects of the hot sun and the wind which came from Africa.

The day before we risked the straits we stood at the steering board. The rest of the crew were asleep. I spoke to Haaken and

Aiden. "I do not wish to be treated as something different. I am still the Dragonheart. I do not want the crew to view me as a walking corpse!"

Haaken laughed, quietly, "Then you are a fool, Dragonheart. Men think that because of the sword you are immortal." He held up his hand. "We know that is not true but these warriors believe that they are stronger because you cannot die. Why do you think that so many men offered to come? It was because the clan cannot afford for you to die. You are, truly, the heart of the clan."

Aiden nodded, "The blow hard is right. You can do nothing about this. Ignore it if you can and if not then pretend to ignore it. Our voyage will be hard. They will need you and your skill before the journey is over."

Even when Sven Stormbringer took over the watch I still stared east. When I first found the blood, I should have ridden off and found someone to fight. I would have died with a sword in my hand and saved my people all of this distress. I had lived long enough.

The crew were ready for the straits. The wind was with us in as much as it was not coming directly from the east but they would need to row. Erik enlisted the help of the ship's boys as well. We needed as much speed as we could. We had anchored off the small settlement David told us was called Tarifa. It was a fishing port and had no wall. Further to the north lay Algeciras. That had a wall. There would be galleys and dhows there. We knew we had to sail to the south of it. We would have a hard row to get through the fifteen or so miles until we hit open water. Then we could turn north and seek liquid gold, and water. Every oar was manned as we waited for dawn. Erik had decided that we could not risk waiting for a call we might or might not hear. We would rush through at dawn.

As soon as we saw the first thin sliver of light Erik shouted, "Now Haaken!"

Haaken had chosen his chant well. It was a chant of the clan's darkest hour when we had almost succumbed to the Skulltaker. We had fought back and we had won.

The Danes they came in dark of night

Viking Shadow

They slew Harland without a fight
Babies children all were slain
Mothers and daughters split in twain
Viking enemy, taking heads
Viking warriors fighting back
Viking enemy, taking heads
Viking warriors fighting back
Across the land the Ulfheonar trekked
Finding a land by Danes' hands wrecked
Ready to die to kill this Dane
Dragonheart was Eggles' bane
Viking enemy, taking heads
Viking warriors fighting back
Viking enemy, taking heads
Viking warriors fighting back
With boys as men the ships were fired
Warriors had these heroes sired
Then Ulfheonar fought their foe
Slaying all in the drekar's glow
Viking enemy, taking heads
Viking warriors fighting back
Viking enemy, taking heads
Viking warriors fighting back
When the Danes broke their leader fled
Leaving his army lying dead
He sailed away to hide and plot
Dragonheart's fury was red hot
Viking enemy, taking heads
Viking warriors fighting back
Viking enemy, taking heads
Viking warriors fighting back
Then sailed the men of Cyninges-tūn
Sailing from the setting sun
They caught the Skull upon the sea
Beneath the church of Hwitebi
Viking enemy, taking heads
Viking warriors fighting back
Viking enemy, taking heads
Viking warriors fighting back

Viking Shadow

Heroes all they fought the Dane
But Finni the Dreamer, he was slain
Then full of fury their blood it boiled
Through blood and bodies, the warriors toiled
With one swift blow the Skull was killed
With bodies and ships the Esk was filled
Viking enemy, taking heads
Viking warriors fighting back
Viking enemy, taking heads
Viking warriors fighting back

When we passed the port we saw that the harbour at the citadel was filled with ships. There were dhows, galleys and merchant men but we were so swift that none stirred. I had no doubt that the sight of a dragon ship would upset them.

Sven Stormbringer shook his head, "Our raid would have ended here. We would have sailed through at full daylight and just used sails. When my brother and our oar brothers died, it was *wyrd*."

Chapter 5

We were down to the dregs in the water barrels. We had rationed but, now that we were through the straits, then we needed to raid and find water. Unless we wished to risk the African coast, it would have to be in the Caliphate. We were in the hands of David ben Samuel. Almost as soon as we were through the straits we noticed a difference both in the water and in the heat. That first day in the Blue Sea, as we headed north to find a river, we felt the effects of the hot sun. Erik had his boys soaking the decks with sea water to prevent them from drying out too much. We passed an island with a small port but there appeared to be no river. We were not concerned about raiding. We needed water. The men were tiring for it was almost noon and they had rowed, in shifts, since dawn. Once we had the water then we could take advantage of the wind which blew from the north and the west.

Ten miles or so north of the island we had passed Siggi spotted the river and the white mud houses which huddled on one bank. "Captain, I see a river. It is two miles off the larboard bow! There is no wall and no tower!"

Beggars could not be choosers. Even if this was a small beck we would have to use it. The men were exhausted. Erik put the steering board over. David stood with Aiden and me. He stared at the straining rowers and asked, "How are these men able to row so long? In the Empire, they use slaves and few last more than a handful of voyages. I did it briefly and look at my hands." His hands were red and raw from the oars

"We are trained to row from an early age. Sámr, my great grandson will probably end up taking an oar before we return home." I turned over my palms. "These have not rowed for some years but feel the skin. It is like leather."

He touched my palms and almost recoiled. "Now I see why you are feared. Even in Caesarea, we have heard of you."

I nodded, "And one day Vikings will come here to raid. It will not be one ship such as I brought, it will be fifty or sixty ships. They will not be crewed by a handful of men as mine is. They will have fifty or sixty men."

David shook his head, "That is a terrible threat and yet, on the voyage thus far, I have met with nothing but kindness."

Aiden smiled, "That is the Viking for you. They make wonderful friends but are the fiercest of enemies."

"You are not Viking?"

"Not by birth. I was taken by the Dragonheart from Hibernia as a child. I have become a Viking in my heart."

"You do not resent being taken?"

Aiden laughed, "It was the best thing that ever happened to me!"

As we had seen in Vasconia the sight of a dragon ship inspired terror. When we neared the handful of huts and tiny fishing ships we saw the people fleeing. They drove animals up the river. There were trees there. We had seen few such stands of trees since we had picked up Sven and his men. If we still needed it we could have hewn timber for the yard. Arne Eriksson hurried back from the prow. "The river is not wide enough for us to sail up it. There is neither quay nor jetty."

Erik nodded glumly, "Then this will take time!" He looked meaningfully at me. We would have to prepare for war. The men were not ready for a hard fight. This was the Norns' web at work.

I turned to Aiden, "I need you, David ben Samuel and Sven Stormbringer to search the village. Sven's men will need clothes. I know these are not what they are used to but they will be better than what they have. Find food and bring any animals."

Aiden nodded, "You fear trouble?"

"Aye."

David said, "But this is a small place. What danger can lie here?"

On our journey from the straits, we had seen at least three citadels. We had only travelled twenty miles since Tarifa. "We are Vikings. We prepare for danger and if it does not come we have lost nothing." I walked towards the seated rowers who were still pulling at the oars. "We are going to land but I fear that you will have no rest. We will have to bring the water to the drekar. We cannot sail up the river. There may be danger. Bring your shields and your swords when we land. If no danger comes then we will have a pleasant afternoon lying on this white sand."

Galmr Hrolfsson shouted, "And that is unlikely to happen."

Siggi Long Face, his oar brother, nodded, "A fight would suit me. I have sat on my arse too long as it is."

They all seemed happy about the prospect of a fight. I hoped it would not come to that. We had been lucky so far and not lost a man but we had barely begun our journey. We had been sailing for less than fifteen days. We still had forty-five days to go and the Blue Sea was a wide and dangerous stretch of water.

There was less movement in the water here in the Blue Sea. Compared with home they barely had tides. Erik laid us parallel to the beach. While the larboard oars kept us steady the steerboard rowers jumped ashore with the ship's boys and pulled the drekar so that she was as close to the beach as possible. When we landed we would have to wade to the beach but our ship could easily pull away when we needed to.

I took my sword and went ashore first with Olaf Leather Neck, Ráðgeir Ráðgeirson, David ben Samuel, Aiden and Sven Stormbringer. Olaf and Ráðgeir Ráðgeirson both had their shields. I did not. The soft sand sucked at our feet as we headed up to the huts. Leaving Aiden and his two assistants to search the huts we went up the slope. Below us, I saw Haaken organising the rowers while Erik had his ship's boys fetching water from upstream. It would take the whole of the afternoon to fill the barrels.

We could see the villagers disappearing into the trees. It was now obvious that there was a road of some description heading inland. Olaf Leather Neck swung his shield around his back. "They are going to a place of safety. That means a wall."

I nodded, "And a wall means warriors. This is a good place to watch. You two stay here. I will have food sent to you."

He nodded and then added glumly, "And these follow the religion that forbids ale! It will be water!"

I laughed, "I fear we will not find ale again for four moons."

Ráðgeir Ráðgeirson was an optimistic warrior. He was more like Haaken than the dour Olaf, "And think how much sweeter it will taste after that time without it! It is almost worth the wait!"

Olaf's snort was eloquent!

I walked back to the beach. No one was slacking despite the exhaustion which was apparent on all of their faces. The ship's boys were all stripped to the waist as they filled the barrels from the human chain of warriors. The weapons and shields lay close to hand. We had hung the horn from a spear planted in the ground. If danger came we could sound it quickly.

Erik shouted down, "They are working hard, Jarl Dragonheart, but this will take time. Are we in danger?"

"Olaf Leather Neck and Ráðgeir Ráðgeirson watch from the west. Let us hope that the men of these parts are cautious." I looked north. We had seen nothing south of us and when we had pulled into the beach I had seen nothing north of us but there was another bay. It was hidden from us by the headland. "Lars Long Nose and Siggi Eainarson, take your weapons and walk to the next bay. I would know if there are enemies there."

Grateful to be relieved of the task of passing pails they took their weapons, and shields and headed north along the beach. I went to the huts to see what my men had found. I saw that Sven Stormbringer had slaughtered an old goat. It had, from the look of one leg, been lame and the villagers had left it. He was butchering it. He grinned as I passed, "Our passenger will enjoy this no matter how tough it is!"

In another hut, David and Aiden had found some pots which would be useful. There was also a quantity of food. I did not recognise it but David did. He said, "This is good food. The rice will need cooking and the Bulgur wheat too but they are both nutritious."

I had tasted the two cereals when in Miklagård but I knew that my men would find it a strange taste. They also found lemons, oranges and pomegranates. These would not last long for I knew that they were delicious. The sack of dried figs and the larger one of dates would last a long time and we would ration those. I left the two of them and returned to the beach. As I passed Sven I saw that he had put the goat on to cook and was drying the skin. We would not fully cook the goat but as with the Vasconian sheep, we would take the pot on board.

Erik shouted as I neared him, "We are halfway there!"

There was no sign of Lars and Siggi. Olaf Leather Neck would shout if there was danger from that quarter. David and Aiden brought down their supplies. It took a few trips for they had found, in what must have been the headman's hut, a chest buried in the floor. It contained dinars! It was probably their tax money. It was not a fortune but would be added to that which we had already collected. The last things they brought down were the clothes for the Clan of the Bear. I smiled for they would be unhappy to be wearing the flowing robes. It would make them look like Arabs. Then I saw an advantage in the disguise for we could use it if we had to enter a town.

We had almost finished when Lars Long Nose came racing down the beach! "Riders! Riders!"

I ran for the horn and sounded it. Everyone recognised the danger. The boys grabbed their bows as the men with the pails raced to the drekar. Aiden and David ran back to help Sven with the pot. I saw that Lars was less than four hundred paces from us but, just two hundred paces behind him was a line of horsemen. They would catch him. I could not allow him to die alone.

"Sámr, to me, warriors follow me." I ran towards Lars. The fact that I could not see Siggi meant he was in Valhalla. We had lost our first man. Sámr easily caught up with me. With my sword and dagger in my hand, I shouted, "When you are in range then kill the leading horsemen. Do not risk yourself. Keep falling back to the drekar. Your task is to slow them."

"Aye Jarl." He stopped.

I continued to run and Galmr joined me. He had a shield and a spear. The leading horseman also had a spear and he was less than twenty paces behind Lars. He leaned forward in readiness to skewer my warrior. I heard the twang of the bow and the hiss of the arrow. Sámr's arrow hit the horse and the rider flew over the head of the dying beast. He did not rise. A second arrow followed so quickly that it surprised even me. This time it plucked a rider from his saddle. The rest slowed and pulled up their shields. Lars reached me and turned. I was now flanked by Galmr and Lars. Others arrived and we made a shield wall. I was the only one without a shield.

Sámr's arrows continued to fall but the mounted, robed warriors used their shields for protection. He only struck the flesh of one of them. He changed target to the horses. We prepared for the shock of the charge. They were all armed with long spears and they rammed them at us. The rest of my men blocked them with their shields. I had none. I fended away the spear head as it came towards me. It nicked my arm. Stepping forward, as the rider withdrew his spear for a second strike, I rammed my sword into the throat of the horse. The blood spurted and the other horses became agitated. I stepped back.

"Walk backwards!"

Even as we began to walk I heard the horn. We had recovered our men. Another rider charged at me and this time it was Sámr's arrow which did the damage. His arrow struck the horse in its head and it catapulted the rider from its dying back. I heard a shout from my right as one of the enemy spears found flesh. Galmr then fended off the strike from the horseman with the mail vest and rammed his own spear into the warrior's leg. He twisted as he pulled it out. The horseman screamed and wheeled his horse away. The movement broke up the press of men and we managed twenty paces closer to our ship. There had been more than forty horsemen. There were still more than twenty-five who were horsed and unwounded. I would have risked glancing over my shoulder to see how close we were but I knew that such a glance could be fatal.

Olaf Leather Neck's voice carried to me, "Two hundred paces Jarl. Bring them a little closer and we will send a shower of arrows!"

Aiden shouted, "Sámr is safe. He is with us!" Aiden could read my thoughts, even in a battle!

I shouted, "On my command, step forward and aim a blow at a horseman and then take ten steps back! Keep in line!"

"Aye jarl!"

"Now!"

The horsemen had grown bold and we all stepped as one. The shields of the others blocked the Córdoban spears. I used Wolf's Blood again to block the blow but this time the spear sliced into my cheek. I tasted salty blood as I swung my sword at the head of the rider's horse. It reared, turned and bucked. The rider was dumped at my feet. I lunged down with Wolf's Blood and sliced across his throat. I stepped back. I was the slowest of my men and it almost cost me my life. The Córdobans came for me.

I heard Olaf Leather Neck shout, "Release!" and ten arrows descended. Four men were struck. Two had mail but the other two did not. Four horses were hit and they careered off. The horsemen halted. Had we wished we might have been able to charge them and make it a true victory. That was too risky and so we marched back to our drekar. We climbed aboard.

As soon as Aiden saw my face and hand he grabbed his satchel. "Those wounds need tending!"

I looked at my kyrtle. It was covered in blood. We pulled away from the beach. The sun was lower in the sky. We had survived but we had been lucky. "Haaken, did we lose any men?"

"Just Siggi and yours is the most serious wound."

Lars came over, "It was my fault Jarl. There was a hut and while Siggi went ahead I investigated. I heard him shout and when I came out I saw him being speared by those Córdoban horsemen. I would have gone to his aid…"

"But it would have been too late and you thought of the clan. This is the Norns' doing. Lars. Had you not gone into the hut then you would have both been surprised and killed. The horsemen would have been upon us and who knows what might have happened. Everything has a purpose. We will honour Siggi."

We gave Sven and his men the robes. Surprisingly the normally dour, not to say unpleasant, Pridbjørn Ellesefsson seemed delighted that he had the change of clothes. Like the others, he immediately took off his dirty, sweat and blood-stained clothes and donned the clean ones. Sven shook his head, "It is a pity we could not have taken the mail from those Moors. I would feel less naked amongst you."

Haaken One Eye shook his head, "I am sorry, Sven, we just thought to save or lives but next time we will strip the bodies for you."

Everyone, including Sven, laughed. We had filled almost all of the barrels. We had food and we had reached the Blue Sea. It was good. With the wind behind, we did not need to row and with three watchkeepers, we could sail all night. David, Aiden and Erik all agreed that the next landfall would be the islands off the coast of Italy and that would take twelve days. So long as the wind held then we had nothing to fear and we would have little to do. My face ached from the stitches Aiden had put in but that too actually helped. The fresh pain took away the gnawing ache in my guts.

Olaf Ulfsson, one of the Bears asked, "Will we land in Italy?"

David ben Samuel answered. He had grown in confidence during the voyage and his Norse was as good as any foreigner I had known. "If we reach the island of Sicily or Italy itself then that will be the land of the Empire. We will be safe." He looked at me, "However, there will be suspicion. Some of the Rus Vikings have raided the Holy City of Constantinopolis. They will be wary. I beg you to allow me to speak when we meet Imperial officials or soldiers."

Aiden nodded, "I have spoken with Erik Short Toe and done the calculations. We have enough water for twelve days. That is how long this voyage to Italy will last. We cannot afford to raid the Empire. Unless we go to Africa then we have made our last raid on this voyage. We will have to visit a port and buy what we need."

Everyone nodded. Pridbjørn Ellesefsson asked, "Then I could go ashore there in safety?"

David said, "Aye."

Aiden had a questioning mind, "I thought you had an oath to fulfil. Is there not a man you have to kill? I assumed he was in Miklagård."

Pridbjørn Ellesefsson gave a thin smile, "I did not say where he was. Let us say that Italy will afford me a better opportunity of fulfilling my oath than Miklagård." Enigmatically that was all he said. I saw Sven Stormbringer frown. I caught his eye and he shrugged. The Clan of the Bear had not been as rigorous in their crew selection as we were.

With little to occupy me, save an increasing worry that my illness was worsening, I spent a great deal of time with David and Aiden studying the map. I had begun to realise that if we sent a couple of knarr and drekar that we could trade in these waters. We had seen little so far that would threaten us. We now knew the problems. On the next voyage, we would take more water barrels. The Blue Sea teemed with fish. We scattered a couple of fishing fleets not long after leaving the coast of Córdoba and caught the fish they had been seeking. They were different fish from the ones we normally ate but the men enjoyed them.

I found that if I ate less then the bleeding was not as bad. It was getting hotter and it was not hard to limit my intake of food. Aiden had told me that the condition would worsen. He had warned me that the potion would lose its efficacy and he was correct. David thought that it would take us just over a moon to reach Miklagård. The time we had lost we had made up with the wind which sped us across the Blue Sea. I found it was better when I had something to occupy my mind and so I sat with David and Aiden.

"Once we have passed Italy then the voyage has fewer human dangers but more natural ones." David pointed to the map.

"Natural ones?"

There are many natural obstacles we have to face. "We have to pass through the Greek Islands. There are thousands of them. The alternative is to sail further south and that risks taking us closer to Africa. We have been lucky so far but the Moors of Africa would like nothing better than to take this drekar. You Vikings would make perfect galley slaves."

I shook my head, "Then you do not know Vikings. You cannot make a slave of a corpse!"

"You would die rather than be a slave?"

"You saw how hard Sven and his men fought. They would have died with their swords in their hands and gone to Valhalla."

"You are a curious clan!"

To take advantage of the wind from the north and west we sailed with Africa just below the horizon to the south of us. Occasionally the lookout would see it a little more clearly and Erik would adjust the steering board to take us further north. It was a fine line we sailed between success and disaster.

We rationed all the food and water. No-one seemed to mind. The men occupied themselves making objects. David ben Samuel, our passenger, appeared almost bemused at the way the mighty warriors he had seen slaying the Moors with such ferocity could carve such intricate combs, love tokens and pins from bones. The goat had provided a much-needed supply. The skin had been cured and given to Sámr. His arrows had saved the clan. The hooves had been retained. When we could light a fire, we would melt them and make a glue and sealant. We wasted nothing. The two horns were made into drinking vessels. Sven kept one and gave the other to Leif. Warriors liked their own ale horn. Even though we were down to water they would still want their own. Siggi's had been given to Galmr. His spare clothes had gone to Haldi Haldisson.

It had been five days since we had left the coast. The wind had veered slightly. Erik rubbed his chin and summoned Aiden and David. He needed David's local knowledge. "The wind is more from the north than the west. Is that a problem?"

"It could be. It will take us closer to the African coast. Here there are many warlords and pirates. I am no sailor but I would suggest caution. It may add time to our voyage but if we head further north and east it will be safer." He rubbed his chin. "Melita was part of the Empire but now it is part of the Caliphate. The Abbasid Turks have a fleet there. They have also invaded Sicily. I have been away too long and I know not how much of the island they will have taken but I do know that it will not be a safe place to land. Italy would be a better landing place." He nodded as though he had just thought something through. "Yes, Captain, my advice would be to sail north and east. It will be slower and may add a day to the journey but it should be safer."

That meant another day of pain for me and a day closer to my death. I said nothing. Aiden looked at me, searchingly. "That may harm the Jarl. Let me look at the map."

He took the chart. I said, "Aiden, I am one man. It is not worth risking the crew just for me. Have you dreamed my death?"

"Since we passed through the straits I have not dreamed. In fact, I feel I am losing my powers. It may be that my strength comes from the Land of the Wolf. That would make sense. The caves of Myrddyn are where I see most clearly into the world of the Spirits."

"Dreamed?"

Aiden smiled, "Yes, David ben Samuel, I dream the future."

I saw the scepticism on his face. "It is true, David ben Samuel. I can swear to it."

Aiden studied the map for a long time. Eventually, he shook his head. "I can see no other course. Erik, you need to get all the speed you can from **'Heart of the Dragon'**. I believe that Jarl Dragonheart's life depends upon it."

His words set a sombre mood. It seemed that the winds themselves conspired to harm me. Their power weakened. Olaf Leather Neck was not the most patient of men. He decided to add the power of rowers and the men rowed for part of each day. It was hard to see how much difference it made but I was touched that they did so.

Chapter 6

Perhaps it was the extra speed which took us to the brink of disaster or, maybe it was the Norns. I know not. Storm clouds were heading from the north and the west. They were some way away but they were the sign of a storm. The waters had been benign hitherto. Now we might see the Blue Sea at its worst. By Aiden's reckoning, we were just four days from port when Siggi Arneson shouted, "Sails to the south." Even as Erik looked questioningly at me Arne added, "And sails to the east."

"Could they be Imperial?"

David had taken to spending more time at the steering board than in his shelter. He listened to the conversation and said, "They could be if they were just from the east but the south? That suggests enemies. I would head north if I were you, captain and, Jarl Dragonheart, I would prepare for war."

"Run out the oars. Let us put some sea room between us and this danger." Erik looked at me apologetically. "I am sorry Jarl, but the Norns are making life difficult for us. I fear this will add a day to our voyage."

I nodded, "And I may yet get to die with a sword in my hand. Whatever happens, it is *wyrd*."

I took out Ragnar's Spirit and Wolf's Blood. I had sharpened them after the last fight. The crew had their weapons strapped to them as they rowed us due north.

Tostig hailed us from the top of the mast. "Jarl, I can see the sails. They are lateen sails and they have oars. They are galleys!"

The sails alone confirmed the identity of the ships. They were from Africa. David came over as they closed with us. He had a sword strapped to his side. It came from the dhow we had fought. I was not certain if he knew how to use it. I suspect we would find out soon enough. "If it is of any use to you I can tell you the name of the man who leads the ships who come for us." I nodded. "He is Ahmad ibn Muhammad al-Aghlabi. He is the emir of the Aghlabid people. They are the ones who are trying to take Sicily. It may well be that we are just unfortunate. They may not even be coming for us. Perhaps they are just sailing to reinforce Sicily."

The identity mattered little to me. In a sea fight defeat normally meant death. Sven Stormbringer had been lucky that we had been so close to them when they were attacked. "Either way it makes little difference. They will not allow us to live. This is the Norns at work, David ben Samuel. We can do nothing about it save to fight for our lives."

It was soon obvious that they would catch us. They had slaves, driven by whips and they had ships closing from two directions. It was difficult to see this ending well. We were in the hands of Erik Short Toe who was a great captain. However, he was not a warrior.

I stepped close to him. "The wind is from the north and slightly from the west. Suppose we turned towards those ships to the east of us?"

"Then they would turn to close with us and would be sailing into the wind. They would have to rely purely on oars." I saw a slight smile appear on his face. "And we would have more speed from the wind." He nodded, "It might work, Jarl Dragonheart, but we would need to sail close to them."

"Would you need your ship's boys?"

"I could do without them if the crew was rowing."

"Then we use them as archers. I rely on your skill with the steering board."

"I will need someone at the prow."

I turned to Aiden, "I need you to guide Erik. I intend to sail through the ships to the east of us."

"Bold!"

"Where the Norns are concerned there is no other way!"

"Ship's boys, get your bows and line the steerboard side."

I saw that the four ships to the east were turning to close with us. They thought we had made a mistake. Perhaps we had but I had cast the bones. We would live or die by the result. There were just three galleys to the south of us. They turned too but because they were sailing into the wind they were reliant on their oars. I turned to David. "Will these galleys have warriors as well as rowers?"

"The rowers are slaves. There will be men with swords and helmets. They will fight you. Dragonheart they are fierce warriors."

I laughed, "They have yet to meet Vikings." Turning to Erik I said, "Aim towards the leading ship. Let us see if he is a married man."

Erik laughed, "You would make him turn?"

"He has two galleys in his quarter. Whichever way he turns he might hit one. Either way, we will have passed the other two and we just have to outrun the galleys behind."

I suddenly realised that I had not felt pain for a while. I looked to the prow and saw Aiden smiling. He was reading my thoughts.

They had four ships but there was not one mind directing them. The captain of the leading galley must have thought he had us. I saw the white around their bow. He had increased their speed. They were leaving the others behind them. I saw Aiden wave his arm and Erik put the steerboard over. We were less than a hundred and fifty paces away.

Haaken had started a chant as he saw Erik put the steerboard over. It was the fast one. Even better, it was the song of the Ulfheonar. We leapt like a greyhound.

Ulfheonar, warriors strong
Ulfheonar, warriors brave
Ulfheonar, fierce as the wolf
Ulfheonar, hides in plain sight
Ulfheonar, Dragon Heart's wolves
Ulfheonar, serving the sword
Ulfheonar, Dragon Heart's wolves
Ulfheonar, serving the sword
Ulfheonar, warriors strong
Ulfheonar, warriors brave
Ulfheonar, fierce as the wolf
Ulfheonar, hides in plain sight
Ulfheonar, Dragon Heart's wolves
Ulfheonar, serving the sword
Ulfheonar, Dragon Heart's wolves
Ulfheonar, serving the sword

Our manoeuvre and increased speed had an immediate effect. The captain of the leading ship pushed his tiller to the steerboard side. Erik had quick reactions. He headed to the larboard side of the ship. There was one galley to the south of the ship which had just turned. If we could disable that one we had a chance. It would leave the last galley to stop us. The captains of the galleys all saw the same manoeuvre from us but each took different actions. They did not use signals. Two galleys were closing with each other. I looked to the larboard side and heard the crash as the two galleys collided. The lading one was struck by the second galley. They would take no further part in the battle for they had sheared oars and become entangled. The other ship could not turn to attack us for fear of fouling the other two.

"Ship's boys! Now is your time. Take out the steering board and there is one dinar for each of you!"

A golden dinar was beyond the wildest dreams of all of them but even more valuable would be the knowledge that they had done that which their jarl had asked and saved their drekar! Sámr had the best bow and I saw his arrow arc before the others were in range. He hit a crewman clinging to the backstay. The effect was dramatic. The galley shifted to the south and a gap opened. When the rest of the ship's boys sent their arrows at the steering board then the turn became more obvious for the steersman tried to avoid the deadly arrows. We had not hit the sailor at the tiller but five men lay dead or wounded. When the next flight struck the ship turned savagely south to avoid the hail of arrows.

I looked astern and saw that the three galleys who had been to the south of us were now following in a line astern. I shouted, "Now, Clan of the Wolf, it is a test. Can you row better and faster than three crews of blackamoors?"

Their response was immediate. Haaken and Olaf increased the rate. Aiden came back to the steering board to join us. He was grinning, "That was an attack that they did not expect!"

I watched the leading galley. It was closing. Aiden had tempted the Norns. Their web was complex. Their captain was not going to allow us to escape. He could afford to have his galley slaves die. He would make them row until they dropped. We did not have that luxury. I was not certain if there were more ships over the horizon. We had to disappear and to do so we had to lose the ships behind.

"Haaken slow the rate!"

"We can out-row them Dragonheart!"

"No, we cannot. We row until they close and then we fight them. The other two ships are falling back. Let them close with us." I waved Sámr over. "Sámr can you organise the ship's boys? When they close their men will gather at their prow. They will try to board over our steering board. I would have you slow down their attack with arrows." I held his shoulders in my hands, "I cannot direct you. This will be your decision. The crew depend upon you."

"I will not let you down great grandfather."

As we slowed, imperceptibly, I saw the leading galley close. The other two had almost given up. I could discount them. "David ben Samuel, how many warriors does a galley hold?"

"To speak truly I do not know. It could be anything from thirty to sixty."

"Thank you! That is all I needed to know. The odds are in our favour!"

"You have less than forty men!"

"I know! They do not know the trouble that is coming their way!"

Haaken was close to us and he shouted, "Slow down the beat. The jarl wishes them to catch us."

I turned and saw that the eager Arab was desperate to catch us. He had seen us outwit three of his companions. He was driving his men hard and I knew that he sought the glory. I had met captains like him before. The others had given up the chase. The four we had confused were dots on the horizon and the other two were turning to rest their rowers and to take advantage of the wind which had changed direction.

"One in two leave the oars and arm yourselves." I turned to David ben Samuel, "It will be hot here. There will be much fighting and blood. I would go to the bows. It will be safer."

"I can fight."

"Not like a Viking. You may be in the way here. Aiden will also be at the bows. If men are hurt then you can tend to them."

Aiden nodded and put his arm around our passenger. "Come. These are warriors and they know what they are doing."

The Arab was now catching us quickly. I wondered how the rowers would be doing. I guessed that many would be dead as a result of the captain's efforts to catch us. Their warriors would be fresh. I saw them at the bow. Aiden told us that they used something they had copied from the Romans. It was called a corvus. It was a bridge which was at their bow. It was not elegant and beautiful like a dragon. It was ugly. There was a spike at the end that would bite into our stern and hold us. The warriors would then run across the bridge. Knowing how they would attack helped.

The rowers we had released took their shields and formed up behind me. The enemy was just four lengths behind us and there was little point in using our oars. "In oars. Clan of the Wolf, we fight."

There was a roar from the men who were behind me. They banged their shields with their swords. I saw Erik's son, Arne, and Sven Stormbringer each take a spear and stand protectively close to Erik. They were in a good position to fend off any attack on our captain. Olaf had his shield across his back and he carried his two-handed axe. The Moors would never have seen the like. The galley now raced close to us. I heard Sámr shout, "Release!"

The four warriors who had the ropes ready to lower the beak to bite into our stern were thrown into the sea. As the bow came even closer I saw men with shields run to protect the next warriors from the arrows. Sámr had done what I asked of him and now he did more. I saw him aim, not at the men on the bow of the Arab but at the helmsman. It was a well-aimed arrow and flew straight and true. It hit him in the chest and threw him from the stern. As he fell his arm jerked over the steering board and the galley lurched. Two of those trying to lower the corvus fell into the sea. A huge warrior stepped forward and hacked at the ropes securing the bridge. It fell with a crash. As it did he was hit by four arrows and he too fell into the sea. We were now bound to the galley. Erik drew his own sword for we were now in the hands of the Allfather. He made the wind and our drekar would follow his course.

Olaf took advantage of the fact that the men who had intended to board us first had fallen into the sea. Their commander was busy trying to have the ship steered once more. Olaf Leather Neck leapt onto the bridge and, swinging his axe before him, ran towards the Moors. It was a move worthy of a berserker and it worked. The Moors had thought they were the hunter and we were the prey. In one move Olaf had reversed the positions. I followed him. It was mad but it was also totally unexpected. We were no longer the victim. We were the attacker. The first two Moors who attempted to face Olaf lost their heads as his axe made a figure of eight swing. He jumped from the bridge and landed amongst the Moors.

Holding my sword and dagger I emulated him. The half-naked Moors were interspersed with Arabs wearing robes and helmets. The helmets would not stop Olaf's axe. Ragnar's Spirit darted forward and struck a warrior in the gut. As I pulled it out I twisted and a mass of wriggling intestines came with it. The front of the galley was narrow and in three blows Olaf Leather Neck and I had made a bridgehead. We waited for our men to follow. Haaken One Eye led the rest of my men aboard. Where Olaf and I had been briefly isolated we were now surrounded by shield brothers. I saw a curved sword rise to strike Olaf on his blind side. The swordsman fell to an arrow. Our ship's boys, under Sámr's direction, were protecting us from dangers we could not see.

The Norns had spun. My plan had been to stop them from taking my ship. Now that had changed. I shouted, "Haldi Haldisson, take your men and release the rowers!" We could increase our strength by letting the rowers get back at their former masters.

"Aye jarl!"

We were tightly pressed together and Wolf's Blood was a deadly weapon in such a battle. Olaf and I were at the fore. Haaken was on my right and Galmr was on Olaf's left. Any flesh before me was a foe. I used my sword to block the enemy weapons as Wolf's Blood sought flesh. The Arab who faced me with a grinning mouth and foul breath suddenly opened his mouth wide as my blade tore into his side. I pulled it savagely towards me and felt hot blood gush. His eyes rolled into his head and he fell dead. As I stepped forward I punched with Ragnar's Spirit. The Arab before me had a helmet but he had not seen the blow coming his way. The guard on my sword took out his eye. Instinctively he lifted his hand and Wolf's Blood ripped across his throat.

There was a roar and feral screams as the rowers were released. They were like an unstoppable tidal wave. Haldi and his men had found a way to get to the rowers' deck. The flood of slaves suddenly erupted behind the men we were fighting. With arrows still striking those at the stern, the Arabs lost their commander. Many of those half-naked men chose the sea rather than the wrath of slaves and blood thirsty Vikings. Those who remained were butchered where they stood.

I saw emaciated slaves hack and chop at bodies long dead. The overseer from the slave deck was literally torn limb from limb by sobbing slaves who had suffered at his hands for so long.

I saw that Olaf Leather Neck had been wounded. That was not a surprise. He had almost gone berserk. He was lucky to be alive at all. "Send for Aiden and David ben Samuel."

I turned, "Ráðgeir Ráðgeirson, take four men and see what we can take from this ship in the way of treasure. Do not take the food or the water. These slaves will need that."

"Aye jarl."

Haaken shook his head, "And we do not?"

"We are not far from Italy and besides," I pointed to the black clouds which were gathering above us, "I think that the Allfather is about to send us a reward in the form of rain."

Haldi Haldisson came towards me. He was blood spattered. He had with him four emaciated men. "Jarl, we have four Norse here. They would come with us."

Just then Aiden and David ben Samuel arrived, "David ben Samuel, speak with the slaves. Tell them that this ship is theirs. Aiden, see to the wounded." They both nodded and I turned to Haldi, "They are more than welcome. The Norns have sent them to us. This is *wyrd*. Get them aboard the *'Heart'*."

I realised that David be Samuel could speak more languages than I had thought. He gave the same message in three different languages. Then he had a long conversation with a slave with skin the same colour as he. Our passenger nodded and they approached me. David said, "This is Yusef. He is of my people. He wishes to thank you for saving him and the others. He told me that eight slaves perished in their chase of us. I have told him your name and he has said that he will spread the word that the Viking with the white hair and beard is a friend."

"Tell him, thank you." He did so. "What will they do?"

After a brief conversation, he said, "There are pirates who are not Moors. They will join with them. Their homes have all been destroyed and their families taken as slaves. They will now prey upon the Arabs."

"And they will die."

David ben Samuel looked at me sadly, "Aye. And I think they know that but at least they will die free men and they will have vengeance on those who mistreated them."

As we went back to our ship I saw the sharks feasting. They had a harvest of corpses. We separated and disentangled our ships. As soon as we did our sail took us north. When it did so the rain began and Erik had the ship's boys grab every container that they could. We had given the sharks their reward and the gods gave us ours.

I saw that the four former slaves had been put under David ben Samuel's awning. Haldi and Leif were giving them food and water. Aiden was mixing a potion. "Is that for me?"

"No, Jarl, yours is already done. This is for these men. They have been mistreated. It will take a moon to make them whole again. This potion will heal the hurts which are within. I have told them that they should not eat too much. It will take time for their stomachs to recover."

I waited until they had drunk the potion given to them by Aiden before I spoke. The rain pattered on the awning. We would be able to collect that precious water too. "What are your stories?"

The eldest of them spoke, "I am Snorri Gunnarson. These are Ulf Galmrson, Sweyn Olafsson and Harald Jorgenson. We are the last of a crew from a knarr. We were trading in Olissipo. We went there in peace. Our ship was taken and we were enslaved."

"When was this?"

He looked up as though trying to remember. "What month is this now, Jarl Dragonheart?"

"It is close to the end of Harpa."

"Then it was half a year ago." He shook his head in disbelief. "It seems longer. We had left the way of the warrior to make a peaceful living. The rest of my crew died and we would avenge them. We would join you, Jarl and become warriors again." He looked at his emaciated body. "If that day ever comes."

"We have a good galdramenn and he will heal you."

The rain, which began as a slight shower, became a veritable deluge. It was as though the Allfather was trying to wash all traces of the Moors away. We managed to fill up the water barrels with the rainwater and every pail we could. We had not taken food from the galley but we had plenty thanks to our one stop in Córdoba. We soaked the Bulgur wheat in water and that made it easier for the former slaves to eat. Their gums had suffered. Aiden said they would heal. The oranges and lemons we had taken would help to cure their hurts but until then they would have to have a diet which was like baby food.

We had taken some of the robes from the Arab ship. The men would not have to be exposed to the sun. With David and Aiden caring for them they improved day by day. Our passenger had proved more than useful. I began to feel guilty about the price his uncle had paid for his passage.

As the last light of the setting sun lit up the western sky I stood with David ben Samuel at the opposite side of the ship to the steering board. Sven Stormbringer was speaking with Arne Eriksson about our course. Sven was healing rapidly and would soon be able to take an oar but there was more to him than a simple oarsman. He was a good navigator.

David's knowledge came to our aid once more. "I think it would be best to head up the coast to Chatacium. It will add a day to our journey but it is a bigger port and we have enough food and water to reach it. More importantly, there is a wall around the city. The Moors are aggressive. They have attacked and conquered part of Sicily. I fear that Italy will be next."

I decided to broach something which had been on my mind for some time, "David ben Samuel, you seem to know a great deal about the Empire."

His face was impassive. "I have one of my homes in Constantinopolis. I keep myself apprised of all that goes on."

"You know far more than a mere merchant would know."

He smiled but it was not with his eyes. He was hiding something, "Let us say I am a very successful merchant because

I keep myself well informed." Before I could ask him more he said, "Your generosity with the galley crew belies your reputation Jarl Dragonheart."

"My own reputation or that of Vikings in general?"

"Vikings."

"It may be because I have no Norse blood in me. I am the result of the union of a Saxon and one who lived in Britannia since before the time of the Romans."

"Yet you lead Vikings."

"This is not like the Empire where it is your father who determines if you lead. I was chosen to be the leader. It is an honour but it is also a burden. Everything I do, I do for the clan. Even if I wished to do other then I would not be able to do so."

"And these new men will become part of your clan?"

"If they choose. The new men have not yet sworn an oath. When we reach Chatacium they may choose, as Pridbjørn Ellesefsson, to stay there. That would not be a problem."

"And this Pridbjørn Ellesefsson, why does he leave? He seems a good fighter. I watched him when you attacked the galley. He fought as well as any."

"He swore an oath to kill someone. I understand that. To a Viking an oath and giving your word are inviolable. A man should never be foresworn. I have taken that oath myself."

"And each time the man died?"

"I am still here and I seek them no longer."

He nodded. "I think that you do not completely trust me, Jarl Dragonheart. I swear on all that is holy to me that I mean you no harm and I will do all in my power to help you and your crew. I will not be, what is your word? Foresworn."

"That is our word and I believe you." I smiled, "Had not your uncle been so generous with the payment for your passage I might have been less suspicious."

"I am Uncle Isaac's last relative. If I die without children then our line ends. When I return to my home I will be married. He would have given you all the gold he possessed to ensure that I reached home safely."

"Yet I will leave you at Miklagård."

"Do not worry about me. Once we reach there then I am as good as home already." He nodded towards the prow, "I will go to see how the sick men fare."

As he headed through the sleeping and dozing men I wondered at his story. I believed that he meant us no harm but that did not mean that I totally believed what he had told me. It was not the whole truth; it was just an acceptable version of the truth. There was more to him than met the eye. He handled a sword better than any merchant I had seen. In all three attacks, he had been both calm and fearless.

The rain brought a fresher feel to both the wind and the weather. We moved along at a healthy pace without the need for oars. We saw our first land when we sailed south of Sicily. It was just a grey smudge on the northern horizon but it was land and it meant we would soon have our first glimpse of the Empire. To our south, we saw the island of Melita. It had been part of the Empire but now belonged to the Abbasid Caliphate. The southern part of Italy was still under the control of the Regent, Theodora. As we sailed north east along the coast we saw many small settlements but nothing that could be called a port.

The four former slaves wished to help. They were grateful to have been rescued. I allowed them to prepare food and take water to the crew. It was almost pitiful to see their gratitude. We had spare swords and scabbards. Each one had been given one. That made a huge difference. To a Viking, a sword made him a warrior. The four of them wished to be warriors. We would have to buy clothes for them when we reached Chatacium. We had taken coins from the Moors as well as some of the bangles and necklaces they wore. The Captain and his senior officers had been richly adorned. We had split the treasure with the slaves. The crew were all in a much happier frame of mind as we sailed towards Chatacium. The exception was Pridbjørn Ellesefsson. If anything, he became more withdrawn and I could not work out the reason. He would be leaving us soon. I had thought he would have spent more time talking to his shipmates for in Chatacium he would be alone. Sven Stormbringer felt guilty about his man departing us. He spoke at length with Pridbjørn. He could get nothing from him save that he had an oath to fulfil and he had coin. We could do no more and so we left him to stew by himself. Any who sat with him for any length of time became infected by his sadness.

Chapter 7

The port of Chatacium was impressive. There were many houses rising up the hill and a good harbour. They had a good wall around it. There was a harbour wall and a safe anchorage. Reassuringly there were two Imperial galleys at anchor in the middle of the harbour. There were many ships at the quay. The efficacy of the security measures was shown when we were hailed as we passed between the two galleys. There was no other way of entering the harbour. David ben Samuel proved invaluable. He understood the questions of the officer. I did not understand David's reply but I did recognise the authoritative tone he took. Whatever he said and however he said it worked for we were waved through. I suppose we were the first drekar they had seen. Soon they would see many more.

As at Bruggas, we had little choice over our berth. There was only one place on the quay large enough to accommodate us. We edged in. David said, "I will go and speak with the port official. We need to pay port dues first and then we can seek supplies."

I handed a leather purse to Aiden, "Go with him and pay. I will work out which crew go ashore first."

They left us and I saw that Sven Stormbringer and his Bears were waiting by the gangplank. Pridbjørn Ellesefsson was leaving us. I saw that he had his war gear in a bag. I guessed he must have acquired it in one of the villages or from the galley. He was wearing the robes we had taken from one of the Arabs. It covered his head. I saw that he would blend in easier than if he had worn his helmet and carried his shield. They would have marked him as a Viking.

He clasped Sven's arm. "Thank you, Sven Stormbringer. I am sorry that your brother died. He was a good man and I would happily have followed him. I will not need my shield. Give it to one of Snorri's men. I have my sword and I have coin. May the Allfather be with you."

He turned to me. There was neither a smile on his face nor in his eyes. He always had cold and unfriendly eyes but he had shown that he was a good warrior. "Farewell, Jarl Dragonheart. It was *wyrd* that we met. I had heard of you and wished to meet you. I can now say that I have met a legend. I never held it but I saw the sword that was touched by the gods. I go now to fulfil my oath."

I nodded and then waved an arm at this exotic place, "Here?"

"Every journey begins somewhere. Mine begins here." With that, he picked up his bag, climbed down the gangplank and disappeared.

Olaf sniffed, "Well good riddance. He did not fit in."

Sven nodded, "I know, I cannot help but think that I have let him down."

I dismissed him from my mind. The crew all wanted to go ashore. This was an opportunity to spend their coin and it was a new and exotic port. I divided the crew into three watches and used the three watchkeepers, Olaf, Haaken and myself. Two of us would remain on board until we were relieved. They insisted that Sven and I go ashore first. I did not mind and I took Sámr with me. The Bears had taken the slaves under their wing. They were a crew within a crew. They had both lost all. They came with us. David ben Samuel and Aiden were still with the port official. I wondered if there was trouble.

When we reached them Aiden read my mind, or perhaps my face, "There is no problem, Jarl Dragonheart. We are just purchasing some charts for the waters through which we will be travelling!"

I decided that we ought to stay together. We had the task of buying the clothes and, if possible, arms, which the new men would need. They were still using the Arab robes and it did not sit well with them. It was a reminder of their six months of pain and degradation. Erik and Olaf would buy the supplies we needed. Haaken and Arne would find the ale, water and wine. They were not hopeful about ale. Thanks to David and Aiden we all had a few words we could speak in Greek. It was mainly numbers and phrases like *'I would like that'* accompanied by a gesture. It was basic but I hoped it would suffice.

The port not only looked different, but it also smelled different. We had arrived at noon when the sun was high and many people were sleeping. I found out why because the heat was oppressive. The heat seemed to reflect from the white houses and buildings. The four ex-slaves were barefoot and the roadways were so hot that they burned. The air was filled with a smell which was a mixture of lemons, oranges and spices mixed with human waste. It was not a pleasant smell. We found a boot maker. His prices were exorbitant and so we bought the four of them sandals. They were cheap and useful. It would stop their feet from burning and when we reached Miklagård we could take some of the seal skin from our hold, give it to them and they could make their own boots. We found a stall selling the local version of a kyrtle and we bought those for the four of them and the Bears. The coin I was spending we had taken. It was booty. We would not have taken it without their help. Sven and his men needed to buy other items as did Sámr. I was still close to death. What did I need to buy? You could not buy life.

We found an inn and ate there. The food was strange and not all of it to our taste but the wine was good and induced a more mellow feeling. Snorri Gunnarson raised his goblet, "Jarl Dragonheart, we would like to thank you again. You have not asked us yet but if you would have us then we would swear an oath to follow you."

"You do not wish to go back to sailing a knarr? That is a more peaceful life."

Ulf said, "That was what we thought until we were taken. We will sail with you. Your men are good warriors. We will strive to be as good."

"Ulf is right. We have spoken with the Clan of the Wolf and they have told us of your land." Snorri waved an arm. "It sounds cooler and more pleasant than here. Wine is all well and good but only when you cannot get ale or beer!"

Ulf nodded, "And, no offence, jarl, but the sooner I get out of these robes the better. It reminds me too much of our time at the oars. I think of those oar brothers who died at the hands of the Moors."

Sven Stormbringer said, "Do not tarry for us. We would get back too. What say we do some cooking? Could we buy some food, jarl? We would like to thank the Clan of the Wolf. I know this is not the end of our journey but it is the end of part of it."

"That is a good idea."

We had had enough fish. We found the meat market and we found some calf meat. The owner assured us, I think, that it had hung but it mattered little. It was a meat we rarely ate. I suspect we paid too much for it but we were in a celebratory mood.

With our purchases, we made our away back to the ship. Arne and Haaken were standing watching as we approached, "You could have spent longer ashore if you had wished, jarl."

I shook my head, "Our new oar brothers wished to cook!"

We lit a fire on the quay. Other ships had set the precedent. I could not see anyone arguing with a crew of Vikings! Aiden and David ben Samuel were also in the town. The sun was slowly descending. We had spent half of the afternoon making our purchases and the other half drinking. At least the men who came with me would not have to have the night watch. That would be the duty of Olaf and Erik's men. Aiden had left me my potion. I would take it when the food was cooked. I had learned that it had a greater effect if I had eaten something first. I did not know why. I left the empty ship and joined Sámr and the others at the quay. Sámr had become something of a mascot to the men, especially the new ones. He was young but his prowess with the Saami bow had earned him their respect. They had an amphora of wine which they were passing around. I did not say anything but I saw that Sámr took just a sip. He would not embarrass himself by becoming drunk.

"Well, young Sámr, you have skills with a bow. How are you with a sword?"

"Not as good, Leif Longshanks, as I am with a bow but I am not fully grown and I practise all that I can." I was pleased that he showed modesty. No one liked a boastful warrior.

"Jarl, will he wield the sword that was touched by the gods when he is older?"

"That is not my decision, Sweyn. The sword will decide that." I smiled, "Of course, if I should die on this voyage then…"

"I am sorry, Jarl Dragonheart. I meant nothing by that. Forgive me."

"There is nothing to forgive. We all know that death hangs over me like an axe. I have lived a long time. I have buried two wives, a son and a grandson. When the Allfather takes me, I cannot complain. I have done all that a warrior can expect."

Sven Stormbringer changed the subject. "I was speaking with the Jew, David ben Samuel. He told me that men can buy good swords in Miklagård."

Harald Jorgensen took a deep drink from the wine skin, "That needs coin and we are already deeply in the Jarl's debt for the clothes we wear and the sandals on our feet."

"The clothes and the shoes are a gift. You owe me nothing for them."

"Thank you. Will we have a chance to raid between here and Miklagård, jarl?"

"I am not certain that we can raid but who knows what the Norns will throw in our way. None of us expected the galley that brought you four to us. The swords we gave you will have to do."

They nodded sagely and Sven sipped the stew. "It is tasting good. By the time the others return it will be ready."

I stood, "I cannot see that being for some time. I will have some of the bread we bought and take my potion."

Sámr looked concerned, "Are you unwell, great-grandfather?"

"Let us say that sleep would not come amiss. Even if I were not ill then I would still enjoy a nap at about this time. The day has been hot and the sun is setting. Sunset is faster here than at home. Give me a bowl of the broth from the stew. I will tell you if it needs seasoning."

Sven had poured in some of the wine from the amphora. I drank some of the wine to slake my thirst. I ate the broth; it needed more seasoning but the taste was good. I dipped the bread into it and finished off the liquor. They looked at me expectantly. "Delicious. When Aiden returns ask him if he bought some pepper. A sprinkle of that would not hurt."

"Pepper?"

"Ask Aiden, Ulf. Now I will sleep. I will have the whole drekar to myself." The gangplank was in darkness. When the crew returned it would be a merry feast. They would not need an old man who was close to death spoiling it. I took off my boots and laid my wolf cloak on the deck. It was a warm night and I would not need any blankets or my cloak. I made water and then drank the potion. I had not been speaking untruths. I was tired.

Placing Ragnar's Spirit and Wolf's Blood next to me, close to my hands, I lay down. Soon I was asleep and I dreamed.

I saw skulls. There was a sea of skulls. They rose around me like the waves of a stormy ocean. Blood oozed from them. The only noise I could hear was the chanting of witches. Four of them danced around a fire. Their faces were half-eaten away. They turned towards me and came closer and closer. I saw worms coming from their eyes and rotting flesh. The blood which oozed from the skulls came like a torrent towards me. I looked down and my kyrtle was soaked with blood. I could not move and then a white shape came towards me.

    I woke. I put my hand down and discovered that my kyrtle was soaked in blood. As I began to rise I saw a sword raised above me. It was wielded by a figure in a white robe. This was no dream. This was real. As the sword descended I did two things at the same time. I reached for one of my weapons. As luck would have it I found myself holding Ragnar's Spirit. At the same time, I swept my feet out. My foot connected with the shin of my attacker. It hurt me but it unbalanced him. Even while falling he still tried to skewer me. I was already rolling away as the sword hacked into my wolf cloak. I scrambled to my feet and lunged at him with Ragnar's Spirit. I had bled but the moment I had touched the sword it was as though I had been touched by the gods again. I felt immortal.

    My would-be killer had hoped that just a sword and a blade in the night would have been sufficient. He had found that it was not. I was a hard man to kill. Now he reached for his dagger. Mine was on the deck behind him. I backed away. I was dimly aware of a great deal of noise and laughter coming from the quay. Someone had told the others something funny and there was a cacophony of roars and guffaws. My men were enjoying the food and the wine. They would not come to my aid. It was up to me. I backed away and reached behind me with my left hand. When I reached the sheerstrake I found a coil of rope. I prayed that it was not tied to anything. I grabbed it and found that it was not. As a weapon, it had little to commend it but it was better than nothing. The deck was in darkness. I could not see my assassin's face for the hood of the Arab cloak they call a *bisht* was about his face. Yet there was something familiar about his movements.

He feinted with his sword. I know not how I knew it was a feint but I did. Perhaps fifty years of such combat had instilled the instinct into my bones. I was backed against the side of the ship. I let the end of the rope slip through my fingers. I did so surreptitiously as his sword and dagger wove intricate patterns before me. I could not see his eyes. If you could see a warrior's eyes then you knew what he intended. I would have to rely on my gut feeling. When I had a length of rope as long as an arm hanging down I feinted too with my sword. At the same time, I whipped the end of the rope across his face. I hit him. Perhaps I struck his eye; I know not but he reeled from the strike. He flailed his arms before him but I did not aim at his body. I lunged at his leg and hit his thigh. I twisted as I withdrew the sword. I swung the end of the rope hard a second time and this time aimed at the right hand which held the sword. I connected. Although he held on to the sword I knew that his hand would be numb. I stabbed towards his middle with Ragnar's Spirit. Unlike most swords, this one, the pinnacle of Bagsecg's skill as a swordsmith, was pointed. His left hand came across to block the blow with his dagger. He did not quite make it. The tip struck his chest and the edge scored a line across the back of his hand. I must have hit something vital for the dagger clattered to the deck. I swung the rope again and hit him on the side of the head. I lunged once more and this time he had no defence. My sword entered his right side and slid through his ribs. He fell backwards, the sword falling from his fingers.

It was only then that I thought to shout, "Clan of the Wolf!"

I felt weak. I did not know if it was from the blood from my body or something else. I dropped to my knees. I saw that the assassin was Pridbjørn Ellesefsson! I knelt over his body. "You! But why?" Realisation came to me. "I am the one you swore to kill, but why? What have I done to you?"

He laughed and a tendril of blood came from his cheek. I was dimly aware of feet thundering up the gangplank. "I could have killed you a dozen times at sea but I wanted to escape with your sword. I would be the warrior who wielded the sword that was touched by the gods."

"What did I ever do to you?"

"I was one of Eggle the Skulltaker's warriors. I swore that you would die when he was killed. When you slew my mother, Ellesef Ship-Breast, then it became a quest which would shape my life. I…" I learned no more. His eyes glazed over. The deck beneath him was covered in blood. He would not be in Valhalla. His sword was lying by his feet. I would not have to face him in the Otherworld.

I looked up and saw Aiden and Sámr along with Haaken One Eye. There were staring at me. They had a lantern and Sámr's eyes and face were filled with horror for the bottom half of my kyrtle was soaked in blood. I smiled, "It is not a wound. It is the illness but I came as close to death this night as ever before. You heard?"

They nodded. Sámr said, "From now on I do not leave your side! I was enjoying myself and you were here at death's door. How could I have faced those at home?"

Haaken One Eye put his arm around my great-grandson, "We are all to blame. We forgot why we were here. Like the rest, I thought that defeating the galleys was the end of the danger. I was wrong. The Norns have spun a web which is so complex that even Aiden our galdramenn cannot fathom it."

Aiden nodded, "You are right. I may gain knowledge here in this land of wonder but the further I am from the Water the fewer powers I have. I saw nothing! I fear that I am only a healer until we return to the Land of the Wolf. You are right Haaken One Eye, we have forgotten why we are here. We all watch the Dragonheart until we return home."

The rest of the crew came aboard. Like Sámr and the others, they stared in horror at the gory mess on the deck. Haaken took charge. "Get rid of this filth. Wash away all traces of him. Olaf Leather Neck, mount a guard on the gangplank. Let no one near. Aiden, Sámr, find the Dragonheart clean clothes. Once more he has borne the brunt of the ire of the Norns! He is their bane! We must become his protectors!"

I was exhausted and Aiden insisted upon a second potion. I slept and it was a dreamless sleep. For that I was grateful. When I awoke it was to the motion of the ship as we headed east. We had left before dawn. All of the crew wished to be away from the place which had almost seen my end. Sámr was close by, almost my shadow. "Sámr, we are at sea. I know that you are concerned but there is no danger here. It is daylight and I am safe. You are a ship's boy. Do not let others do your work for you!"

David ben Samuel said, "I will watch the Dragonheart for you, Sámr. I promise he will come to no harm." Sámr nodded and ran to join the other ship's boys. "He barely slept, jarl, but then few of the crew did either. They blamed themselves."

"They had no need. They could have done nothing about it. This was meant to be. When you kill a witch then the Norns do not forget."

He shook his head, "You are over sixty?" I nodded. "Then you are truly remarkable for Pridbjørn Ellesefsson was half your age and not ridden by a disease. I am pleased that my uncle sent me with you. I have learned much."

I laughed, "As have we all. Now there must be food! I am famished!"

Chapter 8

We sailed south and east for two days. We had the open sea and then we saw the many islands which formed Greece. The first large island we passed was Kerkyra. David ben Samuel pointed to the huge fortification at the north west corner of the island. "That is Angelokastro. If any enemy threatens this island or this side of the Empire then they would have to reduce that stronghold. I do not think it could be done." He looked at me, "Could you take it, Dragonheart?"

I peered at the stone edifice perched high on a rock above the sea. "It would be hard I agree but why would I want to take it? Does it contain treasure? Holy books? Men we could ransom?"

"There would be some."

I laughed, "I am guessing that there would be more on the rest of the islands. I would take them and leave. We are not interested in conquering land unless we would choose to live there. No disrespect, David ben Samuel but we would not wish to live here. It is not green enough."

"Captain, there are ships anchored beneath the stronghold. One comes over to us."

We had not been certain if the Imperial ships understood the convention of shields on the sides of a drekar but, just to be safe, we had then inboard. They did not line the ship. The small galley which came towards us was smaller than we were. The presence of another five larger galleys guaranteed that we would behave.

"Take in the sail."

They bumped gently alongside us. Their captain jabbered away and David ben Samuel answered him. I saw Aiden struggling to keep up. He turned to me, "David is saying who we are." There was a further conversation and this time the captain of the galley pointed south and west. Aiden shook his head, "I did not get enough of that to make sense of it but from the gist, I gathered that there is trouble further south."

The galley left and we used the sail again. The breeze was gentle but, as it came from the west it aided us and meant we did not have to row. The days were much hotter. Rowing in these temperatures was not healthy. It was Skerpla. David ben Samuel told us that in two months' time it would be even hotter. I hoped that by then we were at Miklagård where we would be able to take advantage of cool buildings rather than the open sea.

"There has been an uprising further south in Greece. Achaea is a large province and the city of Kalamata and the surrounding area has risen in revolt." He shrugged, "The local governor was something of a thief. That is normal but he also had an eye for young girls and that offended the locals. There is an army heading south to deal with it but the seaways are no longer safe. We were recommended to head for Corinth and take another ship from there. It would be quicker." He smiled, "I told them you would not agree to that and he said then he could not guarantee our safety."

I nodded, "We mean the locals no harm but if they offer violence then I am afraid that they will suffer."

David shook his head, "It is not the ones who are revolting that have caused the trouble; it is the ones taking advantage of the lack of Imperial ships and troops. There are pirates, brigands and bandits. They prey on those who revolt as well as any traveller passing through their waters."

"And we have to sail through their hunting ground?"

"We do. We would have to sail almost to Kriti to avoid them."

I nodded, "The Norns continue to make our lives difficult. I hope that these doctors in Miklagård are all that Aiden has promised!"

Aiden's face became serious. "They are your only hope, Dragonheart."

We had six days of easy sailing through the safer waters south of Kerkyra. We were able to find deserted islands where we could anchor and cook. We did not wish to risk the islands at night. It was when we turned due east that we entered the troubled waters. Almost as soon as we saw the land of Achaea to the north we were spied by a ship. It was not a galley. It had a lateen sail and a square sail. David recognised it as the type used by pirates. The men prepared weapons but the ship seemed happy to shadow us.

"Erik, tonight we anchor at sea. This ship is a scout. It does not bode well."

David and Aiden joined me as we watched the ship, towards sunset, slip away north. "If it is any consolation, Jarl Dragonheart, we can count the rest of the voyage in days."

I nodded, "Yes, David ben Samuel, but those days have nights too and it seems that we have found ourselves in a world of danger."

What we had learned was that this part of the world could turn from a benign sun-soaked sea into a maelstrom of rain and strong winds. We anchored at sunset. There were too many islands, shoals and hidden rocks in this sea to risk sailing at night time. So it proved. I was awoken by Arne in the middle of the night. The ship was pitching violently. "Jarl, a wind has come from the south. We are being driven north. There are islands there. We saw them as we sailed here. My father says we should man the oars and try to get us south."

"He is captain!"

Arne shouted, "Rowers, man the oars!"

We had sea room to the south. To the north lay Achaea and pirates. We would have to add time to our voyage if we were to reach it safely.

Erik shouted, "Ship's boys get the anchors in and then take an oar. We will need everyone to get us to safety."

I saw him looking at the mast and the yard. We could not afford to lose either of them. As the oars were run out and the anchors taken in the strength of the wind increased. Erik put the steering board over and once the oars began to bite the movement of the drekar became less violent. The oars did not have to propel us south; they just had to stop us from being driven north. There was no chant. There was no song. The crew just kept a steady stroke as we waited for dawn. Once dawn came then we would be able to run with the wind. The lookouts could watch for rocks. It was the darkness which was the danger.

Dawn, when it came, was not blue; it was grey and the wind had not abated but we could now see where we were. Erik sent Lars up the mast. It pitched alarmingly but Lars seemed not to be troubled. "What can you see?"

"There is land to the north, captain, but it is a long way away."

"Ship's boys, lower the sail. Oars, prepare to withdraw."

I saw the relief on the faces of the crew. For the former slaves, this was the first time they had had to row since they had been rescued. I guessed this had felt different. They were not chained and they were surrounded by brothers in arms. I felt some trepidation as I saw Sámr scamper up the yard. In all the years I had been sailing accidents had been few and far between. I did not want Sámr to be one.

Erik turned the steering board. He needed the oars to continue to row to keep the way on her as she turned. He did not wish her to broach. His timing was perfect. As the sail billowed he shouted, "In oars! Take in a couple of reefs! I do not wish to lose the mast." We did not need the full sail. We headed north and east. The wind would try to push us to the mainland but we could avoid the rocks and shallows which might harm us.

All day we were buffeted by the wind. We saw that not all the ships which plied these waters had been as well handled as ours. At what passed for noon we passed some wreckage. It was then that the wind began to abate and our voyage became less frenetic. Erik sought an anchorage for the night. Siggi was the lookout and he shouted, "Island to the south east, captain." Aiden took out the chart we had bought. It was not marked upon it.

"Is there habitation?"

"No, Captain. It has a beach and there are two trees. It is smaller than Whale Island."

Erik nodded, "Then we anchor there. The men need hot food and I need to go over the ship and check for damage."

We saw the island. It was little more than a rock jutting out of the water but there was a beach. As we neared it I saw that it was about two hundred paces by a hundred and fifty paces. One side was a beach and the white water on the opposite side suggested rocks and shoals. We went in very slowly. Lookouts manned the bow but there were, mercifully, no rocks. Erik turned us so that we could be dragged up onto the beach. We hauled *'Heart'* on to the beach. Once ashore we set about collecting driftwood for a fire. Erik and Arne examined the hull for damage. They had to work quickly for night was coming. When they were satisfied we had the task of dragging the drekar back into the water. It was exhausting but necessary. It took so long that we had hot food ready by the time the drekar was tied off the beach and facing the sea. If we had to leave in a hurry we could.

When we had eaten men went back aboard to fetch wet clothes and their weapons. The fire would dry the clothes and weapons could be sharpened, oiled and replaced in their scabbards. Erik Arne and the ship's boys were the deck watch while the rowers, Aiden, David and myself, slept on the island. I placed my cloak between those of Haaken and Olaf. I took off my sword and placed it close to hand. I too was tired and the potion sent me to sleep while the others still sat around the fire talking about Miklagård which now seemed tantalizingly close.

I did not sleep well, despite the potion. Perhaps it was the hard ground. My wolf cloak was drying by the fire and I had just used my cloak. I woke up while it was still dark. I needed to make water. I walked with the dying fire to my left. I head through the trees to the rocks on the far side of the island. It was a longer walk than I had thought. In the dark, it was even harder for the ground was uneven. I had just finished and my eyes were becoming accustomed to the dark when I saw shapes on the water. There were three of them: two small and one large. Almost immediately I knew that they were ships and, here, in this rebellious sea, ships meant danger. I turned and ran back to the men sleeping around the fire.

Aiden was upright, "Danger?"

"Ships. Aiden, wake the men!"

I shook awake Olaf Leather Neck and Haaken One Eye. I fastened my wolf cloak around my shoulders. I would need its luck. As I strapped on my sword and dagger I said, "Ships coming from the south and east. I think it means trouble."

Within a short time, the crew was roused. Aiden led David to the ship to warn Erik. Even as they hurried across the beach I saw a face appear by the trees. Drawing my sword, I said, "Shield wall! Snorri, take your men and help Erik prepare for sea. Have the boys ready with their bows!"

"Aye, jarl."

The boys would not be able to see much but they would be ready. None of us had shields but I suspected that whoever was coming towards us would not either. Only Sven and his men had not fought with us. "Sven, make your men our second rank. We back towards the ship when we are ready."

We did not have the luxury of a leisurely walk back across the beach. The pirates or bandits, it mattered little, suddenly launched themselves at us. Had I not had the men form a shieldless shield wall it might have gone ill but we had thirty swords and axes before us and men who knew how to use them. Olaf's mighty axe smashed into the side of the head of the first foolish warrior who ran at us. I swung Ragnar's Spirit in an arc and tore across the unprotected middle of a second. Then they were on us. They were smaller men than we were and that gave us the advantage for we had a longer reach. Had they used spears then it might have been different but they used short swords and hand axes.

"Walk back!"

Only disciplined warriors can do that. Instinctively we all stepped back on our right legs. The attackers thought we were about to run and they attacked even more furiously. In contrast, we were calm. I took out Wolf's Blood and, as I blocked the sword held in two hands by the Moor, I drove the dagger up through his neck and into his skull. As I withdrew it I lunged with Ragnar's Spirit and it entered the eye of the man behind. Two of the men close by Haaken were wounded and Sven Stormbringer and Leif stepped into the gap as they made their way back to the drekar. Wounded men were a liability. I felt sand beneath my feet and saw, at the same time, the sky was becoming lighter. Dawn was approaching. A couple of arrows flew over our heads and hit the attackers.

Erik shouted from behind me, "Jarl, you have just three paces to the water!"

It was time to show these bandits how Vikings fought. "Clan of the Wolf when I shout I want every man before us slaying and then we board the drekar."

The men all shouted, "Aye, jarl!" and the enemy stopped wondering what the sudden shout meant.

"Now!" I stepped forward and swung my sword to the left and right. My blade bit into the shoulder of one man and the neck of a second. We halted the progress of the pirates. I stepped back and soon felt the water around my ankles. Recovering the wounded, we boarded the ship. I saw that our attackers, seeing that they had lost the chance to hurt us they went back to the camp to pillage what we had left.

Erik said, "Do I set a course for Miklagård?"

I was angry. Angry men do not always make wise decisions. My men had been wounded and someone had to pay. "No, first we teach these pirates a lesson. Man the oars. We row around the island and take their ships!"

The oars were run out and Haaken began the chant. It was a fast one and appropriate for it sang of an attack in the night by Danes.

The Danes they came in dark of night
They slew Harland without a fight
Babies children all were slain
Mothers and daughters split in twain
Viking enemy, taking heads
Viking warriors fighting back
Viking enemy, taking heads
Viking warriors fighting back
Across the land the Ulfheonar trekked
Finding a land by Danes' hands wrecked
Ready to die to kill this Dane
Dragonheart was Eggles' bane
Viking enemy, taking heads
Viking warriors fighting back
Viking enemy, taking heads
Viking warriors fighting back
With boys as men the ships were fired
Warriors had these heroes sired
Then Ulfheonar fought their foe
Slaying all in the drekar's glow
Viking enemy, taking heads
Viking warriors fighting back
Viking enemy, taking heads
Viking warriors fighting back
When the Danes were broke their leader fled
Leaving his army lying dead
He sailed away to hide and plot
Dragonheart's fury was red hot

Viking enemy, taking heads
Viking warriors fighting back
Viking enemy, taking heads
Viking warriors fighting back
Then sailed the men of Cyninges-tūn
Sailing from the setting sun
They caught the Skull upon the sea
Beneath the church of Hwitebi
Viking enemy, taking heads
Viking warriors fighting back
Viking enemy, taking heads
Viking warriors fighting back
Heroes all they fought the Dane
But Finni the Dreamer, he was slain
Then full of fury their blood it boiled
Through blood and bodies, the warriors toiled
With one swift blow the skull was killed
With bodies and ships the Esk was filled
Viking enemy, taking heads
Viking warriors fighting back
Viking enemy, taking heads
Viking warriors fighting back

The pirates had left a deck watch. They were the ones who saw us and we heard them shouting to their comrades ashore. They were not next to the island. They were fifty paces from the shore. I guessed there was a rock shelf.

"Erik, head for the large one. Sámr, have the boys with the bows kill the deck watch!"

The ones on the island now saw the danger. They were hurrying to get to us. We would reach the ship first. The two smaller ships cut their anchors and hoisted their sails. As the crew of the larger one tried the same our arrows struck them.

"In oars!" We bumped into the ship which was as long as ours but wider.

"Half of you board her. Take what you can and then set her alight!"

I lined the side with the rest of the crew. Sámr and the archers were now raining death upon those who were trying to reach us from the island. Snorri and his men had been among those who boarded the pirate ship. I heard Snorri shout, "Back to the ship!" and then I saw flames flickering close to the mast. One of Snorri's men scampered up the forestay and cut one of the ropes holding the sail close to the yard. Half of it fell and, as he slid down to safety the flames caught the bone-dry canvas and flames leapt up. He was the last to board *'Heart of the Dragon'* and we were already using our oars to push us away from the ship which now blazed like a beacon in the dawn's early light. The two smaller ships were well out to sea and I saw the forty or so survivors, on the tiny island, shake their weapons impotently at us.

"Now you can head for Miklagård! We have shown these pirates what a real warrior can do!"

The crew all cheered. Snorri opened one of the chests he had found. He grabbed his hammer of Thor, "The Allfather has provided, jarl." I looked in and saw that it was filled with coins. Many were copper, and most were silver but there were a couple of golden dinars there. The raid on our ship had proved a little expensive for the Greek pirates.

It was fortunate that we had winds for the next two days for our eight wounded men needed time to heal. By the time we turned north for Miklagård and had to row only three men were still unfit.

Aiden and David joined me by the stern rail, "The Norns again, jarl."

I nodded, "It is fortunate that I am old and have a weak bladder, is it not?"

Chapter 9

The last six days at sea were a total contrast to the first ones in the Blue Sea. Then we had seen few ships. Now we had ships on every side. It was not just one or two. On one day there were twenty ships of varying sizes some heading to Miklagård and some heading from. We had to employ every ship's boy to keep track of them. The smaller ones knew these waters and they raced over the sea recklessly close to the bigger ones.

"David ben Samuel, how do they avoid collisions?"

He shook his head, "The simple fact of the matter is that they do not. Often, they strike and the smaller one will sink. It is a hazard of their trade. There are fortunes to be made in Constantinopolis. It can be worth the risk. As a merchant, I can tell you that knowing the political situation can make a man rich overnight. If the army marches north to fight the Pecheng or the Bulgars then you will make a fortune selling carts, wagons, hay and the like. If crops to the north of the city fail then a clever captain can sail south, pick them up cheaply and race back to sell them when there is a shortage. There are many rich people who will pay many times their value just so that they do not starve."

Erik asked, "And what of our goods? We have seal oil, seal skin, animal furs, copper and iron."

"Some of those, the seal oil and seal skin I am not sure of, but the others will fetch you gold. Rich ladies like exotic furs. I will not be heading for Caesarea for a while. I will advise you on the best markets." He hesitated, "I cannot accommodate all of you and your men but my home is yours, Dragonheart."

Erik laughed, "I think that most of the men will happily stay on the ship. There will be inns and taverns close by. That will suit them."

"I must warn you that the authorities do not tolerate unruly behaviour. That is especially true in the city. They are a little more lenient in the harbours." He looked at Erik, "I would suggest you use the Harbour of Theodosius also known as Langa harbour. It is on the Sea of Marmara side. The Golden Horn is a better harbour but it is harder to get in and out. In addition, it is closely policed." He smiled, "And my home is not far away. It is close to the Forum Bovis."

The narrow piece of water they called the Dardanelles was a difficult one to navigate for we had to follow the ship before us. The men had to row. We saw men and ships we had never seen before. Some ships were larger than us but most were smaller. All stared at us as they passed. They knew us for what we were, a predator.

I noticed that the closer we came to Miklagård the more animated David ben Samuel became. It was obvious why. He had managed to avoid death and wounds. That was no mean feat travelling from the cold German Sea to the Sea of Marmara. For myself, I would be glad to reach it too. My reasons were different. Since the attack on the island, my condition had worsened. Aiden blamed the exertion. I knew not why but the bleeding was as bad as ever and the potion did not appear to be effective. If the doctors could do nothing then I would hold Ragnar's Spirit and ask Haaken One Eye to give me the warrior's death. I would not die piece by piece.

Haaken, Aiden, Erik and myself had seen the city before but the others had not and they lined the side of the drekar with open mouths as we neared the harbour and saw the city rose above the walls. The Santa Sophia church and the Great Palace were larger than whole villages and towns in the Land of the Wolf. It even dwarfed Lundenwic. It was the gold of the stone and the white of the walls which impressed them. It was a sight none would ever see again. It humbled me and I knew my men would feel the same. We did not build in stone but even if we did we could not begin to do what these Romans and Greeks had done. Just the sight of the Theodosian Walls made me want to return home. My land was a simpler place. We used wood and turf. We built on a scale which suited our stature. This was not the work of men. This was the work of gods.

The harbour had been enlarged since last we had been here. It meant there was more room and Erik could pick and choose his berth. He wisely chose one which was at the quieter end of the quay. We were not questioned by the guard ship as we entered but I saw six armed men marching with an official towards the berth we had chosen. It took some time to nudge neatly in and the official stood waiting with his clerk and the armed men with a tapping foot.

David Ben Samuel said, "Leave him to me." He turned to Aiden. "Come, let us try your Greek out!" As the gangplank was placed on the ground the two of them strode down to the quay.

Already the men were moving their chests so that Erik could raise the deck and we could take out our trade goods. They would need to air on the quay and be sorted. There would be spoilage. We would sell everything, including that which had been damaged but we would ask the highest price for the better goods. I could see that Erik Short Toe wished to speak to me but was uncomfortable. I guessed it was about my treatment.

"Jarl Dragonheart, how long will we be in port? I only ask because I do not wish to buy anything which might spoil."

I nodded, "A fair question which I cannot answer. It will take time for the musty smell to leave our goods. You can trade for that which will not rot: pots, dishes and the like. I promise that as soon as I can find out how long we shall be here then I will tell you. Aiden has the coin. Ask him for whatever you need. I leave it to you and Olaf Leather Neck to organise the watches." I smiled. "I might be occupied."

"Of course, Jarl."

Everyone was busy and I just stood and watched. Aiden and David ben Samuel returned after a short time. Aiden was smiling, "That was a valuable lesson, David ben Samuel, in how to deal with an official."

He smiled, "They think they are more important than they actually are." He turned to me. "Jarl Dragonheart, if I could borrow six of your men to carry my chests. I will reward them."

I nodded, "Snorri and Sven, choose six of your men to carry our passenger's chests."

"Aye, lord."

David ben Samuel shook his head, "You care about your men even down to the smallest detail. You give this task to those who need the coin the most. I am pleased I have sailed with you. When I have your quarters ready I will send a servant for you. Who will be staying with me?"

I had thought this through. I knew who would enjoy the experience, "Aiden, Haaken One Eye and Sámr."

"No more?"

"Olaf Leather Neck would prefer to stay on the drekar. He will be happier this way."

He nodded and then shouted, "Farewell, Clan of the Wolf. I enjoyed being your shield brother even though it was for a short time. May God watch over you!"

The men all cheered. They had warmed to our passenger.

He turned to me and said, quietly, "And I will seek a healer for you as soon as I can. I cannot promise but…"

I nodded, "Whatever happens, it will be *wyrd*."

There had not been as much spoiled as we had expected. None of the iron or the copper had been damaged. Some of the furs had been used as nests by rats and they had gnawed some of the seal skins. We could trim that off. Erik shook his head, "I will see if I can get a cat while we are in port."

"A cat?" Sámr was curious.

"They have cats here. They are worshipped by some sects, like the Egyptians, and others use them to keep down rats, mice and snakes."

"Snakes, Aiden?"

"Aye, Sámr, this is a new world to which we have come."

Erik asked, "And when we have time, jarl, I will seek Josephus' family. Perhaps they will know where we can acquire a cat."

"You know where he lives?"

"I know where he lived but I suspect his family will be seafarers. If they have moved then I will ask the captains. Josephus' name was known."

The six men returned from David ben Samuel's and their grins reflected their rewards. We had our chests placed on the quay. We awaited David's servants. If the heat at sea had been bad then here it was unbearable. Erik had rigged up the old sail across the deck to keep it cooler but, on the quay, the sun was unrelenting.

I turned to Aiden, "We are good to stay here as long as we wish?"

He nodded, "Our passenger is a man of influence. His name is well known. I think the official saw a chance to make much coin from us. David is a good man. I have learned a great deal.

Had we not had him with us then we might have struggled. My Greek is now much better." He saw me wince as a shaft of pain struck me deep inside. "It will not be long. If you can be saved then David will find the healer."

"And if not, then Olaf can give me a warrior's death."

"Do not talk that way. Life is not something to be cast away so easily."

I snapped back at him, "And until you have endured this pain then do not try to tell me how to live what little of my life I have left."

Sámr had been listening, "Great grandfather, heed Aiden's words. We need you. Ulla War Cry, Mordaf and all your family are not ready for you to go to the Otherworld."

"And that is not my decision, yet, I am in the hands of the Norns." I saw someone approach. They were accompanied by a man with a sort of shade to keep the sun from his bald pate.

Haaken One Eye sniffed, "Your end will not be a mundane one, jarl. The Allfather will see to that."

I could smell his perfume long before he reached us. His head was completely shaven and when he spoke his voice suggested he was a eunuch. He spoke in Greek. I picked up half of the words and guessed at the rest. I could speak but a few words. "Greetings, Jarl Dragonheart. I am Ptolemy. My master has sent me to show you to his home. The chambers are ready."

Sámr whistled and I saw Ptolemy shudder at the shrill sound, "Ship's boys!" The ship's boys would carry our chests. Sámr slung his own over his back. He had gained in strength on the voyage. Olaf had said that he was ready to row on the return voyage. He had left home a boy but would return a man. *Wyrd*.

We did not have far to go. David ben Samuel's house had a gate with a guard. He had a sword at his side and he wore a helmet. The wall was as high as that of the Roman fort in Lundenwic. We were admitted. Once inside we entered a palace of fountains. There were lemon and olive trees. The streets had been filled with the noise of humanity and here it was a paradise of peace. The ship's boys gaped in wonder.

Ptolemy said, "Your boys can leave the chests here. The house slaves will move them." He clapped his hands.

Aiden said, "Leave the chests here."

They looked disappointed. A servant came out with a jug and some beakers. He poured a yellow-looking liquid into each beaker and gave one to each of the boys. They looked to me for instruction. "I think you are to drink it."

Lars said, querulously, "It is not a potion, is it? It will not make us as the man with no hair and the voice of a woman."

I smiled. It was fortunate that Ptolemy did not understand their words. "No, it is a pleasant drink and it is cool. I had it when I came here first. It is called sherbet. You will enjoy it."

I watched as they tentatively sipped and when its sweetness struck their tongue they drank it in one. Ptolemy shook his head and then waved for the slave to refill their beakers. They left us when there was none left. I could only imagine how they would retell the story.

Ptolemy said, "My master has some business to attend to." He sniffed. "He thought you might like to use the bathhouse. The chests will be taken to your chambers if you would follow me."

Haaken said, when Aiden had translated for him, "I suppose we are a little ripe." He turned to Sámr. "You are in for a most delightful experience."

We descended some steps and entered a room which echoed. There was a wooden bench. Ptolemy asked, "You have used a bath house before?"

Aiden nodded, "We have."

"Then I shall leave you." He scurried out. I think our smell and appearance offended him.

Aiden said, "I think he feared seeing our naked, hairy barbarian bodies."

The slaves began to undress us. Sámr looked like he was unhappy about the experience. "Sámr, this is their purpose. Let then undress you."

When we were naked our clothes were taken away and towels were placed around us. We were led to the caldarium. The heat struck you as soon as you walked in. Aiden and I stepped into the hot water. Haaken and Sámr followed. Once in the water our bodies were sponged and washed. Our matted hair and beards were teased and combed. The slaves knew their job for they caused no pain. Sámr still looked unhappy. I saw that the water was now a muddy colour. The slaves stood and gestured. We rose and they wrapped the towels around us. We were led to the frigidarium. We lay on the marble slabs and the slaves took out their strigils to cleanse the last of the dirt from our bodies. The water here was cold. When we stepped into it I was reminded of my bathing in the Water. The icy water cleansed the dirt from us. Finally, we were led to the tepidarium. Here the floor was warm and there were long benches with towels upon them. Aiden and I lay upon them. They combed our hair and then used perfumed oils to massage into our bodies. When they had finished they left us.

Sámr sniffed himself. "I smell like a woman!"

Haaken One Eye laughed. "I confess it takes some getting used to. It is not finished yet, Sámr!"

The slaves returned with a jug and beakers. This was not sherbet. This was iced wine. They had trays of grapes and other chilled fruits. We lay in the tepidarium and enjoyed ourselves. Sámr suddenly pointed, "Great grandfather. Your towel."

I looked. I had bled. Perhaps it was the heat of the water, I know not. I waved a slave over, "Aiden, tell him that I would be dressed."

Aiden spoke and the slave led me to another room where there were clothes. I started to dress myself and he shook his head. He took what looked like a small towel and fashioned it around my lower body. He smiled and nodded. It would contain the blood. I thanked him and finished dressing. Our passenger had provided simple kyrtles for us. I donned the sandals which were there and then the other three joined me.

Haaken said, "I wonder if we could have one built at home? It is a very pleasant experience. I think my wife would enjoy that."

Aiden shook his head, "The system they use to heat the floor and the water is complex. I am not even certain we have the means to keep the water in the bath. This is a different world to ours Haaken One Eye."

He nodded, "Then I can dream. Come, David ben Samuel has been a generous host up to now. I am certain that when we leave here there will be more to come!"

Sámr was just in awe of everything. We followed the slave and he led us upstairs and out into a courtyard. We felt the heat from the walls but the courtyard was shaded and the sound of the fountains made it seem cooler.

Ptolemy appeared. He sniffed and then beamed, "Ah that is better! Now you smell like civilised men. If you wished the slaves would shave you. They are very good and everyone is clean-shaven these days."

Aiden translated and Haaken laughed, "If I did that I might win more battles for my opponents would be laughing so much that I could slay them easily."

"Haaken!"

He shrugged, "He cannot understand my words."

"No, but he can understand your laugh. While we are here try, at least, not to be the barbarian! If you cannot then go back to the drekar."

He realised that he had gone too far and he bowed, "I am sorry, Dragonheart." He turned to Ptolemy and bowed. "And I am sorry that you lost your balls!" He said it with such a serious face that Ptolemy thought he had apologised to him.

Slaves brought more iced wine and a plate of olives, figs and goat's cheese. "Sámr, do not drink heavily. This is wine and not ale."

He nodded, "I know, jarl." He grinned at Haaken One Eye, "I, at least, know how to behave."

Haaken laughed, "So young Sámr has found his voice. You have grown, young one. We still need a name for you. Perhaps Sámr Silken Tongue?"

"Yours is the only silken tongue around here, Haaken One Eye. Now peace and let me enjoy my wine!"

"Yes, jarl!"

I saw him wink at Sámr.

After that, it was a very pleasant evening. The sun lost its heat and the courtyard was pleasant. I knew, from my last visit, that here they ate later. The food they had brought satiated the appetites of even young Sámr. The platters were refilled. David ben Samuel lived well and his servants and slaves were well-trained.

He arrived just as the last light went from the western sky. "Apologies to all of you. I had much business to conduct." He beamed, "Now you smell civilised. All was done well?"

We nodded and I said, "Perfectly!"

"Good. Then I have much to tell you. Firstly, Dragonheart, I have purchased a servant for you who can speak your language and Greek. He is a Rus Viking. He will be waiting for you at your chamber. He will see to your every need but you are Vikings and you must be starving. Our customs will come as a shock to you. Let us go to my dining room. The cook was told to impress the barbarians from the north!" He said it with humour.

Haaken said, "We will make a Viking of you yet!"

He shook his head. "I rowed for an hour and my hands are still red raw. I will continue to do as I have always done."

I smiled, "And what is that, David ben Samuel?"

He gave me an innocent look. "Why, make money of course!" He smiled, "I have been to your ship and told Erik Short Toe which market he should use. I had my men put your goods in my warehouse. It will be safer."

"Thank you, we are in your debt."

"I am still on the debit side of the pact my uncle made with you for I would not be here but for you. A journey across land is fraught with danger. It cost me eight good men to reach my uncle's. I know what you did for me. I now know the value of life."

There were just the five of us at the table. Aiden asked, "Will not Lady Justina be joining us?"

He shook his head, "We are betrothed. Until we are married it would be unseemly for her to dine with me."

I nodded, "Not to mention four barbarians!"

He laughed, "Quite!" He put down the knife he had used to carve pieces from the lamb. "The food is to your satisfaction?"

Haaken nodded, "If I knew what half of it was I would enjoy it even more but a Viking can eat anything. Let us just say that this has tantalised my taste buds." He pointed to my platter. "Unlike the jarl here who appears to have the appetite of a sparrow!"

They all looked at my plate. I had barely eaten. Aiden said a little angrier than he might normally have done for he had drunk well, "Sometimes, Haaken One Eye, I wonder at you! The Dragonheart has not eaten well for the whole voyage. You have not noticed? He has a worm which consumes him from within.

He is in pain and yet he does not wish to burden us with it. Are you so wrapped up in yourself that all you hear are your own inanities?"

Haaken had also drunk well. He looked mortified, "Forgive me, Jarl Dragonheart. You know I mean no harm."

"I know but Aiden is right. Think before you speak."

David ben Samuel said. "I have been absent for a long time as I sought the advice of many physicians. To speak the truth half of the men I spoke with would not consider examining a barbarian. Of the rest, most were pessimistic and would not see you. There is one. He is young but he is talented. Oribasius is a gifted doctor. He said he will examine you but promises nothing until he has done so."

"That is all that I ask. And when do I see him?"

"He will be here in the morning." David ben Samuel looked at Aiden. "He says he wishes to know what you have used to treat him."

"Of course."

There was an embarrassed silence. We all knew that this Oribasius held my life in his hands. If he would not treat me then I would see Olaf Leather Neck. He would give me a warrior's end. I stopped drinking when I knew I was to be seen. Aiden decided that it might be for the best if I did not take the potion that night. I asked, "What about the bleeding?"

"It cannot be helped and I am certain that David ben Samuel will not mind if he has to throw out some bedding."

I went upstairs and saw that there was a somewhat thin and emaciated man sitting on a stool outside my chamber. He stood when I approached. He did so with difficulty. He bowed, "I am Germund and you must be the Dragonheart."

"I am." I entered the room and he followed. He limped. I pointed to his leg. "That is why you are a slave and did not die a warrior's death."

He nodded and gave me a rueful smile. "It was a battle with Imperial marines. I was hamstrung and knocked unconscious. I was sold as a slave. I worked on galleys. I would be there still if my new master had not bought me. I am grateful to him."

Wyrd.

"He has told you about me?"

"You have something which makes you bleed and a doctor will take it out."

"Good. I tell you this, Germund. If I survive then you shall be free. That is my promise."

He nodded, "Then I will pray to the Allfather that he spares you."

Chapter 10

Surprisingly, considering this might be one of my last nights in this world, I slept well. That might have been the wine or exhaustion. I knew not which. When I rose, the bed had red upon it. I felt embarrassed. Germund came in and, with an expressionless face, removed the offending bedding. He returned and proceeded to wash away all evidence from my body. He said nothing. When I was dressed I descended. The others were there already and they were eating. They looked at me as I entered. It was as though they had never seen me before or perhaps, they thought that this would be the last time. I sat with them but I did not eat I just drank. I listened to Haaken's inane chatter without taking in what he said. I knew he did it just to fill the awkward silence.

When Oribasius arrived, with his slave, I was surprised at the youth of the doctor. I had expected, despite David's warning, someone older. He laughed and spoke in rapid Greek. David answered him and then turned to me. "He said your face spoke volumes, Dragonheart. Yes, he is young but that does not mean he does not know what he is doing." He turned to the others. "He wished to examine Jarl Dragonheart in the presence of Aiden alone." They nodded and he turned back to me. "Pray use your chamber and do not be worried about any mess. I have many slaves."

As we went to my room Aiden said, quietly, "I hope that my Greek is up to this."

I was asked to strip. While I did so Oribasius rattled off a series of questions for Aiden. My galdramenn produced his potion. The doctor sniffed it, tasted a little and nodded. Then he came to me. He had me turn around and examined where I had bled then he prodded and poked at me. He asked me nothing. He waved his slave over and scribbled something on the wax tablet the slave held. Then he spoke to Aiden.

Aiden said, "He is going to touch you. If it is really painful then hold ten digits up. If there is no pain then make two fists. Use your fingers and thumbs to indicate the pain between." He nodded to the slave. "The slave will keep a record."

Having been a warrior for fifty years I did not need to use ten digits but on one occasion I held up one hand and two fingers. When he had finished he handed me my shift. He spoke to Aiden. Aiden smiled, "The doctor said that you are a tough warrior, he hurt you more than you said. Being tough does not impress him." I nodded and smiled. "He can help you. He says you have a growth and he can cut it out. He says that it is good that you are tough for you will be awake when he operates. Do you still wish this?"

I said, "Will I be cured?"

Aiden spoke to Oribasius and then shook his head when he was answered. "He cannot be certain. He believes that he can do it but, in his profession, there are no guarantees, just hope."

I nodded, "Then tell him that I will hold my sword while he operates and then I can go to Valhalla if he is unsuccessful."

I saw when my words were translated, that I had shocked and surprised the doctor. He spoke to Aiden who answered him. "I promised him that you would not use the sword on him and he agreed to operate."

"When?"

Aiden looked at me and said, "Tomorrow. He wishes you to fast for the day and to drink only water."

"Where?"

"Here."

"Good."

The doctor spoke again. Aiden translated, "He says you will not be able to leave your bed for at least ten days. You will be as weak as a kitten. There will be no combat for you!"

"I should not need to here in Miklagård!"

I had a day to say my goodbyes. After he had gone I returned to the others. I told them what he had said. Haaken nodded and touched his wolf token. Sámr looked fearful. Then I said, "I will go to the drekar. I need to know how my men are faring."

Haaken One Eye said, "I will explore the city. I will have two months at sea with my oar brothers. That is more than enough time to be with them. Will you come, Sámr?"

"No, Haaken One Eye. When the Dragonheart is recovering from the operation then I will have more than enough time for that. I think I will spend the day with my great-grandfather."

"Suit yourself. Aiden?"

He shook his head. "Oribasius has given me some of his writings explaining what he will do. I will read them." He looked at me. "My powers wane here. I need to add knowledge if I am to aid the physician."

"Then I shall go alone. I will see you all this evening."

After he had gone David ben Samuel said, "This Haaken One Eye, he is a force of nature."

I nodded, "He is that and I am glad that he has been my protector for more than fifty years."

Sámr and I walked in silence through the throngs. We did not have far to go but people were about their business before the heat of the day. It was a relief to get to the ship although the heat and glare from the water came as a shock after David ben Samuel's cool home. There was just a deck watch. I saw Olaf Leather Neck speaking with Arne Eriksson. I would not have as many goodbyes as I had expected.

They looked up as we mounted the gangplank. "Dragonheart! What have they done to you? I can smell you and Sámr from here." He grinned, "Tell me that they have done the same to One Eye! I would love to see him with oiled hair and smelling sweet!"

I laughed; Olaf would never change and for that I was glad. He had always been like a huge bear. Fierce in combat but comforting to have at your side. "Aye, he does. He walks the city."

"Then I will join him when Sven Stormbringer returns." He suddenly seemed to remember the purpose of our visit. "When do you see the healer?"

"I have seen him and he cuts me open tomorrow." Until Aiden had put the metal in Haaken's head such an act would have seemed strange but Olaf just nodded.

"And then you will be healed?"

"I know not. Who knows what the Norns have planned? I will be holding Ragnar's Spirit when he cuts. If he slips or if… well I shall go to Valhalla."

Olaf looked relieved. "I am glad about that, Jarl. I would not wish to go to a Valhalla without the Dragonheart."

I held out my arm and clasped Olaf Leather Neck's, "Thank you for being the warrior you are. Going into battle with you at my side ensured that we always won. I pray you continue to lead the clan into battle after...."

His eyes widened, "With you alongside me eh, Jarl Dragonheart? The last of the Ulfheonar go to war together."

"Perhaps but I will not speak for fear of offending the Norns. What will be will be." I felt his fingers grip my arm and he nodded. Words would not come. A silence lay between us that was filled with the sounds of battles past and the faces of dead Ulfheonar. I nodded and turned to Arne. "Where is your father? I hoped to speak with him?"

"He went early this morning with Siggi to seek the family of Josephus."

"Ah. Tell him I came to speak with him and…"

Olaf Leather Neck said, gruffly, "I will tell him, jarl. I have the words now."

I saw that the chests and goods had gone. "When does your father plan to sell the goods?"

"Tomorrow. David ben Samuel said that it would be a good day for the followers of the White Christ go to their churches on the day after the markets are closed. He said Sabatton was the best day for more people go to market on that day."

"Good, and the men, how do they fare?"

Olaf laughed, "They miss their ale already but Galmr claims he knows of a tavern which has ale and is used by Rus warriors. It is in the north of the city. He and his oar brothers are there now seeking it out. The others enjoy the rest. It was a hard voyage, jarl. We lost but one man and yet much happened. I am surprised that Haaken is not composing a saga about his heroic acts even as we speak."

"He has time. The healer says I cannot move for ten days. Tell the men that their boredom may well continue for some time." In the short time we had stood talking the sun had risen higher and the deck was much hotter. "Come Sámr, we will return to the house. Fare well, Olaf Leather Neck, Arne Eriksson tell my crew… tell them that the Dragonheart says it has been a privilege to lead them!"

They both nodded, tight-lipped, and we turned and left my drekar. I stroked the gunwale as I stepped on to the gangplank and looked up at the mast. She had served me well. I said, quietly, "Farewell, **'Heart of the Dragon'**."

I thought I had said it to myself but Sámr said, "She will be here when you are healed."

As I passed the prow, the dragon carved by Bolli I thought of all the sea miles we had sailed together. She was old and would not have many voyages left in her. I had thought to have her carry my body to the Otherworld. If the Norns had other plans then that would not be. It would be sad if she was just broken up when her days ended. She deserved a warrior's death. As we headed back to the house I said, "Sámr, if I do not survive tomorrow then make sure that **'Heart of the Dragon'** does not have an undignified end. She should be used as the funeral ship for Haaken One Eye or Olaf Leather Neck. She deserves to die with a good warrior in her."

He looked tearful, "You will not die tomorrow! You must live."

"And I hope that I do. It is why I came here but for once I can do nothing about this. I will be in the hands of another. Oribasius, the Norns and the Allfather will determine if I should live or die. I will hold Ragnar's Spirit and perhaps the spirits, though we are miles from home, may also help me see this through."

It was a sombre afternoon but the evening was enlivened by Haaken One Eye's account of his day. He could tell a good tale and he made his encounters with the Greeks he met hilarious. I did not eat, as I had been instructed and I left the table early. "I have a busy day tomorrow. I will experience that which no other has done. I had best be prepared." Sámr made to rise. "No, Sámr, I need to prepare myself."

Germund had laid more towels on the bed. The bleeding had been bad and I felt a little weak. Germund helped me to undress. He did so with great gentleness. I nodded my thanks. "I will see you in the morning Germund."

"I will pray to the Allfather for you."

He left me and I went to my chest. I wished to have Ragnar's Spirit close to hand. I opened the chest and reached in. I suddenly felt dizzy and nearly tumbled over. A hand stayed me. It was Haaken One Eye. He said, gently, "We have watched over each other for most of our lives, Dragonheart, do not shut me out now. Let me help you to bed." I nodded and he took my shift from me and helped me don a clean one. He laid me on the bed and then, after fetching my sword for me, sat next to me. "I know that I joke and I am too loud. I know that but I also know that if I spoke that which was truly in my heart then I would unman myself. I hope this healer knows his business." He tapped his head where the metal plate resided. "Aiden says he does and Aiden saved my life. We have spoken with Aiden. Sámr and I will be there with you tomorrow. Sámr will hold the hand that grips Ragnar's Spirit. He will ensure you do not drop it." He grinned, "Nor skewer the doctor." His face became serious. "If the Allfather takes you then there will be three close to you who will see you safely thither." He took my hand and gripped it. "May the Allfather be with you."

"And with you, old friend. I pray you to watch over my kin. There is none I trust more."

"And know that I shall."

Satisfied I closed my eyes as he left the room. I had said what was needed to be said and I slept. Whatever happened would be *wyrd*.

Germund was standing by my bed when I awoke. He looked concerned. "Jarl, the bleeding looks worse."

"Then it is good that I am to see the doctor this day."

He nodded. "He and his man are here. They told me to remove everything from the bed. They will operate here."

I smiled, "Good then I do not have far to walk. I just need to make water."

He pointed to a large amphora he had brought in. "If you would use that, Jarl Dragonheart then I will empty it." He smiled, "Here they collect it and use it to cleanse clothes. Strange for such a civilised place eh? I smiled.

By the time I had made water he had stripped the bed revealing the wooden slats and he placed white sheets around the bed. Oribasius and his slave arrived. The slave was laden with bags. More slaves arrived with pitchers and bowls of steaming water. Two of them proceeded to pour the boiling water onto the wood and to scrub. They had to have had hands like leather. Another poured more boiling water into the large flat bowl. Oribasius poured in some vinegar. Then his servants began to place thin and pointed knives of various sizes into the bowl.

Sámr, Aiden and Haaken appeared. Sámr said, apologetically, "The healer made us bathe in the caldarium."

"He wanted no risk of badness seeping into the wound I am going to make. He means to save you, Jarl." Aiden explained.

The slaves had finished scrubbing and the healer dismissed them. He spoke to my new servant. Germund spoke to me. "The healer said that I may stay, Jarl Dragonheart. He might need me."

Oribasius spoke. Aiden translated, "You are ready?" I nodded. "He needs you naked."

Oribasius turned to his slave and spoke. I heard the name Leonidas. I was concentrating on the Greek words to take my mind off what was about to happen. I saw the slave take out a razor. I felt embarrassed when I was naked. Sámr and my crew had seen me naked many times when I had bathed after a battle but the healer and his slave were something new. Oribasius did not seem to notice. He spoke to Aiden who translated. "Lie down. If you wish your sword then it first needs to be placed in the boiling water."

Sámr placed it with the instruments. He was going to reach for it when Germund did so. He barely flinched when his fingers touched the water. I saw that Leonidas had a hinged tool to take out the instruments Oribasius would use. Apparently, I needed no shave and I lay down with Ragnar's Spirit in my hand. The pain in my gut abated. Sámr had one hand on my shoulder and one on the hand which held the sword. Haaken was on the other side and he had the same hold. Oribasius must have instructed them. I saw that Aiden was next to the healer. That gave me confidence. The red stone around Aiden's neck would help to protect me.

Germund came towards me with a piece of polished wood, "Jarl Dragonheart, bite upon this it will stop you biting your tongue off." I did so.

Oribasius said, quietly, "There will be pain." I nodded and closed my eyes.

I was not afraid of dying; I had my sword in my hand. I was frightened of letting Sámr and the others down. Whatever pain came my way then I would bear it. I did not feel the first cut. I only knew that he had cut me when I felt the blood running down my side and heard the gasp of breath from Sámr. His fingers dug deeply into my shoulder and my hand. That helped. I know not why but it did. I was aware of a strange sensation. It felt as though there were worms inside me. It was just uncomfortable rather than painful. Time seemed to stand still. I had no idea how long I lay there.

When Oribasius spoke, although he spoke quietly, it almost made me jump. It was fortunate that I was being held down. Then I heard Aiden's voice. It was reassuring but the words were not, "He has found the diseased part of your body, Jarl Dragonheart. It is the size of a crab apple. The smell is not pleasant. He will cut and this may well hurt. Sámr, Haaken, hold him tightly. Germund, be ready."

I nodded. This pain I felt. It was as though all of the worms I had inside me had now grown into serpents and then dragons and they bit me; they burned me. My back tried to arc but could not. I raised my head. It was the only part of me I could move. The pain was excruciating. It felt as though I was being given the blood eagle. No man could stand this pain. I briefly opened my eyes and saw bright blood arcing into the air. I had seen it before when a man had had his throat cut. If I thought the pain was bad before now it was such that, if I had had my right arm free, I would have ended my own life. I wished I had asked Olaf Leather Neck to come and told him to kill me. The pain grew in intensity. I could not bear it.

Then all went black.

The Shadow of the Spirits

I was in a dark room but there was no pain. There was nothing. I knew that my eyes were open but I could see nothing. I could hear nothing. I could smell nothing. I moved my hand and I could feel nothing. Where was I?

Then I saw a light. It almost blinded me. I moved my hand to shield my eyes. When my hand touched my head, I could not feel it. The light grew and I became accustomed to it. I found I could hear. There were noises. There was a steady beat, like a distant drum. It kept the same beat. It was a noise. I could see and I could hear. Where was I?

Then a face appeared. It was Erika. She seemed not to walk but to float. I smiled, or I tried at least to smile. Then I saw Brigid. Brigid looked angry. She held a cross in her hand and she was holding it towards Erika. Erika was just smiling.

Brigid became more animated and angrier. She began to disappear. Her body just faded. Erika continued to smile and she held her hands out to me. I tried to move towards her but it was though I was wading through quicksand. Then, like Brigid, she vanished and I was alone once more.

I was aware of a smell. I could smell! It was the smell of wood smoke. The distant drum beat had faded but it was replaced by the murmur of voices. I found that I could move. I had regained the use of my legs. I tried to shout. If there were voices then, perhaps, when I shouted they might hear me.

Suddenly I saw a door. Perhaps it had always been there and just became clear to me. The door swung open and my son, Wolf Killer, stood there. Next to him were my shield brothers, Cnut and Snorri. They were my Ulfheonar. Behind them I saw a hall. It was filled with warriors. I recognised many of them. They were drinking. Wolf Killer and my Ulfheonar moved aside and I found that I was able to walk through the door. There was a wall of heat which hit me. My sense of touch had returned. There was a fire burning. I could not see it but I could feel it. The heat was intense. It was almost painful. Suddenly the pain became worse as the heat intensified. My senses were returning but I was still unable to speak.

The warriors all stood and the hall became silent. Faces flashed before me. Ragnar, Prince Butar, enemies I had slain. All faced me and then they began banging the tables and chanted, 'Dragonheart! Dragonheart! Dragonheart! Dragonheart!'

Then there was a bang like the crack of doom and all went silent. I saw Odin. He was mailed and he wore a helmet. His long beard hung down and, in his hand, he bore a spear. He held out his hand and said, 'Dragonheart, welcome to Valhalla! There is a place for you at my right hand if you are ready to come!'

I tried to move and take the place of honour and I could not. I heard a small voice. It was behind me and it kept saying, 'Jarl Dragonheart! Jarl Dragonheart! Jarl Dragonheart! Jarl Dragonheart!' It sounded like Aiden's voice. Aiden was not in Valhalla. I was in the world between this and the next. I was in the spirit world. Aiden could not reach the spirit world here. Then it sounded like Sámr's. How could that be?

I felt Ragnar's Spirit in my hand and I gripped it. I managed to raise it. A skull appeared before me and it was shrouded in a cloak. No one else seemed to see it. They laughed and they drank. The shrouded skull cloaked in shadow closed with me. Its gaping maw of a mouth grew larger. I summoned all the strength I had and I struck at the skull.

The hall faded, the heat disappeared and it all went silent. Everything was black and I could feel nothing. Valhalla had been taken from me.

Part Two

Dragonheart and the Shade of the Sun

Chapter 11

"Jarl Dragonheart! Great grandfather! You have slept enough! It has been four days." It was Sámr's voice and there was a catch in it. He could not be dead too, could he? "Aiden, what is wrong. Why will he not wake? Why does he just lie there?"

I was not dead. I tried to speak but I could not.

"He moved! Aiden, he moved."

I felt a hand upon my neck. "Perhaps. Go and fetch some water and Germund."

I heard feet slapping on the floor and then Aiden's voice was close to me, in my ear, "Dragonheart, you are alive. We thought you dead but you have defied death itself. You must try to open your eyes. I will shade them with my hands lest the brightness blinds you."

I felt foolish. Why could I not open my eyes? I was angry with myself and I forced them open. I saw the palms of Aiden's hands. I saw the lines which volvas said could predict how long a man might live. Aiden moved his hands. The brightness hurt at first but he moved them slowly and I saw his face. He was beaming.

"You will find it hard to talk. Your mouth and your throat will need water. Do not try to speak and do not try to move. I will speak. Use your eyes. Blink twice if you can hear me." I had to force my eyes to obey me but I managed it. I saw the relief on his face.

Sámr ran in. His eyes were red. He had been weeping. Haaken One Eye and Germund were there too.

"Germund, bathe his face but do so gently." The cloth felt cool. Germund was as gentle as a mother with her first baby.

"Sámr, put water in a beaker and help him to sip it drop by drop. Germund, support his head. Do not speak, Jarl."

Sámr put the beaker to my lips and Germund raised my head. My lips were so parched that it hurt when I opened them. The water felt like nectar. Drop by drop I drank.

"The doctor is a gifted man. He was gentle and he knew where the problem lay. Cutting out the growth was simple but he had to sew your insides back together. You lost a great deal of blood. At one point we thought you had died for your heart stopped. Sámr called for you and your heart started again. *Wyrd*."

Aiden put his hand on Sámr, "That is enough water for now." He smiled at me. "We have dabbed your lips to keep them moist but you have had neither food nor drink for the last four days. You will be as weak as a new born baby. Germund, go and tell the healer that he has awoken. He will wish to examine you."

Haaken spoke and his voice sounded strangely subdued, "Jarl, when you died did you…"

I blinked twice.

"You saw Valhalla!" I blinked twice to confirm it.

The doctor hurried in. He waved everyone but Aiden from the room. He made me drink a little more. Aiden held the beaker to my lips. His servant lifted the sheets. I saw that I was naked. I had not been bandaged. There was a long and angry looking scar. He put his head close to it and sniffed. He put his hands on either side. He touched but it did not hurt. I saw him watching my face as he did so.

He spoke to Aiden. Aiden asked, "Try to speak, Jarl. How does the wound feel?"

I tried to speak but a croak came out. Aiden handed me the beaker, "Drink more."

I did so and tried again. It was hard to make the words sound. "There is no discomfort. There is no ache. I just feel weak."

Aiden told Oribasius who beamed. He rattled off whole sentences of Greek. Aiden smiled too. "Then it is gone and you are healed. He cannot promise that it will not return. You will be weak until you have built up your strength. He has left instructions for the food you will be given to eat. He says that few other men could have survived what you did. He is writing what he did and placing it in the library so that others may read of the operation."

I croaked again, "How long do I lie here?"

The doctor spoke once more. "He will be back in ten days to remove the stitches. By then you should be able to walk and after that it depends how much work you wish to do to aid your body."

When Aiden had finished the doctor came over and shook my hand. He and his slave left. Aiden returned to the bed. I realised that it now had sheets upon it. They were white and bloodless. "And his payment?"

"He was paid before he made the first incision." He shrugged. "He thought that if you died we might be unwilling to pay. He mistrusted barbarians. He only agreed to operate because of David ben Samuel."

I realised that I had not seen him since the night before the operation. "Where is our host?"

"He left. Ptolemy just said that his master would be gone for a while and we were to treat this as our home." I cocked an eye. "Aye, Jarl, there is more to David ben Samuel than meets the eye. Before he left he was up and down the road to the Palace three or four times a day. He is an important man." He looked to the door. "The others will wish to enter soon. I need to speak. You entered the spirit world." It was a statement and not a question.

"You knew?"

"For the first time since we passed into the Blue Sea I sensed the presence of the spirits. Erika spoke to me. You died, Jarl. The doctor thought he had lost you. It was the spirits who saved you. I know not how but they made your body fight death and you won. The Norns have not finished with you."

He went to the door and let the others in. I wondered at that. I had been ready to surrender. What had made me fight on?

The first ten days saw a succession of visitors. The crew all wished to visit me. Ptolemy insisted on their visits being in groups of five. It made the process even longer but I was pleased to speak with them all. Each had news for me. Haaken, of course, had told them that I had been in Valhalla. Their visits exhausted me and Germund took to limiting the time they had with me. He and Sámr never left my side. Aiden would examine me each morning and evening. Other than that, he left me alone. Erik Short Toe told me that he had a cat. It was a black kitten with a white blaze. If had come from Josephus' family. On its first visit it had killed a rat. The crew liked him and named him Dragon. He seemed to like the name or so Erik Short Toe said. I did not mind any of the trivial conversations for I was alive and they were all the more important for that.

After four days I sensed that Sámr was becoming bored. He stayed with me but I thought that it was out of duty more than anything else. "Sámr, I order you to go and join your oar brothers. This is a fine city. Go with Lars and explore it. You need to buy gifts for your family do you not?"

"But you need me."

Germund said, "Go, young master. I will tend to the Jarl. You have my word." I think that when I had been in the spirit world and then recovering Germund had grown close to Sámr and Haaken. Sámr nodded. When he had gone Germund said, "He is a good boy! You are lucky, Jarl. I have no family and if he is typical of yours then I envy you."

"There is still time for you to have a family, Germund. You are still not too old."

"Who would have a crippled warrior?"

"A woman who could see beyond the wound and into the heart. You too are a good man Germund. If you wish to come back to the Land of the Wolf then I am certain there will be women with eyes clear enough to see that." He nodded and I saw gratitude and hope in his eyes.

Germund kept me apprised of the events beyond my room. He told me that my crew had traded their goods and made a great profit. Erik had confirmed as much. The men had spent much of their gold already. When Erik had visited me had told me that he had visited Josephus' family and discovered that they now had three small ships. I was pleased that we had brought the old man back all those years ago and his return had helped his family to prosper. Germund also brought disturbing news about the city beyond the harbour. There was unrest. It was nothing to do with my men and their high spirits. It was a rival to the Regent. His allies were stirring up trouble.

"I have seen this before, Jarl Dragonheart. The Empress Theodora holds on to power by her fingertips. Her son is still young." Germund hesitated. "My new master is away now seeking alliances for her."

"He works for the Regent."

He shook his head, "His religion makes that impossible. He serves her and that is a subtle difference." He looked uncomfortable. "I cannot be disloyal, Jarl, even for you. He saved me from a life which might have been ended already. I owe him much."

Three days before the doctor was due to return Aiden brought Erik, Olaf and Haaken to see me. "This looks serious."

Erik said, "Jarl, we have a request to make. If you say no then we shall understand."

"Ask."

"Josephus' family wish to trade." I nodded. "The ports they would use are far from here and the waters dangerous."

Aiden said, "The Imperial ships stay close to home these days, Jarl Dragonheart, because of the troubles in the city."

"Aah and they wish *'Heart of the Dragon'* to escort them."

"You are galdramenn, Jarl. Yes, it is so. The men are becoming bored and there would be coin for them. It is your drekar and your decision."

"Erik, your blood is in the drekar too. Take it with my blessing." A sudden thought struck me. "And Sámr?"

Olaf Leather Neck stroked his dagger, "I will watch over him, Jarl Dragonheart. He is to take an oar."

"Then enjoy your voyage and when you return I may be on the quay to welcome you."

After they had gone, leaving just Aiden and Germund in the city I felt lonely. It was fortunate that Oribasius came that day to take my stitches from me and to tell me that I was allowed to walk in the courtyard. Through Aiden he also told me that he was passing my care to my galdramenn. I could see the mutual admiration in their faces. I suspected that they had spent long hours together. Each had things to learn from the other. I was convinced that Aiden had had something to do with the spirits and my return from death. I knew not what but then I did not understand the spirit world. Perhaps the sword was the portal through which Aiden had come for me. Odin had touched it. I had had a glimpse through the door and no more.

It was like being released from prison as I stepped, leaning on the arms of Aiden and Germund, into the lemon scented courtyard. Ptolemy and the servants applauded me as I left the house. I sat and looked at the sun for the first time in almost half a moon. I saw the blue skies and watched the wispy clouds on high. Life was wondrous. I had spoken at length with Aiden. I had been saved for a purpose. The shadow that had hung over me was gone but why had I been saved? Neither Aiden nor I could divine that purpose but we both knew one thing. Life would begin anew for me.

The diet that I had been put on was effective. My strength returned. I began to put on weight. As the days passed I walked more than I sat. By the middle of Sólmánuður I felt the itch of my scar which told me that I was healing. Within a few days I felt much stronger. I asked Aiden if we could walk to the harbour. He did not object and the three of us went. For the first time since I had awoken I carried Ragnar's Spirit. I would not leave it in the house. Germund was protective. He too had put on weight since I had first met him. Good food and security had done that. He and Aiden ensured that there were no accidental bumps to harm me.

The sea breeze fed me. It filled my lungs and reminded me of home. This sea was blue and not grey but the smell was still the same. As we stood at the quayside watching ships come and go I said, "Germund, I would begin to make my arms strong again. I want you to make two practice swords. We can spar."

He looked at Aiden who nodded. "He is growing stronger. His body needs to become what it was and the Jarl has used his sword almost every day for as long as I have known him."

And so my next phase of recovery began. We used the stable area to practise. I knew that Germund was being gentle with me and, at first, that was good for the stretching of my arms made my scar ache. I had had wounds before and knew that it was necessary. When that passed I demanded that he be more vigorous in his attacks.

"Jarl, I do not want to hurt you."

"Then just avoid striking the side with the scar but I would have your full strength, Germund, and not these blows that even Ptolemy could block." I knew my body and I knew what I could take. I was under no illusions. We had found much trouble on our voyage here. I could not see us returning home without some combat. I could not rely on others to fight my battles for me. The practice became more realistic and I felt my old strength return. I had been afraid that I might never recover. Now I saw that I was almost healed.

My ship arrived back before David ben Samuel. Siggi appeared at the door. Ptolemy wrinkled his nose. He allowed him in to the courtyard. "Jarl, we have arrived back in port. My grandfather said you would wish to know."

I nodded, "Tell him that we will be down soon."

The heat of the Miklagård summer and the hot sun meant that we had practised in the shade of the stables. The streets also afforded shade so that when we stepped on to the quay it was like being struck by a wall of fire. I suddenly remembered the spirit world and the heat there. Aiden had said that it was the fire the healer had used to seal the wounds. I was not so sure.

I saw three small ships tied up close to the drekar. All four ships were being unloaded. Olaf Leather Neck, Haaken One Eye and Erik Short Toe strode towards me. As they passed one of the Greek ships they waved a man over. He looked familiar yet I knew I had never seen him.

"Jarl Dragonheart, it is good to see you up and about. This is Josephus' grandson, also called Joseph." The Greek bowed when he heard his name. I guessed he could speak little of our language.

That was when I saw the familiarity. He had the same eyes and nose as my old navigator. "You had a productive voyage?"

"Aye we did. We sailed north to the Hospitable Sea. It is like the edge of the world and filled with wild men. I can see why Joseph and his cousins asked for our help. There were many pirates." I looked at the ship for damage and to see if any shields were missing.

Olaf laughed when he saw my gaze, "They were small boats and the men poorly armed. With two drekar I could conquer the whole sea."

"Were there no Imperial ships keeping the seaways safe?"

Erik shook his head, "That is why they asked for our help, Jarl. The Imperial ships have withdrawn to face the threat of revolt here in the city. It was as David ben Samuel said, we took the risks and the rewards were great. They have had a good harvest there and here is a shortage of grain. We are rich. You are rich!"

I smiled, "Erik, I am alive, what more riches can a man wish?"

"I am sorry, Jarl Dragonheart."

Erik Short Toe asked, "And we can leave now? Soon it will be Heyannir. That would be a good time to leave. If we stay here for longer then we risk the storms of Gormánuður."

"I see no reason why we should not leave. I would like to say farewell to our host but he is still absent."

"It will take seven days or so to refit the ship and load the supplies. With the coin we took we can fill our hold with all that is valuable here. When we were in Bruggas we discovered what fetches the highest prices."

The sun was burning my head. I said, "Good. I will let you know when we can leave. Haaken do you and Sámr wish to stay at David ben Samuel's?"

Haaken smiled. "He has been an oarsman now. I think he wishes to stay here on the ship. Do not worry I will stay with him. We have songs to write." He pointed to half a dozen men who sat by the prow. "And we found these poor souls rowing for the pirates. They were pressed men. Like Germund they are Rus and wish to serve. We will return with more men at the oars than whence we came.

I felt a little excluded as I headed up to the house. Aiden was in the courtyard when we returned. I told him our news. "Then this voyage, risk filled though it was, has been worth it."

"I would not leave without saying goodbye to David ben Samuel."

Aiden frowned, "There is something going on. When I was in the Forum the other day I heard that there was an army camped outside the walls. They are Greek but it is not an Imperial Bandon. There is much tension. From what I can gather, the three who run the Regency, Empress Theodora, Bardas, a general and Theoktistos, a minster, have had a falling out. There was a rumour that Bardas was with the army camped outside the walls. It may be prudent to leave without saying farewell to David ben Samuel. He would understand."

"He might understand but that would not make it right. If there is trouble then we will join the crew on the drekar. You have all that you need from the city?" Since my operation he had spent most days in the library where he had been copying maps and writings which he felt would help us back in the Land of the Wolf.

"I can never have enough! Yet I would rather we were safe and returned home to our families rather than risk all. Without the help of the spirits I am blind here and I do not like it."

I turned to Germund, "The other reason I wish to see David is so that I can buy Germund's freedom."

"You are kind, Jarl, but my new master is a good man. As much as I would like to live amongst my own kind I know that I will not be mistreated if I have to remain here. Do not worry about me."

"Come then, if I am to leave soon I had best spend some of my coin. Let us go to the Forum and see what we can buy." I spent a great deal of coin. I wished to please my family. They would be happy enough just to see me but I was the head of the family and I had coin to spend.

David ben Samuel did not return for another two days. When he did arrive, he looked gaunt. He went to the bath house first and then Aiden and I joined him at his table. "We were concerned."

"And you were right to be so. I wished I had taken your ship. I would have been safer."

"You sailed to Caesarea?"

"No, I sailed to the Hospitable Sea."

I started, "My ship was there too. They were trading."

"I wish that I had known. I was on a diplomatic mission from the Regent. I was trying to make an alliance with the Khazars. The Empress wished them to make war on the Bulgars for they are supporting Patrikios Bardas."

Neither of us said anything but our faces were eloquent.

He smiled, "Yes, I am more than a merchant. I can trust you. In fact, I may need more than just your trust soon. The Khazar leader wanted too much gold and I did not trust him. We will have to come to an agreement with Bardas."

"We were going to bid you farewell, David ben Samuel, and leave this land. I did not wish to go without saying farewell and without asking if I could buy Germund's freedom."

He waved a dismissive hand, "He is yours. He cost me little but I beg you to give me half a month."

I thought back to Erik's words. We could afford to stay until the start of Tvímánuður. We would beat the storms which often made Syllingar so dangerous. "We owe you that at least. You wish our help?"

He gave us a serious look. "More than that, I may need your swords. Your men may be the only ones that I can trust to protect the Empress and her son, the would-be Emperor."

Chapter 12

The next morning, we saw evidence of the unrest. There was a riot at the Forum of Constantine. As that was the closest forum to the Great Palace it was disturbing. The Imperial guards seemed reluctant to intervene and contain it. David ben Samuel said, "Jarl, I must go to the palace. I should be safe enough but would you be able to bring some of your men here? We may need them. I know that you cannot help because…"

"I am a warrior. I am almost healed. If my men are needed then I will lead them. How many would you wish?"

"How many can you spare?"

"I can bring thirty-six men."

"Then I beg you to do so."

Aiden asked, "But it was just a riot. They are not uncommon, are they?"

"No, but it is the coincidence of being so close to the Palace and none of the guards intervening."

"And will you be safe?"

"I have four guards here in my home. They are discreet. I will take them with me."

While he summoned his men, we headed for the harbour. I noticed that the streets seemed quieter. It felt like the sea just before a storm. It was too still. It was the brooding stillness which did not bode well. As the three of us headed for the quay I said, "Well Germund, you have had your answer, you are, to all intents and purposes, a free man."

He nodded, "Freedom, Jarl, is often an illusion. You are free but you serve your people. My freedom means that I cannot be bought or sold. But I am part of you and your world. You have taken me away from a world without hope. I will follow you. Until you tire of me I shall be your lame servant."

I laughed, "I have sparred with you. Karl One Leg, one of my men, still fights and defends my walls. We will get you a sword and helmet when we reach the ship."

The men had fashioned an awning over the deck and the quay so that they could lie in its shade. It was convenient for I would be able to speak with them all. I waved Erik over. "If you and

Arne would have the ship's boys stop anyone listening to us then I would like to speak with the men."

He nodded, "The riot?"

"And other things. What have you heard?"

"Joseph told us that there is a great deal of unrest. The Emperor is but a child. Many people want Bardas to rule. He is a strong man. They think that he would rule with an iron hand." It all began to make sense.

They gathered around and I could feel their anticipation. Since my experience, I now felt like I knew what people might say and even do. This was not the time to speak of it but when I reached my home I would speak with Kara about it. I had much to ask. I would have asked Aiden but he seemed distracted. "We will be going home soon." I saw the relief on their faces. "Before we do that, David ben Samuel has asked for our help. I will not command you to follow me. That is not my way." I had their attention and I saw them all leaning forward to catch my words. It enabled me to lower my voice a little. "There is trouble at the palace. This is not our land but David ben Samuel is our friend. I would not be in this world if it was not for him and his healer." I saw nods. Some gripped the amulet they wore around their necks.

Olaf Leather Neck snorted, "We have never walked away from a fight yet, Jarl. Let us not begin now. It is a bad habit to get into."

Men laughed.

"I will take thirty-two of you with me. All must have a byrnie." I saw the disappointment on Sámr's face and Snorri Gunnarson and his men. The rest will guard the drekar. These are dangerous times and I would not lose all that we have while we are helping David ben Samuel. If any do not wish…"

I got no further. They all stood. To a man, they said, "We will come!"

"Olaf and Haaken will choose the men. Sámr, a word." I saw the disappointment etched all over his face. "Olaf Leather Neck told me that you became a warrior on the last voyage. That is good. You have coin of your own and when we reach Whale Island then you can buy a byrnie or have Bagsecg's sons make you one. Erik and Snorri will have few men left to guard our drekar. I need you here, with your bow, so that we can reach our home."

He nodded, "I understand, Jarl Dragonheart. I am young."

I shook my head, "Age has nothing to do with it. When we go to do whatever David wishes of us then we must look intimidating. We must be mailed, have helmets and shields. They think we are barbarians and for a short time we will be."

He suddenly took in my words. "You will be with them?"

"Who else would lead the Clan of the Wolf? Perhaps you when you are older eh?"

"But your wound."

"Is healed. I shall wear my mail and I will carry Ragnar's Spirit. It is *wyrd*."

The men were mailed and armed in no time at all. Germund fetched me my shield. He had a sword and a helmet which Haaken had found for him. Already he looked like a Viking warrior. Sámr said, "Germund has no mail."

"But he can speak Greek. We will not be taking Aiden with us. Who else can we take?"

He shook his head, "I should have spent the voyage here like Aiden and learned the language. Then I could have come with you."

I waved Haaken over. "Divide the men into three groups. It will attract less attention. I will take the first one." The people who lived close to the harbour were used to seeing small groups of Vikings walking their streets. Thirty odd would be a little too many.

Ptolemy looked shocked as we entered the gate. I smiled, "Your master asked my men to come. There will be more."

Shaking his head, he hurried off to arrange refreshments. Aiden was in his chamber. "I have gathered my things. I think it best if our chests were taken aboard. I know not what he has planned but it may be that we need a hasty departure."

"You have all that you need?"

"This will be my last visit to Miklagård. There is more that I would like to take but I have enough. Perhaps Ylva might come and finish my work."

Just then David ben Samuel arrived. He looked serious. "It is worse than I feared. Bardas has sent men to seize the young

Emperor. They entered through the gate of Charisius. We are fortunate. He will have a longer distance than we to travel through the city."

"And the palace guards?"

"The Empress is uncertain of the loyalty of some of them. I have men on the gate whom we can trust but the palace is large."

"Then you have no time to waste. Lead on." As he waved to his four men I had the opportunity to examine them. They were not young warriors. They were mercenaries. With overlapping mail armour, good helmets and oblong shields they were men who knew their business. They led and we followed in lines of three.

We ran at a steady pace. David ben Samuel's men cleared our path as we ran the relatively short distance to the palace. The ten men at the gate allowed us through. David ben Samuel said to them, "Do not let anyone else in. If Hetaereiarch Bardas comes with his army then you can do nothing. You will have to join us in the Imperial apartments."

As we moved into the palace proper I wondered how he thought a handful of Vikings could hold off an army. I had given my word and I could not go back on it now. Even as we hurried towards the buildings which made up the Imperial apartments I saw Greeks fleeing the palace. They would run now and then return to make their peace with whoever held power. The Greeks were a pragmatic people. This was the world of the easterner and not the world of the Viking.

Our entry to the main quarters was barred. I joined David ben Samuel as he spoke with the officer there. Germund was next to me and he translated. "The officer says that half of the guards who were supposed to be on duty have failed to turn up. There are less than thirty men inside."

David turned to me. "You had better bring your men inside. We will be the last bastion. The guards here and at the gate are loyal. They will give their lives for the Emperor. It will be up to your men to stop the young Emperor being taken."

I had thought David ben Samuel's home was spectacular but the palace and the Imperial quarters were something even more awe inspiring. I had seen them when a young man and they had been improved since then. The Emperors spent their coin on luxury. We had no time for that. They should have spent it on loyal troops.

Empress Theodora, young Michael and the eunuch, Theoktistos, were waiting for us in what we would have called the Great Hall. I knew not what they named it. The latter, Theoktistos reminded me of Ptolemy. He looked dismissively at us, "These barbarians will save us?" Sarcasm oozed from every word. I had enough Greek to understand that.

Empress Theodora had her arm around her son, Michael. She snapped, "Theoktistos!" I could not follow the rest of her diatribe but I got the gist of it. I was looking around the room in which we found ourselves to see if we could defend it. I saw that there were just two doors in and out. One was the large double door through which we had entered and the other was a small, innocuous door at the back. There were eight guards in the room. I was suddenly aware that all eyes were on me.

Germund said, quietly, "The Empress asked what you will do?"

I pointed to the small door. "I want that locked and barred. Put any tables you can find against it." David ben Samuel translated. "The palace guards will guard the Emperor and my men will make a shield wall. The enemy has to come through that door. It is wide enough for four men at most. No matter how many men they have, they have to face us four at a time. We will outnumber them."

When David translated Theoktistos snorted in disgust but the Empress nodded and spoke. Germund said, "She says that you are a confident warrior. She has spoken with your doctor who says you are a remarkable man. If you hold off the enemies then you will need a second ship to carry back the gold you will be given."

I smiled and bowed, "Tell her I will be happy to get home with my life. Now bar the door and form a shield wall." I turned to Germund who had finished translating. "You guard the boy. If we fail then you can die a Viking!"

He nodded, "It has been an honour."

We left the palace guards to bar the doors. David said, "Where would you like my men?"

"They can be between us and the palace guards. We will try to take as many of the enemy as we can. How many will there be?"

"It is a small force he has sent. No more than two hundred men."

"Then let us hope that some of the loyal guards thin their numbers for us." A thought struck me. "There will be loyal troops coming to aid us?"

"The Theme of Thrace and the Theme of Macedonia are both loyal Bandon. They are on their way. You have to hold them until dark."

I saw that my men had formed a shield wall, three men deep. They had not left a space for me. Olaf saw my face and he said, "You can be at the back, Jarl Dragonheart. If we fall then you get to fight. Knowing that Ragnar's Spirit is behind us is enough. The doctor did not heal you just to be killed by a rebel warrior. Trust us."

Haaken One Eye said, "Jarl, you would not want a warrior to die because he relied on you and your wound stopped you being you, would you?"

He was right. There could be no weak links in a shield wall. I could hear commotion in the palace. The doors and the walls were effective at masking it but there were shouts and screams as well as the clash of steel. We had not barred these doors and they were flung open as the last three guards ran in. I saw that they were the ones we had spoken to at the gates. David ben Samuel shouted something. They came and stood by me. We would be the last line before the Emperor and his defenders. I saw that their blades were bloody and their tunics bespattered with blood. One sported a wound to his arm.

There were still men fighting in the corridor. We could hear the sound of sword on sword and men dying. Olaf Leather Neck shouted, "We are the Clan of the Wolf. Haaken let us tell them who we are!"

We had learned that the sound of our chants could put fear in the hearts of our foes. They would wonder what they faced. On an open battlefield it was bad enough but the sound would be emanating from a room. It would echo and be amplified. The first ones in would have to face that fear. Regardless of that, a chant put strength into our men. As we chanted we banged our shields with our sword hilts.

> *Viking enemy, taking heads*
> *Viking warriors fighting back*
> *Viking enemy, taking heads*
> *Viking warriors fighting back*
> *Viking enemy, taking heads*
> *Viking warriors fighting back*
> *Viking enemy, taking heads*
> *Viking warriors fighting back*
> *Viking enemy, taking heads*
> *Viking warriors fighting back*
> *Viking enemy, taking heads*
> *Viking warriors fighting back*

Olaf had placed the men just five paces from the door. There was one row of twelve and two rows of eleven. The first three men ran into the room. They wore scale mail shirts which only came to their waists. On their heads they wore round helmets and they carried an oval shield. Their swords were the long spatha used by horsemen. They had fought with their blades; they were bloody. They would not be as sharp as ours. Olaf had my place in the middle of the front rank and, using his axe two-handed he swept it in an arc to take the heads of all three men. The first had his head removed while the other two were hit in their faces. The first head hit the door and bounced into the corridor. The headless body fell. The other two dropped like stones. The three bodies were a barrier.

"Clan of the Wolf!" When he was in this sort of mood Olaf Leather Neck was the equal of a berserker.

The next skutatos who entered was wary and he stopped in the door. He shouted something down the corridor. The next ones we fought would not die so easily. The Greeks did not use shield wall as we did. Their shields were not locked. They came together and fought as individuals. With the exception of Olaf every other shield was interlinked with their neighbours. Our shields covered most of our bodies and our byrnies hung below the shield to cover us to the knees. They formed their version of a shield wall and stepped forward. I leaned into the back of the third rank and said to the Greeks on either side of me, in Greek, "You too!"

Our lines became one metal mass. I could see, over Halmr's shoulder, the next four men die almost without raising their weapons. Olaf's swinging axe made them raise their shields and Haaken and the others gutted them. Their mail went to their waist only. Outside I could hear orders being shouted. More men appeared and they tried to push into the room. The ones at the front were a sacrifice. Their bodies were held by the ones behind. Our second rank thrust their swords through the gaps in the front rank and Greeks died. They had more men now and gradually our line bowed. I felt my feet slipping back on the marble floor. It did not matter for when the skutatos entered they were surrounded on three sides. Eventually, they would shift us but by then I hoped to have thinned out their best men.

As we were pushed back our lines spread and I found myself, with the three Greeks, in the third rank. Haaken, Olaf and the others in the front rank were still butchering the Greeks but we were also taking casualties. I saw Arne Longwalker fall. He was struck four times and yet he still took two of his killers with him. Others fell wounded and they swapped places with those in the rank behind. When Leif Longshanks was cut in the leg I said, "Change places!" He did so and I was in the second rank. I lifted Ragnar's Spirit so that it was between Haaken One Eye and Sven Stormbringer. I saw a Greek face and I lunged at it. My sword took him in the eye and went into his brain. My scar hurt as I did so but I could live with the pain. Someone had ordered the skutatos to use their spears. One was rammed at Sven Stormbringer's body. He flicked his shield at it. The spear came straight for my head. It rang off my helmet and I saw stars. It was a warning.

Despite the deaths we had inflicted they were pushing us back into the hall. The Greek warriors who were behind us were suited to fighting on a battlefield where large numbers of men would determine the outcome. Here it was every man for himself and we used whatever means we could to attain victory.

A Greek voice from the corridor shouted out an order. Feet sounded in the corridor. He was sending everyman he had. When we were all pushed back I knew what it was. It was a last throw of the bones. He sought to overwhelm us and capture the Emperor. The fact that he might lose most of his men appeared to be a gamble worth taking. The sudden weight of men had an effect. Our double line became single and I found myself fighting alongside two of the palace guards. I could not rely on their shields. I was aware of my scar. On the outside my body was healing but what of inside? Was I risking all by defending a boy? I smiled. I was fulfilling an oath. I had no choice.

The skutatos who ran at me saw a white beard and a man who had been in the rear rank. They were always the softest of warriors. He came at me confidently with his shield held loosely. He struck at me and my shield flicked up to knock the sword away. We were not in a tight formation and I had the room to bring Ragnar's Spirt from on high. He barely had time to block the blow and he reeled. I punched at him with the boss of my shield. The muscle in my side ached but the boss did its job. His nose spread across his face and I lunged at his thigh. Twisting as I pulled the sword out against the bone he fell writhing on the ground. Even as I was withdrawing the sword I brought it up under the arm of the skutatos fighting my Greek shield brother. His arms were bare and my sword tore through muscles and tendons. His sword fell followed, two strokes later, by his body.

The lines were no longer clear. This was a free for all and that would suit my men. I saw Olaf's axe rise and fall. I heard the exultant roar of Galmr as he brought down his blade to take another foe. A skutatos and his shield brother came at me. I was isolated and I stepped back. I knew that there was a palace guard there. One side would be protected. As it happened there were two. I later found that the third had died. Our small shield wall seemed, to the skutatos who were advancing, that we were the last line of defence before the Emperor. Others joined them.

I angled my body so that my shield covered my side and I poked Ragnar's Spirit over the top. I could see that my men were winning but eight men had chosen to break through our shield wall. Jarl Dragonheart might get his wish of a glorious death and a place next to Odin. As they came towards us I knew that I was not ready to die. I had been to the Otherworld and this world had more to offer me.

I took the first blow on my shield and rammed my sword forward. I was rewarded first by flesh and then by bone as Ragnar's Spirit tore into the warrior's mouth. I tore the sword out sideways and it sliced into the neck of the next man. Another warrior stepped forward to take the place of the man I had slain but the press of men was so much that neither of us could use our swords. I pulled back my head. My helmet had a nasal and a mask. When it hit his face, his nose broke as did his cheekbones. A piece of metal ripped out his eye and he fell back screaming. A sword came from behind and scored a line across my helmet.

Suddenly there was a roar from my side and I saw Germund and David ben Samuel lead the men I had left guarding the Empress. They fell upon the skutatos. It was too much. I heard Greek words being shouted. I later learned it was. '*I surrender*'! They were pragmatic warriors. They would now join the winning side. Bardas' attempt to take power had failed.

As the Greeks threw down their swords so my men began banging their shields with their swords and they chanted, "Dragonheart!" Over and over.

Seven of my men lay dead. Others, Olaf Leather Neck and Haaken One Eye included, were wounded. David ben Samuel took charge. He sent men to seal the gates and to fetch a physician. The skutatos were disarmed and the guards mounted a watch on the gate. I took off my helmet and turned to the two Greeks who had fought alongside me. I nodded and said, "Thank you!"

They both grinned and gave a half bow. The captain of the guard shouted an order and they left me to stand watch. For the first time I had fought alongside someone who was not Viking. It had gone well. Perhaps it was a sign for the future. As I cleaned my sword on the tunic of a fallen skutatos I thought back a few moments to the battle. I had chosen life over death. My journey into the shadows had been necessary. I had thought that, because I had a white hair and beard, that my time in this world was done. I had glimpsed Valhalla and knew that a place of honour lay there for me. Yet this world still had more. Sámr and my other grandchildren and great grandchildren were important. I wanted to see them grow.

Germund came over. His tunic was covered in blood and his sword was notched. I nodded to it. "Choose yourself a better weapon, Germund! You have earned it."

He nodded, absent mindedly, as though that was not important, "I have seen Jarl Dragonheart and his men fight. I do not deserve the honour of joining such a clan."

"You deserve it more than any. You could have watched yet, without mail you came to our aid. Yours was the greater act of courage this day."

David ben Samuel came over. He was smiling yet he too had blood upon his tunic. "We could not stand and let you be butchered. The Empress said that we had to join this band of heroes. She called you Spartans! She is right. The Theme of Thrace are at the gates. They will be here soon." He turned as cloaks were laid over our dead. "I am sorry that you lost warriors."

"The men who came with me from the Land of the Wolf chose to come and expected to die. All were single men. The ones who return will honour their memory. I have seen Valhalla and know that they will be happy. They are but a little way from here and the door is opening. They will see old comrades and they will be eager to tell them of this battle."

It was dawn by the time that the reinforcements had arrived. They scoured the palace and captured the enemy who had fled the battle. The leader was dead. Olaf Leather Neck had hewn his head from his body. It had been his death and the attack led by David ben Samuel which had prompted the surrender. As I prepared to lead my men away the Empress came to speak with me and my men. She spoke through David ben Samuel.

"The Empress is impressed with your courage. She invites all of you to be her personal guards. Here you will be given a place of honour and riches beyond your wildest dreams. What do you say to her offer?"

I said nothing. It was not my place to do so. Haaken One Eye looked at my men and they nodded. He would speak for them. "Tell the Empress, David ben Samuel, that we are flattered by her offer and it is attractive." His words were translated and the Empress nodded. "But we swore an oath to Jarl Dragonheart and a man must live by the oaths he makes. We will return to the Land of the Wolf."

I saw the look of surprise on her face and the one of absolute shock on her minister's face. She smiled and came to me. She spoke to me as she held my hand in hers. "The Empress says that you are a lucky man to inspire such loyalty. If you return after noon on the morrow then there will be your rewards."

I nodded, "Thank her for me. Tell her that there are many warriors such as us who would happily serve her. If a Viking makes an oath then he will die for her or her son."

She nodded and spoke to David. "She is in your debt for such sage advice."

We left Miklagård five days later. We had a huge chest of coins. We were allowed to choose the weapons and mail from the dead rebels and we took that too. Our drekar was packed with goods for trade and we had no space in our hold. We had lost men but we had gained warriors too so that we would be well crewed on the way home. Germund and Sámr would be oar brothers and that was *wyrd*.

There was quite a party came to see us off. Joseph and his cousins came as did David ben Samuel and Ptolemy. Perhaps Ptolemy came to make sure that we left. Even though we bathed regularly while we had stayed with David ben Samuel, Ptolemy had always wrinkled his nose when he neared us. David handed me a sealed pouch. "This is for my uncle. It is sealed not to prevent you reading but to keep it watertight." he smiled. "I know the effects of the sea."

"You need not explain."

"I am pleased that you cracked that yard and had to come to Bruggas. Perhaps there is something to this thing called *wyrd*. I do not think that the Emperor would be free today if you had not come for me."

"And you, you will be happy? You will be married now?"

"I will and I have been given a post in the palace. For a Jew this is unheard of. I have you to thank for that. I do not think we will meet again, Dragonheart, but if you do return then my home is yours." His face and his eyes told me that he spoke the truth.

I stepped aboard the drekar and Erik cast off. We headed south and west. There was a slight breeze from the north and so we did not use the oars. The busy Sea of Marmara was not a place for speed. It was a place for caution. There was no hurry. I was no longer dying. We had three moons to make the journey which had taken us two on our way east. We could make a leisurely passage. There was no need for us to court danger. We had a full hold and wanted for nothing. Of course, we had no way of knowing what the Norns had in store for us.

Chapter 13

We sailed home in high summer. It was hot. The canvas we had used in Miklagård was now used to keep us all cooler. There was little breeze as we headed home and it was too hot to row. We edged our way south and west. David ben Samuel and Aiden had procured better maps and we had, from the Empress, an Imperial pass. So long as we were in Imperial waters we would have friends. Once we passed Sicily then we would be amongst enemies. The slow passage on this part of the voyage was not a problem.

Germund and the other new men were getting to know my crew. A voyage was the best way to do so. Sámr and Germund got on well as oar brothers. They had both watched me through my recovery and shared that experience. Other warriors had also found new shield brothers and that engendered an even closer tie. The crew had lost warriors but we were now a compact band of brothers. The new men all needed mail and their own shield but other than that they were prepared should we be attacked. Our experience with the pirates had been a warning. We would heed it. The lookouts now understood the dangers of other ships. Even the smaller ones represented danger.

Once we had passed the narrow seaways of the Dardanelles then we had sea room. The wind, gentle though it was, took us west. It was not fast enough for me but we could do nothing about it. My close encounter with death had made me keen to see my family. I would have had the men row but I knew that was unfair. The heat was almost unbearable and I saw little point in exhausting the ones who had made it possible for the healer to save my life. I knew that they were as keen to return home as I was. Aiden was desperate to pore over the documents he had had copied. Miklagård provided such a service, for a fee, and we were not short of coin. However, they were beneath the decks in waterproof containers. The whole crew wanted to return home. We would all have to be patient.

The seaways were still dangerous. The attempted coup in Constantinopolis had made the Imperial Fleet stay even closer to home. While they were there then corsairs, pirates and even rebels could prey upon helpless ships. We were far from helpless but as we had discovered on the outward voyage there were desperate men who would risk the wrath of the Northman. We kept a good watch.

    I was enjoying life. I had glimpsed Valhalla and it made my home and my comrades even more important. I had almost passed over to the other side and something had drawn me back. It was a voice, Aiden's or Sámr's, which had summoned me but it was not the voice that made me return. The door had slammed in my face. Odin was not yet ready for me. My work was not finished. I knew that now. Sámr would be a fine warrior who would lead the clan in the future but Gruffyd and Ragnar were busy with their own lives. My guiding hand was still needed. I had thought my work was done but with my son and grandson living hard by Whale Island the larger part of the Land of the Wolf needed me and my guidance. While we had been in Miklagård, Aiden had discovered that the island of Britannia was becoming more Norse than Saxon. That was not always a good thing for there were many Danes I did not like. Most were no friends of mine. We had defeated the Saxons at every turn but fighting our own kind was harder. We had beaten the Saxons. Would we need to defeat Danes too?

    One advantage of the slow, steady breeze from the north was that we could sail at night. We had three watch keepers. We were able to head due south towards Kriti and then sail due west. Kriti was hard to miss and we could avoid the myriad of islands to the south of Greece. It added leagues to our journey home but I was no longer dying and there was no rush. Of course, had we known what the Norns had planned then we might have taken a different route. Closer to the Land of the Wolf and Aiden would have been able to see the danger. Here he was so far from his homeland and his roots that he was almost as an ordinary man. All that he could predict were the changes in the weather and Erik Short Toe could do that too. Aiden was a wizard without a purpose. Once we passed the Pillars of Hercules then he would regain his strength.

    We called in at the island of Kriti to top up our water. The pass given to us by the Empress saw us treated as civilized men rather than barbarians. We must have confused the men of Kriti for although we sailed a drekar and they were unmistakable we had all bathed in Miklagård. We had bought fine clothes which were cooler and more refined. Our hair was combed and, as the food we had eaten was Greek, we did not smell the way we normally did. None of us wore mail and our shields were not hung along the side. We were a talking point. I daresay that long after we had left they would be wondering just what we were.

As we had refilled at Kriti with water and fresh food then we did not need to land at Chatacium. Erik, Aiden and I decided that we would sail between Melita and the coast of Italy. It was the most direct route to the Pillars of Hercules. Perhaps it might even save us days. We had enough water to reach beyond the Blue Sea. Once we were through the straits then there would be more rain and more places to collect water. Our slow speed meant that we were able to fish as we sailed ever westward.

The Norns decided that we had had enough peace some seventeen days after leaving Miklagård. We knew something was amiss when the birds which had been following us disappeared. Then the wind veered. Ominously it swung around to blow from the north. We could cope with any wind but that. It would drive us towards Africa. Erik Short Toe consulted with Aiden.

"My skills as a galdramenn cannot help you here but perhaps my knowledge of maps and the weather might. Looking at the clouds we are due for a storm. The air feels heavy."

"Aye, I noticed that."

"Such weather is often violent but does not last long. If you wish my suggestion then we man the oars and row north and east. Melita is close to our larboard side. We do not want to be driven thence and north lies Sicily. There is war there between the Arabs and the Greeks. When I spoke with other scholars they said that the front lines were ambiguous. We should avoid that island too."

Erik shook his head, "Then you wish me to sail a fine line between Melita and Sicily with a wind which comes from the north and threatens to drive us either to Africa or Melita?"

Aiden smiled, "That is about it."

I stepped between them. "We now have more men to row. We do as we did before. We use shifts of rowers. We need not sail into the wind. You can still use your sails, Erik. I admit it is not ideal but once we have passed between the two islands then we have open water. If Aiden is correct then the wind will change direction."

"I am confident that in one day it will swing to blow from the south and east. The Allfather has sent it."

I nodded, "And I pray that this is not a trick of the Norns!" I turned and cupped my hands. "Run out the oars!"

Haaken chose our story. The new men had yet to hear it although I knew that it was told in the inns and taverns of northern Britannia.

> *From mountain high in the land of snow*
> *Garth the slave began to grow*
> *He changed with Ragnar when they lived alone*
> *Warrior skills did Ragnar hone*
> *The Dragonheart was born of cold*
> *Fighting wolves, a warrior bold*
> *The Dragonheart and Haaken Brave*
> *A Viking warrior and a Saxon slave*
> *When Vikings came he held the wall*
> *He feared no foe however tall*
> *Back to back both so brave*
> *A Viking warrior and a Saxon slave*
> *When the battle was done*
> *They stood alone*
> *With their vanquished foes*
> *Lying at their toes*
> *The Dragonheart and Haaken Brave*
> *A Viking warrior and a Saxon slave*
> *The Dragonheart and Haaken Brave*
> *A Viking warrior and a Saxon slave*

Once we had our speed increased then one of the two rowers on each oar stopped. The ship's boys had to work harder. Sámr now rowed with Germund. Aiden had suggested a course of action which necessitated the ship's boys racing up and down the rigging to adjust the reefed sail and take advantage of the wind. Added to that the northern wind brought a storm. It was the kind old sailors called a squall. No matter what they call it, hanging from the yard and trying to reef a sail is never easy and with a shifting wind it could kill an unwary boy. The rain pelted the deck.

Despite our best efforts we were still being driven on to the rocks and small islands which lay to the north of Melita. We had to double up on the oars to maintain our way. I saw that the rowers were becoming exhausted.

"Come, Aiden, you and I will give Sámr and Germund some relief."

"You would have me row?" He was incredulous. I had never asked him to row before.

"There is something else useful that you could be doing?"

Sámr and Germund were reluctant to let us relieve them but I insisted. Part of it was a genuine concern for my great grandson and part of it was to stiffen the resolve of the other rowers. I know not the exact length of time we rowed but Aiden's hands were blistered and bleeding when we allowed Sámr and Germund to relieve us. Aiden was less than happy.

I smiled, "Now you can truly test the efficacy of the salve you give young rowers like Sámr."

As the wind swung around so that it blew first from the north west and then from west we seemed to make little progress. We had to reef the sails. Had we been fully crewed then it might have been different but we had the minimum and we paid the price. It was dark when it swung around to blow from the south. We were able to rest half of the rowers. We saw the dark shape of Sicily to the north of us and we waited until it was well astern before we pulled in the oars and lowered the sail. It was still reefed but the men could rest and the wind, from the south, would take us to open water. The crew, ship's boys and rowers were exhausted. Even Olaf Leather Neck was weary. He had not fully recovered from the wounds he incurred at the palace but he was a hard man and would not show weakness.

I joined Erik and Arne. Sven was now fit enough to row and he lay exhausted. "The four of us will steer the ship this night. I will stand a watch with Arne. Aiden can share one with you, Erik."

"What about lookouts?"

I waved an arm. "Look around you. Do you see boys who can stand a watch? The alternative is to hove to and throw out a sea anchor. We are between Africa and Sicily. We have to make sea room between us and the Musselmen. I cannot see an alternative."

Erik was pragmatic. He nodded, "You are right. I hope the Allfather is with us."

Aiden shook his head, "This feels like the work of the Norns."

Arne and I rolled in our blankets. Erik would wake his son and I when they were too tired to make good judgements. It seemed but moments when I was shaken awake by Aiden and yet the sky was black. It was night time. I joined Arne at the steering board. Handing him a water skin I said, "We should not see any other ships at night."

"You are right, Jarl Dragonheart. Only madmen like us would risk the Blue Sea at night without lookouts."

I pointed west. "There should be nothing until Lusitania and that is many leagues from here."

"You are right but there is a reason that most ships do not sail at night without lookouts."

"Then I will be the lookout. I shall be at the dragon if you need me." I took the spare water skin with me. The storm had served one purpose, at least. It had replenished one of the water barrels. We would not now need water until we had passed through the Pillars of Hercules.

I clambered up to the prow. When I stretched I found it uncomfortable but that, I think, was because of the scar. I had enjoyed rowing with the rest of the crew. Once you were in the rhythm of the crew, even without a chant, it was as though you were one being. The Greeks and Romans built wonderful machines. We had seen some in Miklagård but the machine that was a drekar crew was something special. The common action and motion took away pain and tiredness; for a while at least. I could not remember the last time I had had to row. I would offer to relieve one of the crew the next time we rowed.

After I had made water over the leeward sided I pulled myself up onto the sheerstrake and wrapped my arm around the dragon prow. This was not the grey sea we normally sailed. This was the Blue Sea. At night it was not blue but, unless there was a strong wind blowing, then the waves were not high. It made it much easier to spot rocks and shoals. The maps Aiden had with him did not show any rocks. That did not mean that we did not look. I scanned the water for the tell-tale white marking the presence of rocks. The waves were not normally as large as the ones off Frankia and an anomalous flurry of white would indicate a rock.

I found that being a lookout allowed your mind to wander but kept your eyes sharp. As my eyes looked for the unusual I ran over the events of the last couple of years. There had been a time when I had begun to become an old man. I had been waiting for death. That had been after Brigid had died. A man does not normally bury two wives. I had. Sámr had been my salvation. That was a word used by Brigid. She had always striven to save my soul; whatever a soul was. Taking Sámr with me had been like looking at me when I was young. Old Ragnar had not given up on life when he had taken me in. He had shown me how to be a Viking. I was being selfish thinking of death. I now knew that I had been given a choice by the Allfather. I could have chosen Valhalla and all that meant or I could have chosen life and my family. I had chosen the latter. I had made mistakes with Wolf Killer. I had been less than perfect with Gruffyd. I realised now that perfection did not matter. A man did the best he could. If he was a good man then all would turn out well. I believed that I was a good man. My glimpse into Valhalla had suggested I was.

I was suddenly aware that the back of my neck felt slightly warmer. I looked around and saw a thin light in the east. The warmth was the breeze which had shifted and was now coming from the south and east. That was perfect. It would keep us from the coast of Africa, the pirates and the Musselmen. I lifted my head and, putting my hand on the dragon prow said, "Thank you Allfather and thank you *'Heart of the Dragon'*. When I have the chance, I will make a blót."

The night had passed without incident. The crew, men and boys were all rested and whatever the day brought we would be in a better position to deal with it. It was *wyrd*.

As I walked down the drekar I shook men awake. Dawn was a time of danger. Pirates could lurk in the dark and await passing ships. The wolf sought the sheep! We would stand to and watch for the dawn. The boys would scamper up the mast and ensure that the horizon was clear. Then we would make water, empty our bowels and then eat. I saw that Germund had his body curled protectively around Sámr. When you had an oar brother you were closer than family. For a time, when I was young, my oar brother had been Haaken One Eye. He was as close to a brother as I had had. He had been the one willing to face the Norn in the cave at Syllingar. Since we had stood back to back in Norway fighting other Vikings we had been closer than brothers. We were closer because we had chosen each other.

"Sámr, Germund, it is dawn." I handed them the water skin. "Here is water."

Sámr rubbed his eyes, "You watched all night?"

"No, Sámr, half a night. It was no hardship. The sea is where all the spirits of the world are found. They bring you thoughts which you would not otherwise have. I feel sorry for those who are not close to the sea." I rose and made my way to the steering board.

Erik and Aiden were awake. Aiden was smiling, "Thank you for making me stand a watch, Jarl Dragonheart. A man needs to be alone with his thoughts and standing watch by the steering board allows a man to do just that. Since I learned to control my powers I have forgotten the pleasure of my own thoughts." He tapped his head, "In here I normally compete with the spirits. It can be a very noisy place! I enjoyed the peace of standing a watch."

Lars and Siggi were on the yard and Lars shouted down, "The horizon is clear!"

It meant that we could all relax a little. We could prepare for the day. After he had put out four platters, Siggi brought out the salted ham we had bought in Miklagård and he sliced pieces from it. He laid them neatly on the platters. He did it carefully for his captain and his jarl would eat from them. He returned the ham to the wooden box which he replaced in the chest. It was beneath the awning and would be as cool as anywhere. He took out the cheese and put a slice on each platter. We could not get apples in Miklagård but they had peaches and nectarines. They were not as good but they would do. We missed our bread. We would only enjoy bread if we took it. Finally, he poured each of us a horn of precious beer. We had spent so long in Miklagård that our resourceful warriors had found a woman who brewed ale. She had an inn by the Golden Horn and it was frequented by Rus. We had managed to get two barrels. We eked it out with a horn at each meal. If we could not have bread then at least we could have beer!

The days were much hotter now. After the storm there had been a brief period of more bearable weather but as the morning progressed and we headed west so the heat weighed upon our shoulders. Men lay beneath the awning to get what shade they could. Even Haaken forsook his composing and just lay there unable to move. Erik had picked up a tip or two from Joseph. He had two wide brimmed hats. He could not afford, as captain, to spend all his time beneath the awning. He had to look ahead and at the sea. The hat helped. The ship's boys had also learned to make hats from woven straw. Joseph had told us to rub olive oil on our skin. It would stop the skin flaking from us. We headed back a more experienced crew.

Two days after we had passed Melita the wind shifted. This time it was from the south and south eastern quarter. More importantly it increased in strength. The breeze across the deck freshened us all up and *'Heart of the Dragon'* seemed to relish the chance to speed up. For the first time since we had left Miklagård the drekar flew as only a drekar can. We should have known that it was the Norns.

Not long before noon, as the men were anticipating their water ration, Siggi shouted, "Sails to the west!"

I joined Erik, Olaf, Haaken and Aiden at the steering board. Erik pointed to the pennant at the mast head, "We can turn slightly north or south, Jarl Dragonheart but south takes us closer to Africa and north to the islands they call the Balears. I am loath to change course until Lars can identify the ships."

If the ships to whom the sails belonged were on the horizon it would take some time to identify them. They could have been traders but, in this part of the world, it was best to assume that they were hostile and take the appropriate action. "If they are Arabs or Moors and enemies then we have a slight advantage. The wind is with us. If they turned to face us then we would have the weather gauge and, I have no doubt, that we could slip through them. I do not want to stay in this Blue Sea for one moment longer than we need to. We head for the Pillars of Hercules with all speed."

I could see that, Erik apart, that met with their agreement.

Aiden said, "The wind may change but I believe that it will swing around to come more from the east and that suits us. I have had little to do on this voyage and I have been observing its direction. There seems to be a pattern."

"Then have bows and weapons readied. Put the shields on the sheerstrake. *'**Heart of the Dragon**'* may be going to war." I clutched the wolf I wore around my neck. "We are in the hands of the Allfather now!"

Despite the heat men moved with a purpose. My men were not, by nature, indolent. We liked action. The freshening breeze had made the deck more bearable. I went to my chest and took out my sword and dagger. I did not take out my helmet but I did take out the mail hood I had taken from the dead skutatos in Miklagård. I had seen that they wore it beneath their helmet. My own helmet restricted my vision. The mail hood would afford some protection and yet not restrict my senses. Many of my warriors had also taken hoods. The men who had had no mail not had a mail vest. It only came to their waist but was better than nothing. With the skutatos' knives and daggers as well as their swords, we were better armed than we had been. None would wear mail. It was too much of a risk in a sea which was not ours. The shields would be left at the side of the drekar until they were needed. Armed and prepared we waited for Lars to shout down. He had joined Siggi at the masthead. Two pairs of eyes were better than one.

The sun had passed its zenith when Lars shouted, "Jarl, it is a fleet. I count the sails of ten ships. They are sailing due north."

I turned to Erik and Aiden. I needed their advice. Erik said, "They may be heading for the Balears, they are a group of islands to the north. They have the wind as do we. In fact, they may well be sailing faster."

Aiden said, "When I was in the library in Miklagård I spoke with a man writing about this region. He said that there were many pirates on the islands."

"That would explain so many ships if they were sailing south but not heading north."

Aiden shook his head. "They may not be heading for the islands. They could be heading for the Caliphate of Córdoba. This may be a convoy heading for the eastern coast of the Caliphate. They are sailing due north to take advantage of the wind. They can turn when they are closer." He cupped his hands and shouted up, "Lars, how many are warships?"

There was a pause. Lars was the most experienced of our ship's boys. Siggi might have plucked a number from the air but Lars knew that merchant ships were tubbier to accommodate more cargo and warships, like our drekar, looked like lean and hungry predators. The Arabs, like the Empire, had similar looking ships. The main difference was the lateen sail favoured by the Moors.

"I think there are four warships, galdramenn, one leads and one protects the rear. The other two vessels look like sheepdogs. There are six merchant ships. They waddle in the middle."

Aiden nodded. "You have your answer. If you sail towards the back of the convoy then you take out three of the warships. They will not be able to attack us and we should be able to escape the last one. They would have to turn into the wind to reach us. They might have oars but *'Heart'* is flying today!"

He was right. We could use our superior speed and agility to avoid a confrontation. "Make the adjustment, Erik!"

Erik was a good sailor. He shouted his orders to his boys and then made the slightest of adjustments to the steering board. We were now sailing due east. We had the full force of the wind from our quarter and were rapidly approaching the convoy. I had no doubt that we were seen. That was confirmed when Lars shouted, "One of the warships has turned. She has run out oars and comes to investigate."

I stood by Erik, "You are the captain and you steer the ship but I am a warrior. I would have you sail directly for the warship." His eyes widened. "Hear me out. The wind will be aft of us and we will have more speed. They will be sailing into the wind and will have to use oars. We will try to smash some of the oars and then head south and west. We will try to sail around the convoy."

"That is a risk, Jarl Dragonheart. Perhaps we could sail south and west now."

I pointed, "We know these ships are here. What lies below the horizon? If you were the captain of one of those ships and you saw a single warship heading for you what would you think?"

"That it was a madman." I waited. He smiled, "Or a ship trying to lure us into a trap." He cupped his hands, "Full sail. We are coming about!"

'Heart of the Dragon' leapt towards the Arab galley. I saw flags fluttering from the leading ship. The whole convoy slowly turned to face north and east. If they had to run then they could turn north and west and take full advantage of the wind which pushed us towards them. They suspected a trap. In Miklagård we had heard of Rus ships which came down the network of rivers. They raided in the Hospitable Sea. David ben Samuel told us that some had managed to get into the Blue Sea. There were rich pickings to be had in this rich seaway.

Erik might have been worried but my men were not. Whetstones sharpened daggers, axes and swords. Others donned the mail hoods they had taken from the skutatos. By now all could see the fleet of ships and everyone had heard that there were four warships but none was worried. However many men came at them they were Vikings and they would not give in easily. Now that they had finished doing all that they needed to with the sails the ship's boys took their bows and arrows. We were the Clan of the Wolf and we fought together. I saw Sven Stormbringer speaking to the newest crew members. He had been with us for well over three moons and I think he was explaining how we fought.

We were closing rapidly now and I saw that the ship which was racing towards us was changing course slightly. She was turning to cut us off. I looked to Erik. He shook his head, "She will never make the turn I will turn at the last moment." He smiled and touched his wolf charm. "The Norns make life hard but the Allfather provides. This wind will help us to hit their oars and side hard. When we have struck her, I will turn again to pick up the wind."

Aiden smiled, "*Wyrd*! Their own action, which is intended to hurt us, actually helps us." I saw that he had a sword. He was not the greatest of swordsmen but we both knew how many crew the

Moorish ships held. We would need every man if we were to escape and return home to tell our tale.

We were so close now that I could see the faces lining the side. The oars were driving them through the water as her captain and his crew tried to turn the huge galley. She was far bigger than we were. Perhaps that was why they had turned to take us. They thought that we were a scout. Then I saw agitation at the stern of the ship for it appeared that we were going to ram them. We were travelling as fast as I had ever known my ship to go. Their captain blinked first. Knowing that they had another ship ahead he turned to steer board. That allowed Erik to make a slight turn to larboard. I saw the faces on the side as they realised we were going to strike. Their captain tried to turn even faster but it was to no avail. We hit their oars half way along their length. We heard the splintering of the wood and the screams of the rowers as broken ends of oars struck them. The oars on the steerboard side continued to row and that pushed their hull closer to ours. We still had shields there. At the same time our boys sent arrow after arrow into the men standing at the side. When our hulls collided, many of the Moors and Arabs were thrown to the sea. The lucky ones made the water. Many others were crushed. Our speed took us away from the damaged galley. By the time they had recovered we would be many lengths away and we were faster.

We had one more ship to negotiate and then we would be free and clear. Perhaps the captain of the last galley, which was only slightly larger than we, read our minds. Maybe he was a clever man. He turned his ship as we crashed into his consort. He would be able to catch us.

Haaken saw the manoeuvre and slapped the side of the drekar in joy, "We fight this day! I get to add to my tally of men I have slain!" Haaken One Eye knew to the man how many opponents he had killed. I could remember many of those I had slain but not all of them. I remembered those like Eggle Skulltaker and Sigiberht but the others just melded into one another.

"Prepare to repel boarders."

Haaken looked and sounded disappointed, "We do not board her?"

"We were lucky when we rescued Snorri and the others. Let us not push our luck. Besides the drekar is full. Where is the room for more treasure?"

"Then let us sing as we near them! We will put fear in their veins." I did not mind them singing. It raised the spirits and made men more warlike. It also bound the new ones to us.

Haaken chose the song of Eystein the Rock. It had been a sea battle to, that day, but far to the north in the cold waters off Wihtwara. It was a favourite one of his and he often amended some of the words. As he said, *'perfection was the result of attention to detail.'*

> ***Through the stormy Saxon Seas***
> ***The Ulfheonar they sailed***
> ***Fresh from killing faithless Danes***
> ***Their glory was assured***
> ***Heart of Dragon***
> ***Gift of a king***
> ***Two fine drekar***
> ***Flying o'er foreign seas***
> ***Then Saxons came out full of guile***
> ***An ambush by their Wihtwara Isle***
> ***Vikings fight they do not run***
> ***The Jarl turned away from the rising sun***
> ***Heart of Dragon***
> ***Gift of a king***
> ***Two fine drekar***
> ***Flying o'er foreign seas***
> ***The galdramenn burned Dragon Fire***
> ***And the seas they burned bright red***
> ***Aboard 'The Gift' Asbjorn the Strong***
> ***And the rock Eystein***
> ***Rallied their men to board their foes***
> ***And face them beard to beard***
> ***Heart of Dragon***
> ***Gift of a king***
> ***Two fine drekar***
> ***Flying o'er foreign seas***
> ***Against great odds and back to back***
> ***The heroes fought as one***

Their swords were red with Saxon blood
And the decks with bodies slain
Surrounded on all sides was he
But Eystein faltered not
He slew first one and then another
But the last one did for him
Even though he fought as walking dead
He killed right to the end
Heart of Dragon
Gift of a king
Two fine drekar
Flying o'er foreign seas

The Arab intended to cut across our bows and board us. He had a corvus, a beak. I turned to Erik. "If you are able then avoid the bow. I do not wish us tied to him." I gestured astern where the large galley we had hurt was now using the wind to follow us. She would not catch us unless we were bound to the other.

Erik said. "He will not. She is a fast one, I will give you that, but '*Heart*' is faster and turns on a dinar! I have one hole from a beak in my ship, I will not have a second!"

"Aiden, if you can then use fire. You are more use with magic than your sword!"

He sniffed but had the good grace to nod. "Fire is dangerous, Dragonheart. We do not want to be tied to her when she burns."

"Then use fire at the stern." They were longer than we were and her stern would not be next to ours.

I watched as we closed. The captain did not steer. I recognised him by the plume on his helmet. He stood next to the helmsman and was giving orders. He turned to look at us and then spoke to the helmsman. He was an Arab. He had scale armour; I saw the light reflect upon it. He was adjusting his course to match our own. This would be a battle of wits between the two captains and their ships. Erik had the advantage. The drekar was an extension of him.

"Ship's boys, see if you can hurt their officers!"

The officers were all gathered around the helmsman at the stern. They were an inviting target for not all were armoured and they were standing close together. I saw that Sámr had his bow ready. As the archers loosed Sámr waited and when four of the officers had been hit he sent his at the helmsman. He hit him in the neck. It was a fine strike. We were three lengths from them and I saw the blood spurt and arc. In that moment when the helmsman fell the fate of the Arab was settled. The ship lurched and the rowers were thrown into confusion. Haaken clapped Sámr on the back and gave him the name that he kept for the rest of his life. "You have just ensured that we will win, Sámr the Ship Killer!"

The rest of the crew cheered. We were close enough that the Arabs and the Moors heard us. They looked around. Their loss of rhythm meant that they slowed. I could hear, above the waters, their captain shouting orders. They would not be able to use their beak and so he did the only thing he could. He drew in his larboard oars and brought his ship alongside us as we passed him. His ship was higher than ours. It had a larger crew. They would board us and so we had to make it difficult.

"Olaf, take half the men to the prow side of the mast and make a shield wall. I will hold the rest here."

"Aye jarl."

"Use spears! They will swing down with ropes and they will jump."

I took the nearest spear and grabbed my shield as the galley lurched towards us. It was longer than we were but not by much. As I had expected, even before the hooks came over to tie us together, men had swung across. They were impaled on our spears.

"Archers, clear their stern." If the steering board was covered in their dead then there would be no one to extinguish Aiden's fire.

Then the hooks came over. There was no point in severing them until Aiden had done his work. We had two double ranks; one forward of the mast and the other astern. Erik had left our sail to push us along. It meant we crabbed a little as the larger galley swung around us. Their ship would now be between us and their consort. To get to our larboard side she would have to sail around two ships. It was a small point but it might just save us.

As soon as the hooks bit our gunwale and grabbed then hordes of warriors dropped on to our deck. We had shields braced. All of the shields had a metal boss. We each held our spears above our heads; it was a double row of death. Most of the first ones who jumped were either wounded or died as they found steel tipped ash. Those who avoided a spear were struck in the face by the metal boss of a shield. My spear was shattered by the half-mailed warrior who crashed into it. I quickly drew Ragnar's Spirit and skewered the warrior who had hit Haaken's boss. Our archers did as I had asked. The steering board of the galley was just fifteen paces from us and I saw them fall. The captain, in scale mail and plumed helmet, was struck in the leg but he survived. Taking a shield, he scurried to join those boarding us. The stern was empty.

"Clan of the Wolf, let us send these savages to the bottom of the ocean. Ran must be hungry!"

With a roar of, "Clan of the Wolf!" We all stepped forward, punching with our shields as we hacked and slashed with our swords or stabbed with our spears. The enemy dead provided a convenient step so that we were higher than the men we faced. The mail hood I wore proved to be a wise choice as a spear was thrown from the galley. I saw it at the last moment and moved my head to the side. The spear scraped off the side. Without the hood I would have had a hole in the side of my face! Haaken and I had Sven Stormbringer with us. We were not the youngest of warriors but we were the most experienced and with our huge shields the warriors before us stood no chance.

I heard Aiden shout, "Fire!" He had sent his fire to the ship and now it would begin to die.

Confident that the enemy would not understand the word I turned to Haaken, "Let us sever the ropes which bind us." I sheathed my sword for I saw an opportunity. The captain of the galley was standing above us on the side of his ship. He clung on to the backstay. I picked up a discarded spear and hurled it at him. He was less than five paces from me and it hit him in the middle. He overbalanced and tumbled on to our deck. I grabbed his sword which fell at my feet and I hacked through one of the ropes which bound us. Just at that moment there was a roar as the flaming pot which Aiden had thrown at the stern set fire to the oil lamp which they used at night. The tinder dry deck began to burn. As the galley's crew looked at their burning ship and without a captain to give orders, the last rope was severed and the wind took us away from the burning galley. The other Arab was twenty lengths away. She would no longer be able to attack us. At best she might save the crew of the galley.

"Dragonheart! Dragonheart! Dragonheart!" The crew cheered my name. We had won… again.

Chapter 14

We had lost men. Four had died and we buried them at sea. We wrapped them in cloth and sewed them up with a weight inside so that they would sink to the bottom. We counted thirty-two bodies of Arabs and Moors. After taking their mail, swords, rings, helmets and coins we fed their bodies to the sharks. Despite the four deaths there was a sense of euphoria on the drekar. We had fought and outwitted a greater number of enemies. It was a victory. The Arabs would be wary of attacking a drekar in future; even a single one. Our good fortune deserted us the next day.

A storm began to brew in the night. Arne woke me and his father for he sensed that we were in for a blow. The air felt heavy and the wind had died to a breeze. Erik woke the ship's boys and they were sent aloft in readiness for reefing the sails. Arne asked, "What about the crew?"

"Let them rest as long as we can. We may need them to row and they fought a battle this day." Erik nodded his agreement.

I stayed awake. I had been close to death. Sleep was no longer important. I would live each day as though it was my last and make the most of this reprieve. I felt the breeze begin to grow. As dawn broke it was not the normal blue sky which greeted us but black clouds. Perhaps the god of the Blue Sea was a Moor and he was angry with us for killing so many of his men. When the ship began to pitch Erik ordered the sail reefed. Arne woke the crew. I shouted, "You have time to make water, grab some food and ale and then take an oar. This will be a long day of rowing. The Allfather would know if you are men who can face his fiercest storm!"

The experienced men, and that was most of the crew, took food and an ale skin to their chest. They knew they might not be able to leave the chest for some time. As the winds increased and the sky became so black that it might as well have been night Erik shouted, "Reef the sail. Rowers run out the oars. One man in two to row."

We would use the method which conserved energy. We would not make a great number of miles but we would be able to keep the ship afloat and moving. We had barely begun to row when Lars, who would be the last ship's boy to descend, shouted, "There is a ship in trouble, Captain. She is north of us. It looks like they are trying to run before the storm. She is heading for us."

I went to the steerboard side and peered into the dark. A flash of lightning illuminated the sea briefly. I saw the ship. It was not an Arab, it had the sail of a Frank. Without oars she would be at the mercy of the wind and the storm. The crack of thunder shook us. Aiden asked, "Can we not help them?"

Erik shook his head, "They are doomed." As if to make the point there was another flash of lightning and this time the crack of thunder was almost instantaneous. We saw that the foresail on the Frank had torn loose and was dragging in the water. They were now just twenty lengths from us. I watched as a figure tried to cut away the wreckage. A wave swept him over the side. All went black again until another flash of lightning and crack of thunder showed us that the ship was beam on to the waves and we saw the next wave swamp the ship. The sky became black and waves threatened us. When the next flash of lightning lit up the sea all that we saw were pieces of wreckage. It was a warning.

Aiden came over to me, holding on to the gunwale as he did so. "It seems the Allfather is more powerful than the White Christ."

I shook my head, "That is not the reason they sank. Their ships are not as good as ours. Thank Bolli. It is his work and Erik's skill which will save us."

The day which was like a night eventually became night and the wind finally abated. We had no idea where we were and the crew were exhausted. Erik took the decision to use sea anchors. When dawn came we would be able to use our compass and maps. We were within a few days of the Pillars of Hercules. We had to know precisely where we were before we risked those straits.

We all took turns to sleep. We needed a watch all night. We saw lightning far to the north but the thunder was distant. The storm had moved off but that did not mean it would not return. We ate and we drank. Sámr the Ship Killer and Germund the

Lame needed treatment from Aiden. They had used his salve but the salt water and the rowing had made their hands like pieces of raw meat. As Aiden dressed them and bandaged them he said, "The Blue Sea has more salt than our sea. That is why the wounds are worse."

I shook my head, "What a comfort you are, Aiden!"

He smiled, "I like to inform my patients. These two cannot row again until their hands are healed. That may take half a month."

We four were on watch together. "So Germund, are you sorry you came with us now? David ben Samuel's home was a much safer place."

He smiled, "Jarl, I am back amongst my own kind." He tapped his lame leg. "Here I am useful despite my injury. I like these men. They have made me welcome. David ben Samuel was a good master but his servants did not make me welcome. I was still a barbarian to them."

"And you, Sámr the Ship Killer, do you wish that you had stayed at home with Ulla War Cry?"

He laughed, "You have to ask? My days of staying at home are over. I have coin and Bagsecg can make me a byrnie. I will go to war with my oar brothers."

I looked at Germund, "You cannot stand in a shield wall."

He nodded, "I know but you have a standard. A man does not need two good legs to stand and hold a banner." He smiled. "In fact, it is better if he does not move eh, Jarl?"

I had a good crew!

I was asleep when dawn broke. I had had a couple of disturbed night's sleep and I slept through the crew looking for danger as the sun rose over our stern. I was woken by a call from the masthead, "Wreckage off the steerboard side."

I rose and went to the steering board. Arne was at the helm. He said, "It will be from the Frank we saw sink yesterday. The currents take everything towards the straits."

"There is a body on the wreckage, Jarl."

Arne looked at me. Sailors have an affinity for other sailors. His eyes begged me to sail to the wreckage. I looked up at the sky. It was blue and the breeze was a good one. I nodded, "Go and investigate."

As we turned to head towards the body Lars shouted, "His arm moved! He is alive!"

Olaf snorted, "It will be the wind or perhaps a fish tugs at him. No man can live at sea on a piece of wreckage for this length of time."

We turned from our course. I could see that it was the yard and part of a mast which had broken from the ship. They had formed a cross and, as we neared it I could see that it was a youth or a boy who lay spread-eagled like the White Christ I had often seen in the churches we had raided. I hoped it was not an omen. Three of the ship's boys hung from ropes over the side. We let out the rope so that they could swim to the boy. Lars grabbed him and we hauled on the three ropes to pull them back. Once the body was lifted onto the deck we saw that it was, indeed, a youth. He looked to be about the same age as Sámr but he was scrawny in comparison.

Olaf Leather Neck snorted, "He is dead! He does not move."

Germund the Lame broke through and said, "You are wrong. He has water in his lungs that is all!" He turned him over and began to push on his back. Nothing seemed to be happening and so Germund stood and, holding the youth before him, pulled hard on his middle. Suddenly the youth vomited seawater. Olaf Leather Neck was covered in the sea water and the contents of the youth's lungs. The youth began to cough. He was alive.

Olaf laughed and said. "The Allfather is teaching me a lesson! Do not be so hasty!"

Aiden stepped forward, "Thank you, Germund the Lame, although your name does not do you justice. You have saved this Frank's life." He wrapped a cloak around the youth and lifted him up. We all saw then that this was, indeed a Frank. It should have come as no surprise and yet it did for the youth had survived for many hours at sea. Ran had chosen to save him. Why?

We resumed our course. I stood by the steering board where Aiden was taking the wet clothes from the youth. He looked at me, "He needs warm clothes and he needs to be warmed from the inside. Look at his colour, jarl, he is as blue as the sea."

Sámr and Germund were standing nearby and they helped Aiden to remove the clothes. I took my wolf cloak from my chest. "Wrap him in this while we fetch clothes."

Germund wrapped the cloak around him while Aiden poured some of the wine we had bought in Miklagård into his mouth. Germund stood and said, "This is your wolf cloak, Jarl Dragonheart; are you Ulfheonar?"

I nodded. "As are Olaf and Haaken."

"Does the cloak have powers?"

"It has saved my life many times." A sudden thought struck me and I went to my chest and brought out Ragnar's Spirit. "Perhaps the sword which was touched by the gods may help him." I laid it on his chest.

Germund said, "He is a Frank, a Christian. Why should the gods help him?"

"Because he died and has been reborn. He does not yet know what he is. He can choose the way of the White Christ or the way of the Allfather."

Germund did not look convinced. Sámr and Aiden dressed him in warm clothes and then he was wrapped again in the cloak with the sword laid upon his chest. Aiden fed the youth beer and water. As the rest of the crew went about their duties and he and I were alone with the wolf cloaked Frank I said, "You seem quite worried about someone you do not know, Aiden. Are your powers returning? Is there something you know that we cannot see?"

He shook his head, "Until we pass through the straits then I am as other men." He smiled, "Save that I have a mind, unlike Olaf Leather Neck!"

"Olaf has a mind but it is a mind for war. What does your mind tell you about this youth?"

"There is no cross about his neck. All followers have one even if it is a crude one fashioned from wood.

"It may have fallen off at sea."

Aiden opened the cloak and the top of the kyrtle. "Then how did this survive?" There was a leather thong and a small leather pouch. The youth was still asleep and Aiden removed it. The youth stirred as we took the pouch. Aiden opened it. Inside was a small carved bone horse. "Here is a tale. Why a small carved horse? This is like the bones the ship's boys carve." He replaced it in the pouch and placed it around the youth's neck. "And there is something else. Look at his neck. What do you see?"

I saw the marks of a thrall's collar, "He was a slave."

"Then how did he remove it? My powers have yet to return, Jarl Dragonheart, but when I saw the wreckage and knew how long this youth had floated then I saw the hand of the Norns. We were meant to find him. We had nothing to do with the sinking of his ship but it was sent to us so that we could see it. I know this even without my powers. The Norns have plotted our course since we left Whale Island. I know not their purpose. Even the Allfather does not know that but I can see their claws and their webs at work here."

"Does he bring good or ill to the clan?"

He shook his head, "Good and ill are not words the gods and the Norns use. One man's misery is another man's joy. We fished him from the sea. He is our responsibility. We cannot undo what we have done. We have pulled the root from the ground. We cannot replace it."

It was not until the middle of the afternoon when the youth woke. Aiden had sat by him the whole time. The boy began jabbering. I recognised his words as Frank. Aiden spoke a couple. While we did not understand his questions, he might understand Aiden's. he spoke to him. The youth calmed. "What did you say to him?"

"I said that we had pulled him from the sea and meant him no harm. He needs food. He is as weak as a new born lamb."

Germund had been watching. I think he felt an affinity for the youth. He came over. "He lives?"

I nodded, "He lives and that is thanks to you. He too was a slave. He has the mark of a thrall collar. We saw it when we discovered the horse around his neck."

Germund looked up in surprise. "A horse? Carved from bone?"

My hand went to the wolf around my neck. *Wyrd*! "Aye; why?"

"I thought there was something about him when I fished him out. His eyes and his hair. I think he comes from the land to the west of the mighty river we use to travel south to Miklagård.

There are tribes there who ride horses. They seem to live on the backs of them."

"And he is one of those?"

"He could be."

Aiden had brought over food and was feeding the youth old bread soaked in ale with small pieces of dried meat. He looked up, "Then how did he get to the Blue Sea?"

Germund shrugged, "The same way I did, down the river. Let me try to speak to him. Our peoples use some words which are the same."

When he spoke, I found that I recognised some of the words. The youth's eyes widened and he began to speak. He spoke quickly and Germund smiled and waved his hand to slow him down. The conversation lasted some time. Germund's face was black as thunder when he stood. "The boy was taken six years since by Bulgars and sold to trade slavers. He was sold to a Frank and he lived in East Frankia." He shook his head. "He was not treated well. I was just whipped when I was a slave. He... he suffered much worse. His master... I have heard of such men. They are nithings. If I had the man who had done this then he would have the blood eagle. The Frank tired of him and sold him to a trader who was taking him to Miklagård. There are places there where boys such as this are housed."

Aiden nodded, "How old is he?"

"He has seen thirteen summers."

I asked, "What is his name?"

"Slave! That is all that he knows."

I looked at Aiden, "You say the boy was sent to us. We have a responsibility to care for him."

Aiden nodded, "It is *wyrd*. You were a slave and taken in by Vikings. I was a hostage and taken in by you. He is a slave. He becomes part of the clan; if he will have it so."

I turned to Germund, "Ask him. Tell him he will be free. No one will harm him."

Germund told the young man, for we now knew that he was a man and not a boy, but there was no joy on his face, merely apprehension. It would take time and care for him to recover. I looked at Aiden and he nodded. I had been thinking that Kara was the one who could help him. We did not need rowers and so

I left Sámr and Germund with the rescued slave. They took him to the prow. David ben Samuel's awning was still there. It had all the qualities of a wolf's den and that was what the slave needed.

As we headed west, towards the straits, I said, "He needs a name. We cannot just call him boy or man."

Aiden nodded, "It is out of our hands. The Allfather gave him to us and he will show us where we find his name."

"I thought that this was the Norns."

"The Norns directed us here. We are part of the web but it was the Allfather who made us take him. Do you think the Rus pirates who sail these waters would have saved him?"

Aiden was right.

The rescued slave recovered slowly. His colour returned and he was able to eat more. Germund spoke with him at length. He and Sámr taught him our language. The three of them slept under the awning. I think he found it comforting. Germund and Sámr were seen as friends. The rest of the crew, even when they were smiling looked fierce. We discovered that one of the crew had freed him from his thrall collar when it became obvious that the ship was doomed. There was at least one Frank on the slaver who was a man.

The next day we were approaching the busy waterways of the straits. We saw more ships but, thankfully, there were no war galleys. We had the wind and the current. Erik decided that we would risk using them to fly through. He had had enough of the Blue Sea. The dangers beyond the straits were more familiar. All of us were ready for home. It had been five moons since we had left Whale Island. We had done that which we intended. We had traded well and we had glory. We wanted to get home before the Norns snatched it all from us!

It was late afternoon when we saw the harbour of Al-Jazīra. Just over a mile away it was a busy port. It was filled with ships belonging to the Caliphate of Córdoba. Had the wind failed or turned then we would have been in trouble. Lars reported figures clambering up the rigging to lower the sails. Erik laughed when Lars' words came to him. "With this wind and the current, we will be beyond the straits by the time they reach us. I will back *'Heart'* against any galley in our sea!"

He was proved correct. As we raced out into the more familiar sea of Ran the look outs reported that the galleys had turned and headed back into port. Although not stormy the seas into which we sailed were livelier than the Blue Sea. The waves were bigger and, as we had to head north soon we would need to row for the wind was from the north and the east. That had suited us in the Blue Sea but we did not wish to be driven west. We also needed supplies. We would have to find somewhere to raid. We had been loath to raid Córdoba when in the Blue Sea for we did not wish them to seek us out. Now it did not matter. We would soon be in waters that were Frankish and filled with drekar such as ours.

I spoke with Aiden and Erik, "Do we land sooner rather than later?"

Erik looked at the sky. It was filled with clouds. At this time of year that was unusual and a summer storm could often be more violent than one in winter. "Aye, jarl, I would be happier. Night is coming on. There are some small bays and beaches which will afford us shelter if a storm does break."

We turned north and east to take us close to the coast. Aiden had charts with a couple of beaches marked upon them.

"Out oars! Furl the sail!"

We had not rowed for a while but now we would need to. The coast was visible. It was a dark line on the horizon. I saw our new passenger alone at the prow, under the awning. It was the first time he had been alone since he had joined us. Sámr and Germund would need to take an oar as we were rowing into the wind. It would be a hard pull.

Haaken sang my song, the song of the slave. It seemed appropriate somehow.

> *From mountain high in the land of snow*
> *Garth the slave began to grow*
> *He changed with Ragnar when they lived alone*
> *Warrior skills did Ragnar hone*
> *The Dragonheart was born of cold*
> *Fighting wolves a warrior bold*
> *The Dragonheart and Haaken Brave*
> *A Viking warrior and a Saxon slave*
> *When Vikings came he held the wall*

He feared no foe however tall
Back to back both so brave
A Viking warrior and a Saxon slave
When the battle was done
They stood alone
With their vanquished foes
Lying at their toes
The Dragonheart and Haaken Brave
A Viking warrior and a Saxon slave
The Dragonheart and Haaken Brave
A Viking warrior and a Saxon slave

I walked up the centre of the drekar and stood by the young man. I smiled. I said, "Soon we will be on land." I knew that some of our words were the same and I hoped he understood. He smiled. I had not seen him smile until that moment. It was a beginning.

Chapter 15

It was almost dark when Siggi, at the mast head shouted, "Breakers ahead. I spy a beach."

"Slow the beat."

I gestured for our passenger to rise and pointed. He nodded. Lars and Sven ran forward. They each held a rope, hammer and a stake. After tying the ropes to the two metal hooks at the bows they stood on either side of me. Siggi said, "Haaken One Eye said that you used to do this, Jarl Dragonheart."

I nodded, "Aye except the waters were the waters of Norway, Hibernia and Mann. They were a little colder than here."

"There Lars, one day we could be jarls too!"

I laughed, "You are Vikings. You can be whatever you choose!"

They both clambered up and held on to the prow. Lars shouted over his shoulder. "Back water, Captain, we are there!" Without waiting for the oars to stop he and Siggi leapt as far forward as they could. I heard the intake of breath from our passenger. Lars was taller and the water came up to his waist. Siggi was smaller and a wave washed over his head. Undeterred the two of them struggled up the shingle and sand beach. The drekar had way upon her and continued to follow them. It was as though she was alive.

I peered into the gloom of dusk but I saw nothing. The wind was from the land and I smelled no smoke. I had known of ship's boys who had been killed as they had attempted to secure a drekar. When I heard the sound of mallets driving the stakes into the sand then I knew it was safe. Other ship's boys came and ran out two gangplanks into the sea. They gestured for me to leave. I took our passenger's hand, "Come, this can be tricky." I was not sure if he understood but he clambered up and followed me through the sea to the beach. I smiled as he wobbled once we were on the sand and shingle.

With swords drawn Sámr and Germund joined me. Our passenger let go of my hand and walked with the two of them flanking him. They were well on the way to becoming oar and shield brothers. When Olaf Leather Neck landed he led twenty men to scout out the land beyond the sand dunes. Meanwhile a fire was prepared but not lit. Although the wind was blowing from the sea we would not risk a fire until we knew we were safe.

Even as we gathered driftwood the first signs of the change in the weather and the storm appeared. The wind increased. Erik ordered the ship's boys to run two more lines from the stern to secure the ship. He had an old sail brought from the ship to provide shelter in case it rained. When Olaf returned he had with him the butchered carcasses of two goats.

"You can light the fire. There is no-one who is close. These two were wandering. We found no water!"

Aiden pointed to the skies, "I would not worry about that. Rain is coming."

Our galdramenn made the fire while the goats were butchered. The sail was secured over twelve spears. It would sag if it rained but that would give us water. We brought a pair of small empty barrels ashore to fill. As the wind increased in force so the rain began. We huddled under the awning while the goat stew cooked. We would have been as dry on the drekar but we would not have had a fire.

Sámr, Germund and our passenger were talking. Aiden joined them. Haaken came over to me. Haaken asked, "What do you think will happen to him?"

"He can stay with us or we can leave him with Isaac in Bruggas." We had letters from David ben Samuel to deliver.

"Would he want that?"

"The old man is a good master. That is some time off, Haaken. We have many leagues to sail. You know the Norns."

He touched his head where Aiden had placed a small piece of metal, "Aye I do, jarl."

The stew took some time to cook. Olaf Leather Neck came over, "The men need beer or wine lord. We have had enough water. Could we not raid? We could have the better part of a moon before we reach home"

Haaken nodded his agreement, "Olaf is right. We do not seek Holy Books nor glory. So long as the town does not have a wall we can be in and out quickly. Take food and wine and make the last part of our voyage a little more pleasant."

I saw no harm in it and so I nodded my agreement. I should have been warned by Aiden's face. We had passed the Pillars. His power was returning. He sensed danger in that course of action.

Sámr came over with his platter and that of our passenger when the food was ready. "We have a name for the slave we rescued."

Aiden frowned, "How so? Has the Allfather spoken? The Norns? Has he done something to merit a name, Sámr Ship Killer?"

The grin did not leave his face, "Aye, galdramenn. We heard more of his tale. His people were horsemen. They raided the Bulgars from the north. He remembers that his father led his people and that he lived in the largest hall. His father was a king and he was a prince. He is Baldr!"

I smiled, "He has you there, Aiden, Baldr is Norse for prince and it suits. How does he feel about that?"

"Germund told him what the name meant and he liked it. He said it was a link to his past."

"Then it is so." I suddenly stopped, "He is a horseman? Like Hrolf the Horseman?"

"His people ride horses. He remembers riding before walking. Why, Jarl Dragonheart?"

I shook my head, "Nothing but it is *wyrd*, is all. To have two horsemen come into my life is unusual."

Olaf Leather Neck had brought his bowl of stew over. "That does us precious little good. We need warriors and not horsemen."

Sámr had the confidence now to argue with Olaf Leather Neck. "His people are fierce warriors. Germund had heard of them. He may not be a warrior like us but he will have it in his blood to fight."

I had much to think on. That night the storm burst upon us. Erik and his crew of boys and navigators went back aboard but the land anchors held. We were dry but as the sail filled with water I wondered if we would have a soaking before dawn. Aiden had anticipated the problem and he had the barrels filled. The awning dipped but held when we tipped the water into an empty barrel. We boarded the drekar with blue skies above us and an almost benevolent sea before us. With a wind from the south and west we could sail north and find a town or a village to raid. We would avoid the walled city of Qādis. It was one of the most powerful of strongholds. We decided to raid further north. If we raided south of Qādis then there was a chance that they could block our escape north.

When the wind shifted a little and was blowing east north east, it allowed us to cut across the bay of Qādis. We would be out of sight of land and away from the main seaways. It took a day and a half for the winds were not strong. Having had hot food and filled our water barrels we were not overly concerned. Baldr's lessons continued. It was not as hard as might have been expected as there were many words he and Germund shared in their own languages. It helped that Sámr was keen to be able to speak directly with Baldr. They were of an age.

We were not far from the place Sven Stormbringer had been attacked. The people here were not friendly. We hove to just below the horizon. With sail furled and sea anchors out we waited for darkness. The lookouts had spotted the land and the tell-tale smoke from homes. Aiden had found the place we would raid: Cerro da Vila. There were risks involved as there was another mighty Arab fortress just twenty miles up the coast. Al-buhera was almost as strong as Qādis. We had not had to row and the men were rested. We donned our mail. We would be going ashore and there might be men defending the town. According to the information we had there was a harbour but no wall and no castle. The fortress of Al-buhera was deemed enough to deter attackers. They did not know Vikings. When darkness was complete and we deemed that all of those in the small town were abed, Erik ordered the sail lowered and we headed into shore.

Sámr and Germund would not be coming on the raid. Neither had mail and I wanted them to watch over Baldr. He had been sent to us by the Allfather and until we reached Bruggas we had to do all in our power to keep him safe.

We did not smell the town as we approached. The wind was behind us but we saw the dots of lights where doors opened and revealed the fires glowing within. The town rose on the hillside above the small harbour. I stood at the prow and saw that there were ships in the harbour. Most were small but there was one larger merchant ship. Even as we edged closer I saw the hand of the Allfather in this. We had payment for the lives of the men we had lost or perhaps the Allfather was paying us for carrying out his wishes and saving Baldr.

As we ghosted towards the harbour the watchman they had there, or perhaps he was a fisherman, spotted our dragon. He let out a yell. Olaf grunted, "Well they know we are coming."

"Olaf Leather Neck, take the younger warriors and close off their escape. Watch for any enemies."

It was unfortunate that we had been seen but it was not a disaster. We were after ale or wine. We wanted food. They would not flee with those. They would try to save their coin and their lives. The danger would be if there was a stronghold inland to which they might flee. There was no spare berth and so Erik laid us alongside the merchant ship. Olaf led my men across it. The ship had the crew aboard. As they heard the sound of our hull striking them they poured onto the deck. Olaf and his men contemptuously slew them and did as I had ordered.

I led the rest across the deck. As I clambered over the gunwale I said, "Aiden, check the hold and see if there is anything on board which we can use."

He said, "Why not take the ship? We have Arne and spare crew."

I did not answer him but it was a good idea. Smaller than us it would only need a crew of eight. We had enough spare men now. Screams from the hillside above us told me that Olaf and his men had been seen. I saw two bodies close by the largest building in the small town.

"Sven Stormbringer, search the buildings with your men. Take what we need back to our ship. Haaken, take four men and search the buildings to the east of the town. The rest, follow me."

As we worked our way through the town which had less than forty buildings we found occasional bodies. All were armed. Men had tried to delay Olaf and his men. They thought we sought slaves. In this part of the world that was a common occurrence. I took off my helmet when we reached Olaf. "Have four men keep watch here and take the rest to search and sack the town. It is a little bigger than I thought. I cannot see such a place being unguarded. The Franks in Leon would raid it."

I turned and descended. Ráðgeir Ráðgeirson, Lars Long Nose, Siggi Eainarson, Ráðulfr Magnusson, Siggi Long Face and Galmr Hrolfsson were still with me. Although I carried my helmet I still had Ragnar's Spirit in my hand. Ráðgeir Ráðgeirson and Lars Long Nose flanked me. We heard the sound of combat from the east. That was the direction Haaken One Eye had taken. There were narrow passages between the houses in this part of the town and we hurried down the nearest one. We could hear the sound of steel on steel and the sound of shouting. We burst out into an open square. There were a dozen horse warriors. They wore helmets and they had short mail shirts. I saw that Haldi Bollison lay either dead or badly wounded and the four who remained were in a tight circle. I had no time to don my helmet and I dropped it as I took out my dagger.

The warriors were not Moors, nor were they Arabs; they were lighter skinned. When I heard the horses neigh then I knew them to be cavalry. Even as I blocked a blow from a sword with my dagger I took in that we were in a stable area with fields for grazing. I swept my sword in an arc towards the horseman's middle. His head barely came up to my chest. He had a small shield. He managed to block my blow but I knew that I had hurt him. He was not a Viking and he cried out. As he pulled back his sword for a second blow Wolf's Blood darted forward and I ripped through the back of his hand. He tried to turn and run. A huge bearded Viking wielding a deadly blade was not an opponent to face willingly. He had seen the grey beard and thought I was an easy foe. I brought my sword down across his back. He fell to the ground. I did not wait for a horseman to seek me I ran towards the ones surrounding Haaken. As one turned to face me I swept my sword across his unprotected thigh. Bright blood spurted and as he dropped to his knee I tore Wolf's Blood across his throat. Ráðgeir Ráðgeirson and the others had all slain or wounded some of the dismounted horsemen. The few survivors tried to flee to their waiting horses. Haaken and I apart, our men were young and fit. All were slain before they reached the stables and the horses they sought.

Sheathing my sword, I walked back and retrieved my helmet. Haaken was kneeling over the body of Haldi. "He died because I was careless, Dragonheart." I cocked my head to one side. "We heard the horses and I just thought that we would have horsemeat to eat." He shook his head. "Four escaped and the others, who must still have been saddling their horses, burst upon us. Haldi stepped forward to protect me."

"It happens and Haldi was a warrior. Ráðgeir Ráðgeirson, collect what you can from the bodies. Put Haldi on a horse and bring him to the drekar. We will bury him at sea."

"Aye, Jarl."

By the time we reached the harbour the first grey of dawn was in the east. We were the last to return save for the four sentries we had left. Olaf was enjoying some ale he had found and looked in high spirits. "This is fair ale! A good raid!"

I shook my head, "Haldi Bollison is dead and four horsemen escaped. Get the drekar loaded."

"Aiden has begun loading the merchant ship."

I shook my head and snapped, "Then perhaps instead of speaking of the ale you might have told me that first!"

"Sorry, Jarl Dragonheart."

"And have you called in your sentries or has the ale driven them from your thoughts?"

In answer he shouted, "Galmr, fetch the men. The rest of you get this loaded on the drekar!"

I crossed the merchant ship, which was being loaded and went to the drekar. I put my helmet in my chest. "Erik, you had better prepare for sea. Four horsemen escaped. Haldi Bollison is dead." He nodded. "Is your son going to sail the merchant vessel?"

"Aye. Lars and Snorri Gunnarson and his men will be the crew." He saw my face, which was as black as thunder. "You could have done nothing about Haldi. It is the Norns and their webs. The Allfather gave us Baldr. There had to be payment."

Just then I heard Galmr's voice as he ran down the hill with the four sentries. "Arabs are coming!"

"No one else leaves the drekar. Prepare for sea!" I shouted, "Get the drekar out of the harbour. The merchant ship cannot leave with you in the way."

"I will take her next to the fishing boats. You can board over them. We can give you arrows."

I unsheathed my sword. I hurried back across the merchant ship. I saw Arne. "Prepare for sea. Anything we have not yet taken on board, leave. Enemies come. We have lost one too many men already!"

"Aye, Jarl. Lars, get up the mast and lower the sail."

"But we are still tied up!"

"If we sever the ropes then so be it. I want to be ready to sail as soon as all of the men have boarded."

"And what about you?"

"We will use the fishing boats to escape!" I joined Olaf and Haaken. They had with them just ten men. Ráðgeir Ráðgeirson and his men were leading the laden horses. I ran to take Haldi's shield from the horse. He would need it no longer. I shouted, "Get everything on board the merchant ship now! If you cannot carry it then leave it! The enemy comes! We hold them here until we have our dead loaded."

Olaf nodded and said, "I am sorry, Jarl."

"Your need for ale has proved expensive. Let us hope that we pay no more. When Arne has gone we climb down to the fishing ships and use them to board our drekar."

We saw the horsemen appear on the road which led down to the harbour. They were led by four men who had mail shirts. I could see, from the sun glinting on them, that they reached to their knees. There were just thirteen of us. There were seven of us in the front rank and six behind. I had a shield and that made me feel better.

The horsemen galloped down the road. I saw that some had bows. It would take a phenomenal archer to hit someone while galloping down a cobbled surface. There was, however, always the chance of a lucky arrow.

I heard Sámr the Ship Killer shout, "Draw!" The horsemen were closing with us. The four with mail would strike us first. They had lances. The horsemen with bows were further back.

"Brace!" I felt two shields press into my back. I held Ragnar's Spirit over the top of Ráðulfr's shield. As I had counted on the horses did not charge into us. We were a solid wall of wood and metal. Instead they turned as their riders rammed their lances at us. They must have been used to charging unarmoured men who fled when horses approached. We were Vikings and we stood. At the same time arrows flew from behind us to hit the horses and men attacking us. I saw a horse's head and I rammed my sword towards its eye. It reared and, as it did so an arrow hit its chest. The horse and rider fell to their right. They crashed into the next two horsemen. Olaf swung his axe and took a rider's head. Haaken struck at the horse before him and its throat spurted blood. Horses do not like the smell of blood and panic ensued. I took a chance and, punched my shield at the rider who tried to stand. He tried to sway out of the way. I swung my sword at a rider who groggily rose. His head flew backwards.

As our bow men thinned the ranks behind I heard Erik shout, "You are clear, Jarl!"

I shouted, "You six jump into the fishing boats and tell us when it is clear for us to do so." The horsemen, I could see now that they were Arab mercenaries, were wary. Three of their mailed men lay dead or dying. The fourth had crawled away from his dying horse. Some of those without mail lay dead. There were dead and dying horses littering the quay. Those with bows were the targets of my bow men. They hesitated. A real warrior does not hesitate.

"Clear, Jarl. You can jump!"

Slipping my shield around my back, I said, "On three. One, two, three!"

We turned and jumped into the boat which was just below us. The enemy horsemen rode towards the quay. Arrows thudded into our shields and then the archers died as my own slew them. We huddled beneath our shields. One of the ship's boys had tethered the fishing boat to the stern of the drekar. The drekar pulled us out of range of the arrows. We climbed the rope onto the deck of our drekar. As we landed on the deck I turned to Olaf Leather Neck and said, "No more stops for ale!"

He grinned, "But think how good this will taste!"

Ráðgeir Ráðgeirson was the last aboard and I saw him raise his sword to sever the rope we had just climbed. "Hold! Leave the fishing boat tied there."

"But it will drag us, Jarl. It will be like a sea anchor."

I pointed to the merchant ship, "Erik, that will determine our speed not the fishing boat. It does not have the lines of a knarr. We know not yet how we may use it but we are tethered to it."

We headed west along the coast. As we neared their fortress and citadel we saw that the riders had reached it. It looked like someone had disturbed a wasp's nest. Ominously there were ships in the harbour. The merchant ship, Erik had named her, somewhat ungraciously, as the Cow, waddled along. She was not as slow as we had thought but we had to reef our sails. Even with a fishing boat astern we were still far faster.

Erik complained, "This will add days to our voyage."

I smiled, "Then bring aboard the cargo and we will sink her!"

He looked appalled, "You cannot deliberately sink a ship which is undamaged!" He was a sailor and, to him, all ships were living things. The fishing boat we pulled had no spirit. The fishing boat was dispensable but a shipwright had fashioned the hull of the merchant ship. The prow, small though it was, had been carved carefully. Part of the builder was in the hull. I smiled. He would not complain again.

We had left the town by the third hour of the day. We passed their citadel two hours later. The sun baked down and there was a haze upon the water. Men languished beneath the awning. I looked at the masthead. The wind was easing and changing direction. What little breeze there was pushed us towards the shore. It came from the south and west. Aiden said, "We will have to row."

"The wind will return."

"Aye, Erik, but we do not have the luxury of time." Aiden pointed to the land, a mile or so to the north of us. There were towers. "They will signal back to Al-buhera. Their galleys will come and they will take us. Besides the further west we are the more chance there is of picking up a wind. Remember when we came south? The wind lessened here. It is something to do with the shape of the land."

He acknowledged defeat and he took us next to his son's ship. "We will tow you." He looked at me. "Do we abandon the fishing boat?"

"No, she may still serve a purpose."

Erik Short Toe shouted to his son, "Tie the fishing boat to your stern."

It took some time to accomplish the task and then the crew took to the oars. We had some of our crew on the merchant ship and we had lost a warrior. It would be a hard row. Aiden had to use a chant to build up the speed. Snorri had his men using the sweeps on the merchant ship to make our task easier. The song was a fast one. It was the song of the Ulfheonar.

> *Ulfheonar, warriors strong*
> *Ulfheonar, warriors brave*
> *Ulfheonar, fierce as the wolf*
> *Ulfheonar, hides in plain sight*
> *Ulfheonar, Dragon Heart's wolves*
> *Ulfheonar, serving the sword*
> *Ulfheonar, Dragon Heart's wolves*
> *Ulfheonar, serving the sword*
> *Ulfheonar, warriors strong*
> *Ulfheonar, warriors brave*
> *Ulfheonar, fierce as the wolf*
> *Ulfheonar, hides in plain sight*
> *Ulfheonar, Dragon Heart's wolves*
> *Ulfheonar, serving the sword*
> *Ulfheonar, Dragon Heart's wolves*
> *Ulfheonar, serving the sword*

Once we had way we stopped singing and one man in two stopped rowing. Snorri's oars on the merchant ship made it easier for us. There was less drag and we edged west. Erik took us slightly south and west to move us away from the coast. With sails furled we could sail into the slight breeze which was taking us north and east.

The ship's boys took food and water to the rowers. We had some ale but that would be saved for the time when they could cease rowing. The sun passed its zenith and the heat grew. The ship's boys took to pouring seawater over the rowers to cool them. We still had a look out as did Arne. It was Lars on the *'Cow'* who shouted the warning first, "Galleys to the north and east. There are three of them."

I looked at Aiden, "They are following. We should not have stopped."

Aiden laughed. Since we had passed the straits his powers were returning and with his powers came confidence, "Jarl Dragonheart, this is the work of the Norns. I can feel their web. Had we not raided then something else would have happened. All is not lost. I cannot see the ships. They are too far away. They will have a long row to reach us." He pointed ahead. To the west were clouds. They were moving. "There is a wind to the west. Olaf Leather Neck will row until he drops. He feels guilty about Haldi. The other men feel the same. They all wished to raid."

I looked at the crew. Men were swapping places with their oar brothers. There were no complaints. Even Baldr was part of the crew. He had taken a water skin and was helping the ship's boys. The danger and the hardship were tightening the bonds of brotherhood. Baldr was becoming part of the clan. I could now see the Allfather's hand in this. The Norns had spun the web and it was there to make my warriors like a mail byrnie. We would be bonded and harder. We sailed west by south.

Inexorably the galleys closed with us and we were still far from the clouds and the elusive breeze. I shouted up to Siggi, at the masthead, "How far to the coast?"

"I can see it no longer."

Aiden's voice came from behind me. "We have another ten miles of rowing, Jarl. It will be close but I have a plan." I turned, "The fishing ship we tow can be used as a fireship. They will be upon us just before dusk. We have Arne light a fire in a pot. He has the sails raised on the fishing boat and cuts it adrift. The fire will spread. The wind will take the boat towards the galleys."

"They will be able to avoid it."

"Of course, but to do so they will have to alter course and that increases our lead. If the Allfather wills it then we will catch the breeze and can sail north. We should have cleared the coast and the wind will aid us and deter the galleys."

"Then you had better explain to Arne exactly what he must do when they close. It will take time to prepare a fire pot."

We had used a fire pot before. We had a supply of candles. They were the ones we took from smaller churches. We used them to signal at night and to make fire pots. They would be placed in oil-soaked cloth. When the candle burned down and ignited the flames then they would leap up the mast. The wind would do the rest.

Arne understood what he had to do and I saw Lars and Arne as they prepared the pot. Siggi was now our only lookout. The afternoon was passing quickly. He shouted, "Captain, the galleys are closing. I think they have upped the beat."

We could do the same but, unlike the galleys, my men were not slaves and if the galleys closed we would have to fight. Aiden read my mind, "By the time they close with us the wind will be with us and we will have cleared the coast. Look!" He pointed to the masthead. The pennant fluttered faster than it had. The wind was freshening. Once we had cleared the coast then our two ships would fly. It would, however, be close.

Lars came forrard and shouted that they had the pot prepared. I cupped my hands and shouted back, "Listen for my signal. When you have raised the boat's sails, lit the pot and severed the rope then have Arne hoist the sail. We head north. You will sail to larboard of us and we will protect you from the galleys."

"Aye, Jarl!"

I turned to Aiden, "We are in your hands, galdramenn."

He smiled, "I am getting closer to home. My powers grow. I see dimly but at least I can see here. I am not living in the fog of the Blue Sea."

We could all see the galleys now. As with all ships they were not identical neither in their handling nor their crews. One was tardy and three lengths from the second ship. The leading ship was well handled. The oars rose and fell in unison. We could see that the third one had a slightly ragged stroke. The second was the smaller of the three galleys. The wind was stronger now. I could feel it on my face. I looked at Aiden and he smiled, "Now, Jarl. Now is the time."

Cupping my hands, I shouted, "Light the fire!"

Erik shouted, "Prepare to lower the sail."

I watched as Arne sent Ulf Galmrson to the mast with Sweyn Olafsson. They would lower the sail. Meanwhile Snorri Gunnarson ran to the prow to slip the cable. Galmr stood ready to retrieve the rope. We could not see the fishing boat but we could see that the galleys were just ten lengths away and closing fast. As soon as Snorri threw the tow rope into the sea and the sail was lowered we knew that the fireship had been launched.

"Lower the sail. In oars. We come about!"

The father and son, Erik and Arne were a little like Aiden and me. They understood each other without words. As we headed north Arne took his ship west. It would allow us to be between him and the galleys. As soon as we had cleared *'Cow'* I saw the fishing boat. She was heading north and east. With no one at the helm she was going where the wind took her. She was sailing across the course the three galleys wished to take. I watched as the leading galley increased the stroke rate as the captain tried to cut us off. The other two turned south to avoid the fireship. It was one to one and I would take those odds any day.

My crew, relieved from the oars lined the side to look at the galley and the fireship. The sail caught fire and the fishing boat slowly settled in the water. She had done her part. The galley was now less than five lengths from us. She was using her oars and her sails but we were faster. I glanced to larboard and saw that Arne was two lengths from our side but four lengths astern. He was struggling to keep up. I saw the coastline ahead. It was just a mile away.

Erik glanced behind us, "He is sailing too close to the coast. He must be desperate to get to us." He pushed the steering board a little more to larboard. It meant we were slightly slower but we would be heading away from any rocks and it would allow Arne to catch up with us. The galley closed to within three lengths and disaster struck. We saw the ship suddenly slow and then the mast shuddered. Oars flew in the air.

"She has struck a reef."

Aiden pointed over the side. "And we came within a length of disaster."

I could see the rocks. We had a shallow draught but even we would have struck them. Erik turned further west and Arne mirrored our course. We watched the galley as she broke up and her consorts raced to get the survivors before they drowned or were devoured by the shoal of sharks which raced towards them.

Chapter 16

With the wind from our larboard quarter and the coast of the Caliphate to the east we kept a good watch as we headed north. We were on the last part of our journey and it would not do to be careless and run aground. Olaf Leather Neck avoided me. I had a sharper edge to my tongue of late and he was not afraid of any enemies but he feared upsetting Jarl Dragonheart! The men did not have to row. Now that we were in the grey ocean the sun burned less fiercely. In the Blue Sea the sun seemed to reflect off the water and make the ship hotter. Here the ocean absorbed the heat in its dark, grey waters. Men no longer stripped to their breeks. They wore their kyrtles. We divided the crew into three watches so that we could sail without stopping. On the merchant ship Arne and Snorri would have to go watch and watch about. At night we would hang a lantern from our stern. It had been one of the purchases we had made in Miklagård. Although expensive it allowed us to read charts at night. It was safe. A candle burned in the opaque glass. The glass was fragile and when not in use it had a sheepskin lined basket. It would pay for itself on this one voyage.

So long as the wind held we kept to our northerly coast. We were soon in familiar waters. Once we passed the Caliphate then we had the waters of Vasconia and Frankia to navigate. The seas around Frankia would be dangerous. There were pirates, enemies and rocks. They were a lethal combination and we would be forced to stay close to the coast for fear of running foul of Syllingar.

During this part of the voyage Baldr came out of his shell. Helping the crew during the pursuit had made him less afraid to smile and to use the new words he had learned. Like Germund and me, he had been a slave and a slave had to learn to pick up languages quickly or suffer a beating. There were no threatened beatings but he still learned quickly. From Germund we gathered that he was looking forward to a new life. His family was so far away both in time and distance that he had forgotten them.

Sámr said, one night as we stood a watch together, "He does not wish to leave us at Bruggas, great grandfather. He wishes to go to the Land of the Wolf."

"We could take him to Hrolf the Horseman. His land is now the Land of the Horse. Perhaps that would be even better for him."

He shook his head, "He is like a young deer. He is shy. Germund and I have tempted him from the woods. To him, we are not hunters. We are friends. Hrolf and his clan might be kind but to Baldr, they would be hunters."

I ruffled his hair, "You have become wise, Sámr the Ship Killer."

"I did not kill the ship!"

"And Olaf does not have a leather neck. You killed those who steered the ship and we won. Accept the name for it is honourable."

The journey north was slow but uneventful. Erik was pleased that we were not moving too fast for we had had so many collisions and been subjected to so many storms that he feared for the integrity of the drekar. "I will be happier, Jarl, when she is out of the water and we can give her a good examination."

And so we plodded north at the pace of the **'Cow'**. When we found deserted beaches and could land for a night ashore Arne found virtue in the Arab merchant ship. "She is not as fast as **'Kara'**; that I will grant you but she can take far more cargo."

His father looked at him, "You would think to sail her in home waters?"

"She is the Jarl's ship, it is for him to decide what happens to her save that I do not like her name. She is no cow!" Normally we would not rename a ship for it was considered unlucky but, as this one had an Arab name we could not decipher we had no other choice.

"For myself, Arne, she is yours. You have done us great service on this voyage and I would reward you. If you wish the ship for your own then it is done. But I would heed your father's advice about her suitability for our waters."

"We took her in our sea and not the Blue Sea. I admit that her sails are not what we are used to but Lars and I have found that we can sail closer to the wind than **'Kara'**."

His father shrugged. "If Jarl Dragonheart wishes you to have her then so be it. I thought to sell her in Bruggas but if you can crew her then have her." It was not the most gracious speech that Erik had ever made but it was prompted by what he saw as a question over his judgement.

Arne was not put out by the tone, "I have a crew, until we reach the Land of the Wolf at any rate. Snorri and his men are happy to sail on her."

Aiden had been listening. "Then what do you name her? Before you answer think hard. This is not something trivial. The name will be hers until she dies."

"'**Kara**' is a good ship and she is named after a volva. I would name her Ylva in honour of your daughter."

Even Erik liked the name and so the ship built by an Arab ended her days in the black and grey waters off the Land of the Wolf and she was named after a volva. *Wyrd*.

We were off the coast where Hrolf the Horseman had settled. I was tempted to visit him at the Haugr but Aiden had dreams which worried him. "All is not well in the Land of the Wolf."

"There is danger?"

"We are too far away but I think so."

"Then perhaps we should forego Bruggas and sail directly home."

"That would mean sailing close to Syllingar. Besides we have goods which we need to trade and we must take on ale and supplies. We cannot stop in Wessex or Om Walum."

Aiden shook his head, "Go to Bruggas. We have promised David ben Samuel to deliver letters for him. I would not be foresworn for he helped me greatly. I just have a bad feeling. I do not sense disaster but I feel that there is danger."

His words meant that we did not see Hrolf the Horseman. That was sad for our webs had been linked. I believed they still were but I never saw him again in this world and that was sad. In light of subsequent events it would have been better if we had seen him. The Norns, however, had other plans; for both of us.

We stood well out to sea when we passed the Breton coast. It was a graveyard of ships. There were islands, rocks, shoals and pirates. The deeper waters of the ocean were a better choice. It added another day and it meant that we reached Bruggas in the middle of Tvímánuður. We had stood off the coast and waited for dawn. The estuary was not one to risk at night. The delay benefitted us for we arrived at high tide when ships were leaving and we found two berths close together. They were also closer to the *'Saddle'* and that suited the crew who were looking forward to Freja's ale and food.

Aiden and I took the letters and headed for Isaac's home. Half of the crew went to the inn. The other half would have the evening there. We had nothing of value and so we did not feel the need for a bodyguard.

Oddvakr opened the door and his smile was genuine, "You live, Jarl! That is good news! When you left I feared that the legend would end."

I smiled, "It goes on. Is your master home? We have news from his nephew."

"Follow me, Jarl. You have just landed?" I nodded. "I will have food and ale fetched for you. My master will also be pleased that you live."

Isaac was a dried up old man but his smile when he saw me was genuine and he suddenly looked much younger. He clapped his hands together. "I thought you were gone forever, Jarl, and yet you look hale and hearty. All went well?"

"It did and we are indebted to your nephew."

He shook his head, "He carried valuable information." He cocked his head to one side. "You knew that. Oddvakr said that your face, when you received the chest, told of your disquiet. I am sorry but, as you know now, my nephew is not just a merchant."

I nodded, "Let us say that I am disappointed that you did not trust me." I shrugged. "I suppose to you I am still a barbarian."

"To one who is descended from Abraham, most people are barbarians but you are right to admonish me. How may I make it up to you?"

"We have goods to trade." Just then food and drink arrived.

Isaac did not wish to speak in front of the servants and so he asked, "Tell me about your visit to the great city." As the food was laid out I told him what he really wanted to know; the political situation in Miklagård. Isaac waited until we were alone before he spoke. "I do have some news for you but that can wait until you have broken bread with me and told me how I may be of service."

"We have many items we wish to sell. You know the true value in the current market. Your advice would be welcome. We wish to get the best prices."

"What are your goods?"

I turned to Aiden who handed him a list he had written. We ate the bread and cheese. I did not expect ham at the home of Isaac.

He studied the list. "Most I will take off your hands. The spices, especially, are very expensive here. In fact, the problems you alluded to in Constantinopolis may explain it. Few ships have arrived from the east and nothing over land. You and your people will be rich."

"I am rich, Isaac, because I am alive. This news you said you had, what is it?"

"It concerns Wessex mainly. The Danes are making inroads into the land of the East Angles. Some say that the land is theirs already. That means that Wessex cannot be complacent. They prepare for an attack from the Danes. That, in turn, means that the Mercians have some respite. They have suffered at the hands of the men of Wessex for many years. Now they are no longer threatened they seek to extend their land."

"Towards Wales?" I had a sinking feeling in the pit of my stomach.

"Partly but I heard, from a Saxon captain, that he heard that Mercia sought to retake their lands in the north."

"My land."

"And have you heard when?"

He shook his head. "I am a merchant and not a warrior. War is your business. When would you attack, if it was you?"

"Haustmánuður, after the crops have been gathered in."

"Then you have answered yourself. When is this Haustmánuður?"

"A moon from now."

"You have time. They are subjugating the Welsh now and gathering their crops in."

"How do you know all of this?"

"I have Oddvakr and my other men frequent the taverns and inns by the river. They listen. I piece together information. That knowledge can help me. I can predict which prices will rise and which will fall. The margins are narrow." He smiled, "I prosper. When you return to the Land of the Wolf send your captains to me. I will make it worth their while."

"I will do so."

"Oddvakr will come with the chest of coins and take the goods away. The market is not until the morrow. Will you stay?"

I shook my head. "The goods are on a merchant ship. Arne can wait to sell what remains. After your news we fly."

"You are a good leader. Would that the Franks had such a leader. I fear that Charles has little of Charlemagne's blood in his veins." He stood and clasped my arm. "I can say no more than this. You are my friend and we are bound. May Jehovah watch over you."

As we headed back to the ship I turned to Aiden, "Your powers are returning."

"So it would seem."

"It is worrying though. The Mercians have been quiet for many years. Why are they becoming belligerent now?"

"When I was in Miklagård there were some penitents from England. I met them in the library. King Beorhtwulf is the new King of Mercia. Wiglaf was a weak king, we all know that. Perhaps this new king has decided to show his power by defeating barbarians. If he attacked Wales then he must be confident."

"He will have a large army."

We were approaching the **'Saddle'** and Aiden laughed, "Since when do large numbers worry Jarl Dragonheart? If we get back in time then you can meet him in the field. We know where he must march."

I nodded, "The land of Sigtrygg Thrandson."

"We have fought there before. Erik Short Toe will need to sail like he has never sailed before. You will need to sail on the morning tide."

"Then the men can have one night in port. I will not risk the river at night."

"The voyage home has not been as hard as it might. Besides Ragnar and Gruffyd might have had a whisper of the attack and be preparing."

It was my turn to laugh, as we entered the inn, "You know that is not true!"

Erik, Olaf and Sven were in the inn. Arne, and Haaken would be along later. The whole inn cheered as we entered. Freja walked up to me and kissed me. My men cheered even louder. "You live! When you left here I feared for your life. I have heard of your deeds." She squeezed me, "Vikings now visit here because they know that you are my friend and wish to know about you! How long do you stay?"

"I sail on the morning tide!"

Her face fell. She turned, "Ale over here! I will sit with the Jarl Dragonheart until he leaves!"

I sat on the seat which was vacated by Arne Thin Hair. Erik Short Toe and Olaf Leather Neck leaned over, "We leave so soon?"

"We have information that there may be trouble at home." Erik's eyes widened. He had a family at Úlfarrston. "We have time but we need to be home in less than a month."

"We can be there in fourteen nights... if the Norns permit it."

"Aye and there is the rub. We leave on the morning tide. Your son can sell the trade goods we carry. Will he have enough crew?"

"He will. I will go back and have the cargo offloaded and the supplies loaded."

"You have time enough. Stay."

He smiled, "Jarl, it is my ship and my son. I can drink at home." He left.

Freja handed me my ale. "You have loyal men."

"And that is why I have white hair and I am not in Valhalla!"

Aiden and I were assaulted by questions from Olaf and the others. When we had answered them Olaf said, "And now we go back so that the other half of the crew can enjoy Freja's food and ale. There is work for warriors and it is in the Land of the Wolf."

Haaken and Arne also had questions. We answered them and then Freja stood and shouted, "Enough questions! Dragonheart and his wizard need food and they need peace." She was so intimidating that all of my warriors save Haaken melted away.

Haaken smiled, "If I were not married, Freja, then you would make a woman fit for me!"

She laughed and pushed him off his seat. "There is only one man for me and that is the Dragonheart!" She stood and went to fetch more ale.

Haaken said. "She would take you to her bed, Jarl!"

It was my turn to laugh, "And at my age that would involve sleep and nothing more!"

When she returned with the ale Freja sat close by me. "I was listening to your words. I too have heard of this King of Mercia. Beorhtwulf wishes to impress the other kings of Britannia. He would be high King. Egbert was strong enough but his seed is not as strong as he was. Beorhtwulf sees this as his chance. Northumbria is almost gone. If Beorhtwulf takes your land then Northumbria would rise and follow him."

I laughed, "You have much knowledge for an inn keeper."

She smiled and looked, suddenly younger, "Why do you think I have such a successful business? My ale and food are good but I keep my ears open. Others pay me for information. For you it is free!" She became serious. "Be careful, Dragonheart. I have heard that this Beorhtwulf hires mercenaries. Danes and Hibernians fight for him. He will recover the lands he lost to the men of Dyfed. When that is done he will head north. He will come for you."

After making some last purchases from the market, Aiden and I left in the late afternoon. Freja made it quite clear that I could have her and I was flattered. Erika and Brigid were the two women with whom I had shared a bed and they would remain the only ones. Aiden and I had much to do. Isaac would be sending payment and I was honour bound to make sure that he received what he was owed.

Sámr greeted me. "We leave on the first tide?"

"Aye so if you have anything you wish to buy then now is the time."

He shook his head. "What I need is Bagsecg's mail. Germund and I bought clothes for Baldr. He had little."

My great grandson had learned much on this voyage. I knew, in my heart, that the clan would be safe in his hands. I knew not how he would lead the clan but lead it he would. The evening passed in a blur. Goods were transferred to '*Ylva*'. Coin was stored in our hold. Ale and food were brought aboard. Erik had bought as much rope as he could and a spare yard. He then went to '*Ylva*' and spoke to his son. I saw him hand over his charts and maps. Erik had them in his head. The night passed quickly for there was much to do. When the tide turned we were ready and we headed down the river with the sun peering over the eastern horizon. The men did not need to row. We had the tide and we had the current. There was even the hint of a wind from the east. We were going home.

As we neared the coast of Wessex Aiden stood with me at the stern. Erik Short Toe had rarely left it. He was asleep beneath his cloak and Aiden and I were taking a turn at the steering board. "Now you know why you returned from the Otherworld. You were needed in the Land of the Wolf."

"I thought you called me back. It was your voice I heard or perhaps Sámr's. I am becoming confused. I knew the voice when I was there but now...."

He shook his head, "I told you, in Miklagård, I had no power. The voice you heard calling you was in the room at David ben Samuel's house. Sámr and I sat with you. Sámr held the hand which grasped Ragnar's Spirit and I held the other. We called for you to return to our world but we were not in the spirit world." He looked up at the masthead and then back at me. "It was the Allfather allowed my voice to go to you. You say the doors were closed on you?" I nodded. "Then the Allfather was telling you that it was not your time." He nodded ahead, "Now if we can get by the isles and make a swift passage then we can meet this King Beorhtwulf and you can show him why your name is feared."

"It was but I am an old man now. Men will not fear me."

"Then they are fools! I have watched you as you fought the enemy in the Blue Sea. You may have lost some of your speed but you have made up for it with cunning. The old wolf is the most dangerous. You know that."

I nodded. I remembered hunting with my son and the Ulfheonar high in Lang's Dale. It had been the old wolf which had nearly done for us. The young ones were reckless and came at us quickly with teeth bared and snarling jowls. The old wolf sneaked upon us and chose his moment to attack. He had been hard to kill and his attack almost saved his pack. Aiden was right, I would be the old wolf.

We landed on a beach on the south coast of On Walum. We would not risk either An Lysardh or Syllingar at night. The crew did not leave the ship save the ship's boys who sought shellfish. We lit no fire and we kept a good watch.

Just before dawn we were all awake. We had bought a goat. We would make a blót. Aiden believed that it would make Ran, the god of the sea, protect us from the malice of the Norns. It could not hurt. I slit the goat's throat at the stern. "Ran, we give you this sacrifice so that you will watch over us as we sail through your waters. We need your protection to help us save our home."

The carcass was lowered into the water and the crew stood, watching the sun rise in the east. If the blót had been successful then the wind would be in our favour and the sun would break over a calm sea and with blue skies. A thin grey line appeared as we watched. Erik glanced up, as did I, when the pennant fluttered slightly. This was a new one. We had replaced it in Miklagård for the old one was a little ragged. This one was still bright red and it showed the wind was from the south east. Erik nodded but I saw that he still clutched the wolf charm around his neck. We still needed clear skies. The last thing we wanted would be a cloud filled day and squally rain. A hint of pink edged with blue appeared. The pink and blue became red and suddenly the sun burst over the eastern horizon. The water appeared bathed in blood. Aiden peered aft. The body of the goat remained beneath the waves. Ran had accepted our blót. The red sea, reflecting the setting sun, was like the goat's blood.

"I think, Erik Short Toe, that we can now risk Syllingar."

Even though we had the wind the men took their oars. We would not use them until we neared An Lysardh. Our intention was to race around the headland and take advantage of this precious wind and clement conditions. Who knew when they would fail us?

Baldr had become a ship's boy. We did not risk him in the rigging. That took skill and practice. He was willing but having plucked him from the sea we would not put him in danger. He acted as lookout at the prow and he took ale and food to the rowers. He had picked up many more words. He could even curse in Norse! He was popular with the crew. They knew that he had been chosen by the gods. To have survived as long at sea as he had done was nothing short of a miracle. We still did not know why he had been saved or why we had been sent to find him. Perhaps there was no reason and the gods just wished him saved. It mattered not. We were now responsible for him.

As An Lysardh drew closer Erik shouted, "Run out the oars!"

As Haaken began the chant the oars bit into the sea. It was not the normal grey. There was a green hue tinged with blue and we took that as a sign that the sacrifice had been a good one. I wondered if Haaken had lost his mind when he began the chant. It was the story of Ylva. As I moved to stop the chant Aiden restrained me, "No, Jarl Dragonheart, this is good. The Allfather will approve. It shows that we are not afraid of the Norns. We showed respect to Ran with the blót and now we show him that we are Vikings. Your crew are warriors. It is *wyrd*." He pointed to Baldr. "And there is another that we saved. The song could equally be about him, could it not?"

I nodded. He was right.

The Dragonheart sailed with warriors brave
To find the child he was meant to save
With Haaken and Ragnar's Spirit
They dared to delve with true warrior's grit
With Aðils Shape Shifter with scout skills honed
They found the island close by the rocky stones
The Jarl and Haaken will bravely roar
The Jarl and Haaken and the Ulfheonar
Beneath the earth the two they went
With the sword by Odin sent
In the dark the witch grew strong
Even though her deeds were wrong
A dragon's form she took to kill
Dragonheart faced her still
He drew the sword touched by the god

Made by Odin and staunched in blood
The Jarl and Haaken will bravely roar
The Jarl and Haaken and the Ulfheonar
With a mighty blow, he struck the beast
On Dragonheart's flesh he would not feast
The blade struck true and the witch she fled
Ylva lay as though she were dead
The witch's power could not match the blade
The Ulfheonar are not afraid
The Jarl and Haaken will bravely roar
The Jarl and Haaken and the Ulfheonar
And now the sword will strike once more
Using all the Allfather's power
Fear the wrath you Danish lost
You fight the wolf and pay the cost
The Jarl and Haaken will bravely roar
The Jarl and Haaken and the Ulfheonar

    We stopped rowing when we passed the rugged rocks of An Lysardh. There were few people who lived on this exposed headland but once we turned north then we would have to keep watch for the men of Om Walum. They had no love for Vikings. The daughter of their last king now lived with my son in the Land of the Wolf. It would take many ships but if they saw **'Heart of the Dragon'** then they might think the risk worth taking. We stopped rowing and thanked the Allfather for the wind which sped us north towards the Sabrina. We were on the last leg of our journey home.

    Our luck lasted until we neared the isle of the puffins; Ynys Enlli. The skies darkened and a storm came out of nowhere. With a swirling wind and seas as high as our mast we hove to in the lee of the island. We ran out sea anchors and rode out the storm. It lasted the afternoon, the night and into the morning. When it stopped we noticed a list. Erik said, "We have sprung some strakes. We need to beach her and make repairs. I am sorry, Jarl."

    "It is no one's fault. At least we are close to a beach that we know is safe."

The only people who lived on the island was a colony of monks. These were not the rich monks of the Saxons. They came from Hibernia and lived a simple life. We did not bother them.

It took all of the crew to drag the drekar on to the beach. While the crew took out the cargo to make certain it was not damaged Erik and I went around the hull to inspect it. The strakes by the keel were the ones which had sprung. They were below the ballast and I hoped that our cargo had not been spoiled. Isaac had taken much of it but we had spices and the ingredients which Kara wanted not to mention the oils and fine cloth we had bought.

Erik looked relieved, "I have enough pine tar for this and we have the glue made from the goat's hooves." He pointed to the sheep which grazed on the slopes of the rocky hillside below the monastery. "And the Allfather has sent us the wool."

I nodded, "We will not slaughter the sheep. Aiden and I will visit with the monks and we will buy the wool and not harm their animals."

When I told Olaf Leather Neck he was surprised, "They are not of our people. If they complain then we kill them!"

I shook my head, "And what would that gain us?" He looked confused. "Since we have sailed these waters we have used this island. The Allfather has smiled on us by giving us a haven where there are birds and fish for us to eat. I know not why he allows these followers of the White Christ to live but I see no reason to hurt them. We have things to trade for the wool."

Aiden nodded, "They lead a simple life but an amphora of wine would be welcome, I am thinking."

We took Baldr with us and we carried the amphora up the hill as Erik lit the fire to heat the pine tar. Baldr asked, as we neared the simple conical huts, "Why do men live here? What do they do?"

Aiden answered, "They meditate and they pray."

He looked confused, "Why? Do they not have families? Where are the women?"

It was a good question and I could find no answer. It seemed to me a pointless existence. I admired their hardiness and the simplicity of their lives but at the end of the day their line was gone. Their god could not possibly want them to be the end of their blood. I shrugged, "There are many types of men. They are just different from us."

Despite my weapons they did not seem afraid of us. There were six who came to greet us. Four others continued to tend the garden. I saw there were beans which were being harvested as well some greens. They lived a simple life but with sheep's cheese, fish, eggs and puffins, they ate well. Aiden spoke their language. He had been born in Hibernia which was their home too. The conversation went on for some time. He took the jug of wine from Baldr and gave it to them. I saw the ghost of a smile on the oldest of the monks. They gave a slight bow and then returned to their huts and their gardens.

Aiden translated his words as we headed back down the hill, "He said we are welcome. He was surprised that we asked. The old one said he had been watching us come here since he was a young monk. He recognised our ship. When others come they hide. He did not say where they hide."

We returned to the beach and sent six men to shear as many of the sheep as we could. Others hunted some of the puffins while the ship's boys collected shellfish. Until we had the wool then Erik could do nothing. The pine tar was still heating. Erik shouted to the men who would harvest wool. "Bring back the wool as soon as you have some. I do not want to waste the tar."

It was noon by the time they had cornered and shorn the sheep. Erik summoned his boys and they began the messy task of filling the cracks in the hull with wool and then coating them in pine tar. We were lucky that it was just down one side of the drekar. I realised it was the side which had hit the galley in the Blue Sea. We had won but there had been a price.

When we had finished and were waiting for it to dry we ate. Erik said, "I told, you, Jarl, that we needed to maintain our ship. Had they sprung off An Lysardh then we would all be in the Otherworld."

Olaf nodded, "Aye, the Allfather has protected us and now we just have a couple of days of hard rowing before we reach our home."

Erik Short Toe said, "We have to wait until morning. I want this repair to be dried and watertight."

Viking Shadow

    We left in the third hour of the day. It took that long for us to pull her off the beach. We headed north and west. There was open water and the wind was from the west and the south. We rowed for a short time until we could turn and head north with the wind making our sail billow. We would pass between the Angle Sea and Hibernia. I held my wolf amulet tightly for, with luck and a continuing wind, we could head for the land south of the Land of the Wolf. It would give us a better approach to our home and allow us to see if the Mercians were on the march.

Chapter 17

It was dark by the time we had passed Man and reached the coast of the land to the south of the land of the Wolf. Once there had been many people who lived by the rivers here but after Sigtrygg Thrandson and his men had been killed there were fewer. Perhaps that would now change. We hove to. As much as we wanted to hurry home I wanted to ensure that the Mercians were not camped within marching distance of our home. We were a day's march from Úlfarrston and Whale Island. If there was no sign of them then we had time. We did not land but used a sea anchor. As the sail was furled for the night I peered landward. A light appeared and then disappeared. It was night time and distance was hard to estimate. I waved over Galmr. He had better eyes than I did. "What can you see?"

"I think it is a camp fire, Jarl. Men are moving in front of it."

"Thank you." I turned to Aiden. "Aiden?"

He closed his eyes. His power was returning. "I sense danger, Jarl Dragonheart. The spirits tell me there are enemies close."

I turned and walked down the drekar. The sound of the surf on the shingle would mask any sounds from the drekar. "Olaf, Haaken, choose four men who have knife skills and can easily move in the dark. We are going ashore to investigate the fire yonder."

Olaf stood and peered over the side. At first, he saw nothing and then saw the flash of light. "It is a camp fire. Mercians?"

"It could be. It will cost us wet breeks to find out." As he went to find the men I turned to Erik. "Have us taken in close enough to wade ashore."

He ordered the crew to man the larboard oars and he had the sea anchors raised. I went to my chest and took out my wolf cloak and Ragnar's Spirit. Sámr saw me and came over. "You are going ashore?"

"There may be Saxons close by. If there are then I would question them."

"I will come with you!"

"No, you will not. You have not the skills." He looked hurt. "This is work for Ulfheonar. There are just three of us and so we will take other warriors who have knife skills. Do you have knife skills? Can you walk at night without being seen?" He shook his head. "You have done well on this voyage. One day, when you have developed such skills then you may well be able to sneak ashore, walk up to a sentry and slit his throat. But at the moment? I fear you might jeopardise the raid." He nodded.

Erik said, quietly, "We are as close as we dare."

"Then wait here. We will not be long." Turning to the men I would lead I said, "If they are Saxons then I want one prisoner!"

I slipped over the side and the others followed. Olaf was an Ulfheonar but he was not as silent as I was. He would bring up the rear. Lars Long Nose and Ráðgeir Ráðgeirson would be behind me with Haaken One eye in the middle. That way the three Ulfheonar would be able to manage the other four. They had skills but we had the skills of the wolf. The water was cold and came up to my waist. None of us wore mail. It might make a noise and I did not think that whoever we found would be wearing mail. The dunes and the undergrowth hid the light from us but I had marked its position and I lead my men over the dunes and scrubland towards it. I could see the light better now. I spied the fire. Whatever had been in front of the fire had moved. By my estimate it was six hundred paces or more from us. I waved Lars Long Nose and Ráðgeir Ráðgeirson to my left and right. We moved closer and I was able to discern shapes around the fire. We were on track and so I held my hand up and paused. The sounds of voices drifted to me. I also heard the neigh of horses. That made it more likely that they were scouts and Saxons. Who else would be camping here? The wind was from our right and so I moved further east so that he would be able to smell them before they could smell us. As we approached the camp I saw one of the figures moving. They were not asleep yet but, from what I could see, there were no sentries. That made sense. We were more than thirty miles from the nearest of my people and that was just an isolated farm where Sigtrygg Thrandson had had his hall. I turned and pointed to Haaken. I pointed east. He nodded and touched Arne on the shoulder. He moved off. I pointed to Olaf and he led Galmr to the west. I drew Ragnar's Spirit.

Viking Shadow

The three of us moved towards the camp. I had seen more than sixty summers but I knew how to move silently. I could hear the two warriors with me. I knew that they were trying to be quiet but they were failing. I held my hand up and gestured for them to stop. We were less than fifty paces from the fire. If they made a noise then the Saxons might grab horses and flee. I did not want that. I moved so slowly that I knew my movements would not alert the Saxons. They were all facing the fire and they would not be able to see me in the dark. It took time for eyes to adjust to the dark. The conversation around the fire had ended which meant that they would be able to hear me. The firelight illuminated the camp. I halted and counted. There were eight men. Four lay sleeping. I saw that they had their horses, three of them, tethered close to the fire. I had Olaf Leather Neck and Haaken one Eye approaching from the east and the west. I could count on those two. I waved my arm for Lars Long Nose and Ráðgeir Ráðgeirson to follow me. I rose and stepped towards the Saxon who had just risen with his back to me.

In two strides I was upon him and I swung the flat of my blade into the side of the head. He fell in a heap at my feet. Even before he had hit the ground I raced in and hacked into the neck of the man seated to my right. The other six leapt to their feet. Scouts were usually good warriors with quick minds. In normal circumstances they would have survived but they were facing Ulfheonar. Olaf's sword came out of the chest of a Saxon who stared at me as though I was a ghost. Haaken's sword was rammed into the side of a warrior who was drawing his own weapon. Galmr leapt towards the horses as Lars Long Nose and Ráðgeir Ráðgeirson charged into the camp. Within a few moments it was over.

The man Galmr had hit was still alive. I ran to him, "Who is your master?" I spoke in Saxon. He spat bloody phlegm at me. "Tell me and you shall have a warrior's death."

His hand went to his cross, "I am not pagan! I am Christian and…." The light went from his eyes and he died.

I turned and ran to the man I had struck with my sword. He was trying to rise. "Seize him. Haaken, fetch a brand. Lars Long Nose and Ráðgeir Ráðgeirson, take the horses back to the drekar.

We will take them home with us. We cannot have them running back to the army."

Olaf said, "You are sure that there is an army?"

"Why else would there be eight Mercians this close to the Land of the Wolf?"

The Saxon was not a big man. He was young. He had seen perhaps twenty summers and he looked fearfully at us as he was pinned. I took out Wolf's Blood. I realised that Christians would not wish a warrior's death. I had to offer something else. I would offer life. I did not press the dagger to his neck. I held it behind my back. I smiled, "What is your name?"

He seemed confused that I spoke Saxon but he answered, "Ethelbert."

"You are Mercian?" He nodded. It seemed I knew all the answers anyway. I spoke Saxon well and that had him confused. "Your king is Beorhtwulf and he has just subjugated the Welsh. He is at the fortress the Romans called Deva." All of this was guesswork on my part. I was using the information we had already and joining it together. If I was wrong then his brow would wrinkle and his eyes would give him away.

"Aye, lord." He looked more bemused than confused. I seemed to know all.

"Then how many men make up the army?"

His eyes narrowed and he stiffened. "I will not tell you. I will die first."

I nodded and brought out Wolf's Blood and held it before him. The firelight made it sparkle. I moved it close to his manhood. "There are worse things than death. Haaken One Eye." Haaken appeared with the torch. "We could take your manhood or your eyes. Then we could let you go. Imagine the terror of wandering in a world of dark with no manhood. If you tell me what I need to know then you shall be whole and you will be taken with us to our home. You will be a slave until your king comes and then I will sell you back to him if he lives. Is that not better than death?" He hesitated. "I know your king comes to the Land of the Wolf. He comes to my land."

"You are the Dragonheart?" He tried to push himself into the earth.

I nodded. "And you know I can change into a wolf." I played on the legend of the warriors who were shape shifters. Even the Christians were worried by that concept.

"The priest said you could not. He told us that you were just men with a wolf cloak."

"Then how did we get so close without your guards or horses seeing us?" His eyes told me that he had no answer. "How many horsemen does he have?" I saw doubt in his eyes. "How can that hurt your king?"

He bit his lip and Haaken lurched towards him with the burning brand. "A hundred! I did not count them all! Do not blind me!"

"There, that was not so hard. And I assume he has called out the hundreds, the fyrd?" He nodded. "Then that would give him a thousand men." He nodded, "And hearth-weru and thegns?"

"Fifty thegns and forty heart-weru."

I nodded, "Galmr take him back to the ship."

Olaf said, "You will let him live?"

"I told him I would. He may yet serve a purpose. Arne collect the weapons. Let us go. Leave the bodies here. It will be a few days before the Saxon army reaches here and by then we will be at home."

By the time we reached our ship they were loading the last of the horses. I stood in the water as the last one was hoisted aboard. I shook my head, "How did you load them so quickly?"

Sámr grinned, "Baldr. He spoke to the horses and they allowed the men to put the slings beneath them. He is a galdramenn for horses!"

Wyrd! The Allfather had sent him to us with a purpose. Perhaps I now saw that purpose. The men were all awake and there was little point in waiting. We had learned all that we needed to learn. The wind was from the east and so we rowed up the coast. This was our land and our waters. We were familiar with every rock, shoal and current. The wind helped us. We did not row hard. We did not chant. With one man in two resting it was just a way to reach home sooner. As dawn broke we saw, in the distance, the mountains of home. Soon we would be able to make out Old Olaf. Baldr and Sámr stood with the three horses keeping them calm. They were typical Saxon horses; small and hardy. We used horses more than most Norse. Now that we had Baldr we had someone who understood horses. They were in his veins. As we headed up the coast the wind veered slightly so that it was coming more from the south and we stopped rowing. Men prepared for our arrival. All had family waiting for them. Only Haaken and Erik had wives but there would be mothers, sisters and grandparents. Only a few would be at Whale Island. Our watch tower would see us before we saw them. Our drekar, with the wolf on the sail, was unmistakable. I knew that Ragnar, Gruffyd and their families would be there to greet us. A rider would head to Cyninges-tūn. He would tell Kara and Uhtric that we were returning. It had been half a year.

Aiden stood next to me. "There has been trouble at home." I looked at him. He nodded. "I felt it last night when you went hunting Saxons. Today it has grown. The spirits are sad. The people who greet us will be sad."

When we had left I was the one they were concerned about. What had happened? The joy of my return disappeared in an instant. We lowered the sail and the oars took us the last half mile into the harbour. I saw my son and grandson waiting for me. Their wives and their families were not there. What did that mean? My men did not know of the sadness and, as we tied up they began to chant, "Dragonheart!" Over and over. They beat their shields with their swords and stamped on the decks. The horses became agitated.

I raised my hand, "Peace! Save your joy for your families. Remember we have but a short time and then there will be war!"

I saw Ragnar and Gruffyd exchange glances. I stepped ashore when we were tied up. Ragnar said, "War?"

I nodded, "First give me the news that makes your faces dark and your hearts heavy."

Gruffyd said, "Aiden?" I nodded. "My sister, Erika, her husband and their children are all dead. Hibernians attacked the hall in Dyflin and slew them and most of the other Vikings there. The ones who survived fled to Veisafjǫrðr. Is it a war with the Hibernians?"

I shook my head, "That vengeance is for the future. For now, we have a greater threat. The King of Mercia comes north with an army of more than a thousand men. He is on the road from Caestir. We must summon the clan; all of it."

Ragnar, who was older than Gruffyd, put his arms around my shoulders. "And we have been remiss. The disease is gone?" I nodded. He beamed. "Then we should be celebrating."

I shook my head, "That will have to wait. I will ride back to Cyninges-tūn with Aiden. I need to summon Ketil, Ulf and Asbjorn. I leave you two to raise the bondi. Have the knarr sail south to find out where the Mercians march. I believe it will be along the coast. I will return within two days."

Baldr had brought the horses from the drekar. I turned to Ragnar. "Have a couple of saddles brought. Baldr, you will come with Aiden and me. We ride to Cyninges-tūn."

Baldr looked confused until Sámr said, "It is his home. He will return with you will he not, great grandfather?"

"Aye we will all be back here. Within seven days we will have a fight to save the Land of the Wolf."

When the saddles were brought Baldr said, "I need no saddle."

"Then you are a true horseman."

I donned my cloak and strapped Ragnar's Spirit to my side. My chest could stay here. We mounted and headed up through the darkening gloom of late afternoon to Cyninges-tūn. I had much to do. This was not the homecoming I had anticipated when we had left Miklagård. Of the three of us, Baldr seemed the happiest. No doubt that was because he was on a horse. Aiden was wrapped in his own thoughts. Dyflin had been a place where we could trade and find allies. If the jarl and my daughter were dead then we were even more isolated. The shadow grew over the Land of the Wolf. Our enemies grew and did not diminish. The Danes had not finished with us. Pridbjørn Ellesefsson had shown me that there were still Danes out there with vengeance in their hearts. With Man a den of pirates and now Dyflin bereft of allies there were few that we could turn to. Empress Theodora was many leagues hence. By the time we reached my hall the gates were barred. The rider with the news of our arrival would have beaten us by many hours. None would have expected us to ride for home.

"Open the gates. It is Jarl Dragonheart."

It was Karl who opened them. Karl was the captain of my guard. An Ulfheonar, he had been wounded and, like Germund, was lame. It did not stop him wanting to serve the clan. "We heard you were back, Jarl, but we did not expect you so soon."

I nodded. I could speak plainly with Karl. "The Mercians are coming. War has returned."

Kara was wrapped in a wolf cloak as was Ylva and they came out to us. Kara threw her arms around me, "I am happy that there is a magic stronger than mine. I could not save you but now I see that you are whole again."

Ylva hugged her father. He said, simply, "The Mercians come. They are just days away."

Ylva smiled, "I sensed danger. Now that we know whence it comes we can put our mind to defeating it."

"I think, granddaughter, that it will be the steel of my men which will defeat them."

Ylva kissed me on the cheek, "But a little magic cannot hurt." She saw Baldr for the first time. "And who is this?"

"This is Baldr, we gave him that name for he was a slave. He was a prince of the horsewarriors in the steppes to the east of Miklagård. We found him floating on a pierce of driftwood in the Blue Sea. He had been there for more than half a day. The Allfather sent him to us."

Ylva walked up to him and put her hand on his forehead. She closed her eyes. Baldr seemed both bemused and bewitched. Ylva opened her eyes, "Here is a tale. He was sent to us. You saved him just as you were saved by Old Ragnar. You must train him to become a warrior."

I shook my head. "It is too late. You begin a warrior's training when he has seen seven summers. Any older and it is too late."

She smiled, enigmatically, "Then this will be your challenge. Besides it will occupy you and stop you becoming so melancholic!"

My granddaughter had the power to bewitch even me. She had taken my mind from the task in hand. I shook my head and turned to Karl. "At first light send riders to my jarls. I need every warrior gathered at Úlfarrston in three days. Every farmer from around here is needed too. We have to fight an army of a thousand men. This will not be easy."

"Aye, Jarl!"

I turned to Baldr, "Come you shall stay in my hall."

He shook his head, "First I will see to the horses. They have been ridden hard. Do you have a stable?"

I saw Karl smile as he put his arm around Baldr's shoulder, "Come with me, young horseman. I will take you to the Jarl's hall when that is done."

Uhtric stood in my door. I saw tears in his eyes, "You live, Jarl. The Allfather heard my plea."

"Thank you for telling my daughter and Aiden of my problem. I was foolish. We have a guest. He is far from his home. He was a slave for many years and he was badly treated. Make him welcome."

"Always, Jarl."

It felt good to be back in my hall. Before I had left it had felt cold and melancholy. Now it felt warm and welcoming. It was the same hall. It was me that had changed. The healer had cut out more than the disease. He had cut out that part of me which looked inward. I had not been the leader I once had and I was diminishing. I was become less than I should. Now I had purpose.

Uhtric brought me ale, bread and cheese. I smiled, "You will no longer have to wash bedding each day, Uhtric."

"Good."

Karl brought Baldr. I said, "This is Uhtric, he looks after me and my hall. He will show you to your chambers. There is ale, cheese and bread if you wish it."

He nodded, "I would like that."

Uhtric smiled and pulled another chair so that Baldr could sit close to the fire. He tasted the beer, "This is good beer."

"It is made from the water here and that is the finest water anywhere. We have good ale wives."

"Will I be with you, when you go to war?"

"Would you like to be?"

"I am part of this clan. I like what I have seen and the land, the little I have seen of it, looks like it is worth defending."

"Then you will be with me but I will try to keep you from danger. We have many enemies to fight."

"And you do not fight on a horse."

"No, Baldr, but when we fight we fear no horsemen."

"On the ship coming here I spoke with Sámr. I know that I have little skill in war. Had I still been with my father then I would be a warrior who was to be feared. I know how to fight but I have not the body nor the skills yet. Give me time and you, Sámr and Germund will be proud of me."

We spoke long into the night. He told me of his family and how they fought. I told him of Wolf Killer and the battles we had fought until Uhtric said, "Jarl, he is asleep."

"Then put him to bed. I have much to ponder."

As I finished off the ale I devised a way to defeat an army that would be twice as large as mine. If I took every warrior from my land then I might be able to have parity of numbers with his levy. I could not do that. Ketil and Ulf would need to leave men guarding their stad. The Northumbrians might have heard of the Mercian attack. They might take advantage of our dilemma. We could muster, perhaps, six or seven hundred men and still leave my stad protected. Of those only four hundred would be warriors. Less than half of those warriors would have mail. We would have to use guile, magic and the Land of the Wolf to defeat the King of Mercia.

Even though I had been up late I was still awake early. I had eaten already when Baldr entered. "I have much to do. You can occupy yourself until I return?"

"I will see to the horses." He dropped to one knee. "Thank you for taking me into your clan, Jarl Dragonheart. I can speak your language now and I would swear an oath to serve you."

"You know that an oath is a sacred vow which will bind you to me."

"I do and I wish to do so freely."

"Then I will take you as an oathsworn. When I return we will go to the Water and you shall swear there."

I wanted to speak to Kara and Ylva but I had men to find. I spent the morning in the stad and the farms which were close by, speaking to the men I would take and giving instructions for the ones I would leave behind. I sent the men who would fight off to

Úlfarrston. The gathering had to begin as soon as possible. I was on my way back to my hall and Baldr when I met Aiden and his family. They were heading for my hall.

Kara was smiling and her smile was like dawn on the Water. It lit up the valley. "This is the father we thought we had lost. He has purpose and a spring in his step. His eyes smile and his head is held high."

"Thank you, daughter. It is strange. The disease was in here," I touched my middle, "and yet I feel like a weight has been lifted from my shoulders."

"And what do you do now, father?"

I will go and fetch those who live in the Lang Dale. Then I will spend one more night here and head to Úlfarrston in the morning."

"Ylva will come with you. You will need one of us on the battlefield."

I looked at Ylva. She seemed so small and helpless. The three of them laughed as they read my thoughts, or perhaps my face. She shook her head. "I have been in the depths of the earth and faced a Norn. I think I can face Mercians for they are merely men and I am a witch. I will be safe."

"Then I will be glad for Ulla War Cry, Mordaf and Sámr will be there also."

"With the power of their spirits combined with my power this Mercian king knows not what awaits him."

Kara nodded and slipped her arm through Aiden's. "And we will stay here and use the power of Old Olaf and the Water to protect this land."

When I reached my hall Uhtric was laying out food and Baldr was helping. "We eat quickly and then we ride. We have much to do this day."

I could not persuade Baldr to use a saddle. We headed up towards the dale where my best Ulfheonar lived. Aðils Shape Shifter had taken a wife and made a home in the wildest and most remote part of my land. He was the most skilled Ulfheonar I had ever had.

Baldr had not seen my mountains the night before. He had seen the forest and the Water only. From what Aiden had told me he had been born in the flat plains. He had lived in the rich valleys of Frankia and now he saw the wild and untamed mountains and crags that made up the Land of the Wolf. He twisted and turned to take it all in. I saw wonder on his face and in his eyes. My land did that to all who saw it.

It had been some time since I had visited Aðils Shape Shifter. His stad had grown. There were now four or five huts around his hall. He had senses which even I did not understand and he was waiting to greet us as we descended from the forest. He smiled, "You live, Jarl Dragonheart. The Allfather heard our pleas."

"Thank you. This is Baldr. You will hear his tale in time but time is a luxury for us. The Mercian king marches north with an army to take the Land of the Wolf from us. I need you and as many men as you can bring to gather at Úlfarrston."

He nodded, "I will do so. The Ulfheonar will fight once more eh, Jarl Dragonheart?"

"They will. Can you gather those who live twixt here and my hall?"

"Aye. It was good to meet you, Baldr the Horseman."

Baldr started, "How did you know I was a horseman?"

Aðils laughed, "The way you sit upon the horse and the way that your hand has not stopped stroking her since you arrived."

As we headed south Baldr said, "Jarl, what are the Ulfheonar?"

"We are warriors with special skills. We can move in the night like a wolf; silently and with deadly purpose. We are a weapon of terror. When we fight on a battlefield then we are hard to defeat for we are all brothers of the wolf." I touched my wolf cloak. "We all have to kill a wolf as part of our initiation. I killed my first one when I was about your age." He nodded. "There is a reason I would like you to use a saddle. When we ride to war we need to take weapons with us. It is easier to do so using a saddle. If you are to come with me to war then you will be armed. There will be a banner to rally my men."

He nodded, "Then I will use a saddle even though I do not need one."

"And we need a helmet, sword, shield, spear and leather byrnie for you too. I do not expect you to fight but I do not want you hurt."

When we reached my hall, the sun was setting and it was a perfect time to go to the Water and for Baldr to swear an oath. There were just the two of us and as the sun made the waters red and bathed my wife, Erika's grave, in a warm glow, Baldr the prince from the east, swore to be my bondsman. I now saw the Allfather's purpose. The Norns had conspired to put obstacles in our way but the Allfather had used them to help me.

We had the weapons and mail for Baldr in my hall. My son and my grandsons, not to mention my great grandsons had all left mail, weapons and armour in my hall. Brigid had complained frequently about the mess. She had never understood the martial nature of our clan. Now Baldr had a wide choice from which to choose. He did so well. He might have been a slave for half of his life but warrior's blood coursed through his veins. He knew what he wanted even though he had never used weapons in anger. It boded well.

We left the next morning just after dawn. Ylva rode the third of the Saxon horses. She wore a wolf cloak about her and a seax hung from her belt. I had offered her a shield and helmet but she had laughed for her weapons were less obvious and deadlier; it was her magic. Rolf Horse Killer and Rollo Thin Skin rode with me. They too were Ulfheonar. They had their own men now for both lived in their own stad. In all I led fifty men south. More than that had already gone. Over half of the men I led were mounted. We would not fight from the backs of horses but we would reach the place I had chosen to fight, quicker.

I called at the shipyard where Erik had the **'Heart of the Dragon'** out of the water for repairs. The threttanessa, **'Red Dragon'** was in the water next to her. She had just had her hull recaulked. Our larger drekar were moored at Whale Island. I spoke for some time with Erik and gave him instructions and then we carried on to the armed camp.

A huge camp was already in place just north of Úlfarrston. The men from the south and west of my land were already there. Leif Ulfsson, Ketil, Asbjorn the Strong and Ulf Olafsson would be the last to reach us. They had the furthest to travel. In fact, I feared that Ketil would not reach us until we had left the camp. Time, as I knew was not on our side. I saw that Mordaf ap Gruffyd and Ulla War Cry were with their fathers. Both had leather byrnies. Sámr was with the men who had sailed on ***'Heart'*** and I saw that he wore one of his father's old mail byrnies. He looked like an oar brother now. Ragnar and Gruffyd came to greet me. They were with Raibeart ap Pasgen who was the jarl of Úlfarrston.

"What did the knarr report?"

"That the Saxons have still to cross the Belisima. They have not yet reached Prestune." The Belisima was the name the Romans had given to the river which was well south of us. It was further south than where we had found and killed their scouts. That was good for it meant they were still blind.

"Then they are still more than two days from us. We leave in the morning. I hope that the other jarls will have reached us here but if not then we will go without them. I intend to hold them at the river the Welsh called Ēa Lōn. There is no bridge but the ford is sandy and they cannot cross quickly. We will use our men with bows to thin their numbers. There is an old abandoned priory close by. Further east is the old Roman fort. We will make our stand at the old priory. It is on a small hill. Sigtrygg Thrandson repaired the ditches and the walls. We can use that for our horses and our bondi. They will fight better behind a little stone wall. There are trees there for I would disguise our numbers."

Raibeart ap Pasgen said, "A good plan. I have a man who knows the way across the sands." I looked up from the map I had been using. "The sands were treacherous and could swallow up whole armies". He smiled, "Do not worry, Jarl, he collects shellfish and knows the sands. He can find us a way. It is but twenty miles across them. We can be there in less than a day. If we go by safer routes it will take more than one day."

Ragnar nodded, "I know the place you have chosen to fight. It is a good site but we will need to do work."

It was my turn to laugh, "Now do you read my mind too?"

Ylva said, "The blood of Erika the matriarch of the family courses through our veins. All of us have inherited some of her powers." She shrugged, "I have more than most but we know your thoughts."

"Aye, grandfather. We cannot defeat the Saxons with the numbers of men available to us. We must use the land and our cunning too."

Wyrd; Ragnar had come to the same conclusion as me. The land would be safe in his hands and Sámr's.

"Good then you and your people will lead Raibeart ap Pasgen. My son and grandson will accompany you. Galmr Haldisson will wait here for the other jarls and he can bring them to meet us at the deserted priory which lies close to Cynibald's cross. We can use the old priory grounds for our camp. Rollo and Rolf can head south and scout out the enemy. If the Ulfheonar fight with us, let us use them."

Chapter 18

Haaken and Olaf Leather Neck arrived just a short time after dusk. Asbjorn the Strong was with them and brought the men of Windar's Mere and the dale of Grize. Our numbers were growing. I told them our plan. Olaf Leather Neck did not care so long as he got to fight. He was pleased to be fighting with other Ulfheonar once more. He and Rolf the Horse Killer used the same weapon, the Danish axe. They were a formidable pair in a shield wall. Raibaert's people had prepared food. The harvest had been collected in. They were grateful that I was fighting south of their land. I could have chosen more favourable ground to the north. That was not my way. I wanted the battle to be as far from my people as possible. We ate in the open. It was a pleasant evening and it was good that the army could see that their leaders endured the same conditions and food as they did. There were many farmers who had never had to fight before. It was rare for me to ask them to do so. They knew that it was a serious threat we faced.

I saw that Sámr did not sit with Ulla War Cry and Mordaf ap Gruffyd. He sat with Germund, Baldr and the other warriors who had been on the voyage to Miklagård. It was sad but understandable. Sámr would be in the shield wall when we fought. He would not be in the front rank. He and Germund would be in the third. Sámr's inexperience and Germund's leg determined that. My two grandsons would be used as messengers. They sat close to their fathers. My son and grandson would be discussing the battlefield. Their sons were hanging on to their every word.

Ylva sat by me. Haaken One Eye was on the other side of her. Haaken had been with me when we had rescued her from the witch and there was a bond between the two of them. I saw some of the newer warriors like Snorri Gunnarson and Sven Stormbringer observing her. They had never see a woman go to war. Ylva smiled, "Your men do not know what to make of me, grandfather."

"They are new to the land. It has yet to grab and hold them. The Land of the Wolf is special." I shook my head and laughed,

"What am I doing telling you that? You know better than any. It will soon seep into their heart and they will be attuned to it. Then they will understand that here the power of the spirits and the land is as powerful a weapon as Ragnar's Spirit."

She shook her head, "I do not mind the scrutiny. It allows me to read their minds. They are good men and they will not crumble when they are attacked by overwhelming numbers."

"You can see that now?"

"They are less than three days from us. I can feel them. I could not give you a precise number but I know that they will outnumber you."

Haaken picked his teeth with the small bone he had taken from the chicken. "That is nothing new for us but I am intrigued, Jarl Dragonheart, how do you plan to defeat them?"

"Raibeart's short cut will help us. The river where we will make our stand is wide and it has mud banks and shoals. The Mercians will cross the river close to the sea at low tide. At this time of the year it is not deep."

Ylva asked, "How can you be certain that they will cross there?"

"It is the more direct route north. His scouts were heading up the coast. To the east is the forest and high ground that is Bogeuurde. It forces any large army west. When he sees me he will be confident for I will have just a hundred men in byrnies there and a hundred archers. They will not recognise them as archers for their bows will be hidden. They will see what they think is my warband. Their King will seize the opportunity to kill me and take my land quickly. I will have my banner and I will be standing at the fore. When they try to cross we will use our archers to thin their numbers as they cross the river. It is muddy close to the north bank."

"How do you know?" Ylva could read my thoughts but Haaken could not.

"When I arrived, Haaken, I spoke at length with Raibeart. I know this land well from the time of Sigtrygg but I asked if it had changed. It has not. The course of the river is slightly different but the conditions are still the same. The priory was north of the river. Sigtrygg destroyed it many years ago but the some of the stone foundations remain. As the river sometimes flood the monks built up the ground. It lies less than half a mile from the river. The sea is also less than half a mile away. We hold them between the sea and the priory. We hide the bulk of our warriors in the ruins and behind the hill. We will feign a retreat towards the sands. They will think we are trapped and they will send all of their men to follow us. That is when Ragnar and Gruffyd will lead the bulk of our men to attack their rear and to catch as many as they can in the river. By then we will have precise numbers for Rolf and Rollo will have returned from their scouting expedition."

My two Ulfheonar had eaten already and they would retire early. We would leave at dawn by which time they would be heading down to scout out the Mercian army. We needed to know their numbers and their position. Both were crucial.

Ylva asked, "Where will I be?"

"Where you can do the most good."

She nodded, "Then the high ground would be the best. I can confuse the minds of their leaders and disguise the ambush." She smiled, "A clever plan but it relies on the Saxons doing exactly what you expect."

I drank some of the excellent ale Raibeart had provided, "And if they do not then I will change my plans. If they come to my land on the road which is further east then we have the opportunity to get behind them. The last thing they would expect would be an attack on their baggage. I have fought Saxons before. They like their comfort. They will have tents, wagons and carts. But I do not think they will come from the far road. Their scouts were close to the coast. That will be their route."

Before we went to bed and with plenty of sentries patrolling I spoke with the jarls who had arrived late and told them of our plan. Asbjorn asked, "And who will make up the two hundred men who will be live bait?"

"The Ulfheonar, the men of Cyninges-tūn and those who were in Miklagård with me. There are archers in numbers amongst my men. It will make it easier when the ambush is sprung for each jarl will lead their own men. Ragnar son of Wolf Killer will lead the rest. There will be five warbands who will fall upon the Saxons. Five warbands with a snout of mailed warriors and the ones without armour supporting. The five warbands will slice through the Saxons. You and those who attack will be like a Viking shadow. You will be attacking men from their right. They will not have shields to protect them and you will drive them back towards the mud and the sands of the river. I will lead my warband to complete the trap."

Asbjorn said, "You have just recovered, Jarl. Is this wise?"

"What has wisdom to do with this? I am Dragonheart and it is the right thing to do!" I smiled, "Asbjorn, when I was in Miklagård I almost died. I saw Valhalla and Eystein the Rock." His eyes widened. Eystein had been his friend and shield brother. "I do not fear death. This Mercian king thinks that I am old and that he can claim a great victory. He sees this as his chance to become as great a king as Coenwulf or even Offa. His arrogance will be his undoing. The Saxons think that we are all barbarians. They believe that they know how to make war. They are wrong."

More men arrived during the night. There were just the three northern warbands to come. Galmr would bring them to us but not across the sands. That was too risky. It meant they might not arrive in time. That could not be helped. This was the Norn's web. We left at dawn. There were nine miles to go before we reached the sands. Our guide had chosen low tide for our crossing. He knew the sands well. I had seen the sands many times. They looked deceptively solid but they were not. More importantly the sea could quickly sweep in. When we began to cross we would have to do so quickly.

After we reached the sands, we dismounted. It was not worth risking the weight of a mailed warrior and a horse. We sank a little in the soft sands and the sands threatened to come over my seal skin boots. My dream came back to me. We followed the footsteps of Raibeart and his guides. The four or five miles we trudged through the wet and cloying sand seemed to take forever. But when I saw Raibeart and his men ahead of us on dry land then I knew our ordeal was almost over. Once on dry land we rested and drank from our skins. When we marched south the sands and the incoming tide were to the west of us. I would not wish to make the journey a second time. We mounted our horses. It was late afternoon when we reached the deserted priory. All of us went to the river to wash the mud and sand from us. I took my mail off too. I would not need it until the battle. I was one of the first to return to the priory. I examined it as though I was King Beorhtwulf. The men would have to lie down if they were to remain hidden. There were a few places where they could watch from but I could not see how they would know when to spring the trap.

The ground between the old priory and the sea had been farmed until seven years ago. Since then it had been left to its own devices. It was weed covered. The grass was as high as a man's waist in places. Scrubby brambles and elder had sprouted as well as all manner of weeds. It would not hinder us for the land was largely flat. It rose towards the mound on the hill where the old priory and the scrubby trees stood.

Ylva joined me. She smiled. "You have read my thoughts?"

She nodded, "It is simple. I shall sit here and watch the Mercians approach. They will not fear a young woman. When the time is right I will tell Ragnar and Gruffyd and they can begin their attack. It will also help me to use my powers." She tapped the stone. "This stone was quarried from Old Olaf. I can feel the connection. I will use these stones to channel my power. It is *wyrd*." She took out a piece of wool. I saw that there were knots on it. It was a hex. "I wove this when I knew I was coming with you. It will frighten the Danes and the Hibernians."

I had my jarls organise the men so that the camp was hidden behind the hill and the trees. We would have cold fare. "No fires. We have water and cold rations!" I wanted no smoke to tell the Saxons that my army waited behind the hill.

Ylva laughed, "Grandfather! Have your men by the river do the cooking! You wish them to be seen."

I felt foolish. This young woman of twenty-seven summers was teaching me how to make war. "You are right and I am a foolish old man."

"You have much to think of. Ragnar and Gruffyd should do more. I will speak with them." They were both older than Ylva and yet they were in awe of her. I headed back to my men. Sámr had been delighted when I had told him he would be with me. Even though he knew that he would be in the third rank he was happy. Baldr was also waiting for orders. He carried the banner but it was furled.

"Olaf Leather Neck, get a fire going. We, at least, will have hot food. Baldr, take our horses to the camp. We will not need them until the battle is fought and won."

"I will come with you." Sámr led one of the animals.

Just then Haaken shouted, "We have company!" and pointed north. It was Aðils Shape Shifter and his band. It was the smallest contingent. There were just twelve of them but I knew that they would all be good archers. Aðils was the best that I had.

I smiled as he approached. "How did you know we would be here? Did you not go to the gathering?"

He looked a little sheepish. "I came to scout ahead, Jarl. My men are not the warriors for a shield wall. They are archers and scouts."

"Fear not I have Rolf and Rollo scouting and your men will be needed as archers," I told him my plan and he nodded.

"I will head up the river. If the Saxons have sent scouts by the other road then I will find them." He spoke briefly with his men and then loped off.

Haaken shook his head, "That one never changes but I am glad that he has come. He might make all the difference."

We lit fires and laid nets across the river. We would enjoy fresh fish. The sun had just set when Rolf and Rollo rode in. They looked weary. Olaf and Haaken joined us. Rollo pointed south. "They are at Prestune. There are no scouts." He smiled, "Not anymore. We found four of them. They were on foot. We counted forty thegns and another forty who looked to be housecarls. They are all mounted. There are seven of their hundreds."

Haaken nodded, "Then that is less than the prisoner said."

Rolf said, "Aye but he did not tell us about the fifty Danes and sixty odd wild Hibernians."

"Do you think he lied?"

"No, Haaken One Eye, I think he did not know about them. King Beorhtwulf would save them for us. If he has them with him then he will use those to attack us first. If they die then he does not have to pay them."

"But it makes out task harder."

"And the task of the rest of the clan easier. They will be attacking the fyrd. It is we who will bear the brunt of the attack of these mercenaries. We have to be strong and to hold a little while longer than we might have expected. Rolf, Rollo, you have done well eat."

Aðils Shape Shifter arrived much later. "I have scouted as far east as Bogeuurde. I saw nothing. I even climbed Clougha Pike. They do not have scouts out."

"That confirms what Rolf and Rollo said. Then they could be here tomorrow. It is twenty miles up the Roman Road." I was thinking as I was speaking. The tide would be on the way in and they would be keeping their scouts close to their army. I guessed the scouts would be within hailing distance of the army. They would see us at the end of the day and would think that they had caught the Dragonheart with just a few men. It might just make all the difference. If they waited and camped then they would have to endure a night of the Ulfheonar. Leaving my men at the riverside camp I went to the main camp to speak to the others. I would hold a council of war.

"Danes will be with them?"

"Aye, Ylva."

"Then I can use my power against them. They will have priests of the White Christ but the Danes believe in witches. I will give them the evil sign." She held up the hex.

"That might make them attack you."

"No, grandfather. Snorri, Haaken and yourself were the only men foolish enough to attack a witch. The followers of the White Christ might but not Danes."

Ragnar said, "The fact that it is the end of the day will help us. We will be in the east and harder to see." I should have known that the Norns would be spinning. They would not allow me so cheap and easy a victory.

Gruffyd nodded, "The Allfather helps us as I knew he would."

That night I felt more confident about the outcome. I would take nothing for granted but the Saxons were approaching from the direction I had predicted. My plan could still succeed. It would come down to the steel of my men!

I woke before dawn. Now it was because I had so much to do and not because of blood or the need to make water. Mornings were now a joy. We still had food we had cooked the night before and some bread we had brought from Úlfarrston. The men were in good spirits. That always helped before a battle. I sent Aðils Shape Shifter with four of Raibeart's men who knew the area. They would scout and give us warning of the enemy's approach. They did not need to remain hidden but I sent Aðils Shape Shifter so that it would be an accurate report. We had the whole day to prepare. Ragnar had had some caltrops prepared. If the fyrd attacked us then they might not have shoes. We seeded the grassy bank by the river. When they emerged from the mud it would be another shock. We had learned that distraction often paid.

Ylva prepared her surprise. She had already woven the piece of wool, the hex, and was now knotting it. She would place it on our side of the river. When the Danes came they would see Ylva weaving. The Saxons might not worry about such things but the Danes and the Hibernians would. It was one thing to face a warrior but quite another to face a witch.

We had brought with us fifty or so boys. They had a number of purposes. One was to fetch and carry for the warriors. They would also use their slings to not only annoy the enemy but to actually hurt them. They were higher up the river collecting more stones when there was a shout from the west. "Jarl, it is '**Red Dragon**'."

I saw the drekar anchoring just off the river mouth. None knew of this surprise. Raibeart ap Pasgen took a horse and galloped from the camp. "What is this, Jarl Dragonheart? Does it mean my home is threatened?"

I shook my head. "I planned this with Erik Short Toe. He has twenty ship's boys aboard. They have bows. When we retreat towards the sea the Mercian king will think that I mean to flee, by sea."

"But you would never do such a thing."

"He does not know that! In addition, the arrows they will send can protect us."

"How do you think of such things? Where do the ideas come from?"

I touched my chest, "Perhaps I do have a dragon's heart for we know that the dragon is the most cunning of creatures." I led him back to the camp. "Our plans are all made. Now we wait for

Leif Ulfsson, Ketil, and Ulf Olafsson. I fear that without them then all my plans will be in vain. We need five warbands and not two."

It was late in the afternoon when the three warbands arrived. They were weary. Galmr had led them the long way, the safe way. It had added more than fifteen miles to the journey. I let Ragnar son of Wolf Killer give them their instructions. He would be leading them. When Aðils Shape Shifter arrived a short time later it was with the news that the Saxon army was hard on their heels. They had been seen. I had Sámr sound the horn. That was the signal for my warband to form up and the rest to hide. Would King Beorhtwulf take the bait?

Baldr had asked me if he could hold my banner sitting on a horse. He said that it would make him feel more confident. I was going to say no and then I realised that this was meant to be. He was a horseman. That was how his people fought. He would be higher and, if things went against us then he and my banner could escape. He held my banner high. He was with Sámr in the third rank. He was safer there and yet my banner could be clearly seen. *Wyrd*. We were in the front rank and we were close to the river. Fifty paces east of us was the hex which Ylva had placed there. When the enemy came then Baldr would take his place at the rear of the warriors with the spears. Behind him would be the men with bows and on our flanks were thirty boys with slings. I hoped King Beorhtwulf and his mercenaries would not smell a trap.

The Saxons were slower to reach us than we had thought. They arrived when the sun could still be seen in the sky to the west but the light did not last long. When they saw our camp, their king had his two bands of mercenaries form a shield wall on their side of the river. They were out of range of our bows. No one would risk crossing a river at night. The leader of the Danish warband stepped into the shallows. He shouted, "Jarl Dragonheart, know that Einar Man Splitter comes to take your magic sword and your head! Flee now, old man!"

Such an insult could not be ignored. Flanked by Olaf and Haaken I walked to the water's edge. "And know this, Einar Man Splitter, that I have slain more Danes than you have lived years upon this earth. When you come, Einar Taker of Saxon Pay, then we will slaughter you. I pointed upstream, "And know that I have a witch and she has already woven your deaths."

He looked upstream and saw, for the first time, the woven wool between the two spears. The light from the setting sun seemed to make it appear blood red and the black knots stood out clearly. He should have replied to the insult but, instead, he and the rest of the two warbands ran back to the main camp. The light was fading but I could see the Dane in conference with mailed warriors. One of them had to be King Beorhtwulf. A short while later and when the sun was illuminating the evening sky blood red, four priests came to the river and they began to chant. Ylva had been watching. I had no doubt that the Danes would also be watching. They would not believe that the priests could do anything about the spell but they would be interested.

Ylva faced the priests. She spoke in our language for her message was for the Danes. She spoke, as all witches do, in riddles. A witch is like a dragon. She never tells more than she has to. Her words were like the chant of warriors on a drekar. They were hypnotic.

> *"I am she who is born of a slave and lives like a princess.*
> *I am born of the blood of a wolf.*
> *I am she who died and yet lived.*
> *I am she who defied the Norns.*
> *I curse you Einar Man Splitter!*
> *Your warriors are dead men walking!"*

She went to the wool and tied another knot. As the sun dropped below the sky she turned her back. I smiled. She was wearing a black cloak and it was as though she had disappeared. I heard a hubbub of noise from the Mercian camp. We had caused a stir. Even the followers of the White Christ would be worried now.

Haaken laughed, "Dragonheart, your granddaughter is the equal of Kara. The Danes will get no sleep this night."

"And we will ensure that the whole army gets little."

Olaf asked, "We slit a few throats?"

"It is not worth the risk of crossing the river. No. When all is quiet and their camp is dark the wolves will come." I turned and shouted to my men, "First blood to us. Back to our camp!" They cheered.

We reached our camp. "We set sentries. Sámr, go and tell your father that this night the wolves will howl. They should not be afeared." I told my Ulfheonar my plan and we slept. Nothing that had happened had changed save that they had not arrived and rushed over to attack us. They still had the river to ford and now the mercenaries had fear in their hearts. We had lost the ally that was the dark from the east. Ragnar and his men would not be attacking from the shadows. We were going to aggravate that fear by making them lose sleep.

I was shaken awake by Rollo. "Ready, Jarl. Aðils Shape Shifter and Rolf Horse Killer have set off already." He loped off east. I knew that Haaken and Olaf would be to my left. I walked to the river. I could see the glow of the enemy fires. They were well back from the river in case we attacked at night. I waited. Aðils Shape Shifter would begin the howling. As my eyes became accustomed to the dark I saw their sentries. They were black shapes which passed before the fires. They would be Saxon. The Danes would be as far from the hex as they could get.

Suddenly the night's silence was torn apart by the howl from what seemed like Clougha Pike. Even as it died Rolf's howl began and when that faded Rollo's. Olaf's followed. I heard Haaken, just a hundred paces from me. I howled. It must have seemed like a wave of wolves came down the river.

I heard a Saxon voice shout, "Stand to!"

A Danish voice shouted, "It is the Ulfheonar! They are in our camp!"

I heard a clash of steel and a scream. There were more shouts and cries. It had worked better than I had hoped. We had often sent Ulfheonar into the camps of our enemies and we had slit throats. Our howls and the dark had done enough. Someone had been killed by a Dane fearful of the knife in the night. The noise and confusion lasted some time. I saw lighted brands as the camp was searched. All became quiet and so I howled again. This time the howling went upstream. No one shouted this time but I knew that the Saxons and their allies were not sleeping. They were mailed and waiting for an attack which never came. I turned and headed back to our camp.

Haaken caught up with me, "This will be a tale to tell at Samhain! How the howls of a handful of men made Danes slay each other."

I rolled up in my wolf cloak and slept well. I doubted that the enemy would.

Baldr shook me awake before dawn. I heard his horse neigh. He held its reins. "I was told to wake you, Jarl. I have an ale skin and the last of the bread."

"First I will make water and you can help me don my mail." I was glad to see that he had his leather armour on already. I did not want the Allfather's gift to die in his first battle in the Land of the Wolf.

By the time dawn broke we were already in position and the Saxons had formed up. As I had hoped Ylva's curse and the hex had made the Hibernians and the Danes form up closer to the sea. The river was wider here. There were more sandbanks but the water was deeper in places. My drekar had also taken advantage of the night and Erik had brought her closer. She was the smallest of my fleet with the shallowest draught. She was now as close as she dared to be in the mouth of the river. They might not have seen her the night before but they saw her now.

Behind the Danish wedge and the Hibernian warband the priests of the Saxon King were intoning their prayers and chanting. They held banners which had the White Christ embroidered upon them. I smiled for the Danish banner, a crudely sewn man split into two, had skulls hanging from it. King Beorhtwulf was being cautious. No doubt the Danes had told him of my tricks and they waited until the sun had been in the sky for an hour before his horns sounded and his army advanced. While the Danes and the Hibernians came further downstream, the fyrd marched to cross the river by the hex. I could not see the thegns but I did see the housecarls. Their wall of spears gathered around the banner of Mercia. It was a yellow diagonal cross on a blue background. It looked to be a finely made banner. What they would see would be a shield wall. It would look like the normal Viking formation. The archers were hidden behind three rows of shields. We would look like a small and vulnerable warband. Just over thirty men made up each rank. When the first of the fyrd hundred and the mercenaries hit us then they would outnumber us two to one. I glanced to my left. There stood Ylva. Sitting on the side of the hill she was weaving using a spindle. The Danes would see it and would keep clear of her. She looked so vulnerable. She was just six hundred paces from us but it seemed further. I feared for her.

The Danes and Hibernians stepped into the river. They would not be able to keep their formation while crossing it. The river was relatively low for it was not the wet season and the tide was out but they were still in danger from the deeper parts. I saw one mailed Dane disappear beneath the waters. Men struggled to keep their balance. The fyrd was having an easier time of it. They had reached the middle without losses. The Danes were less than a hundred and fifty paces from us while the Saxons were at the extreme range of my archers. They were two hundred and fifty paces away. It was time. I raised my spear.

Sámr's voice came from behind me, "Release!"

A hundred arrows flew over our heads. They were spread out along the river. They could not see the enemy but we had marked out the range and they knew their business. The arrows rained down. The Hibernians bore the brunt of the deaths and wounds. They did not wear mail. The fyrd suffered too but three Danes were hit in that first strike. Shields came up as the second and third arrow storm struck. As the fyrd came closer so they took more hits. I saw King Beorhtwulf point his spear and shout something. The next two hundreds raced forward to follow the first. The Danes were the only ones who were approaching in any kind of order. The first warriors were struggling through the mud but would soon be upon us.

I donned my helmet and shouted, "Shields and spears!"

The Danes and Hibernians had now come into the range of my slingers and stones began to rattle like hail on helmets and shields. Men fell. Hibernians died. I had endured such storms. They were deadly at worst and disconcerting at best. The Danes with open face helmets were at the greatest risk.

As one our shields were swung around. The middle six warriors in our front rank were all Ulfheonar. Next to us were Sven Stormbringer and Snorri Gunnarson. All of us were mailed and we were ready. The Danish wedge had disintegrated. Eight of their number did not make the northern bank of the Ēa Lōn. They wore sealskin boots and the caltrops did not affect them but the Hibernians, who had lost twenty of their number, did suffer. As they were disrupted then the arrows found more flesh. Instead of being hit by more than two hundred and twenty men we were hit first, by forty Danes and then thirty Hibernians.

Sámr's voice came from behind me. Baldr on his horse had a good view of the battle. He was advising his friend. "Archers, switch targets."

With my slingers and archers concentrating their missiles on the hundred, the fyrd broke and fled. They took the shortest route back. They ran across the river. They broke up the next one hundred crossing the river. The Danes formed up. The Hibernians did no such thing. Enraged by their losses they hurled themselves at us. They struck Sven Stormbringer and his men. Sven's men's spears darted out and impaled the wild men who literally threw themselves at our shields. I have fought these men before. When fighting other Hibernians such tactics worked. Against stout Vikings they were doomed to failure. They did not have the numbers they had planned and our wall of spears defeated them. With the next two bands of the fyrd making their way across the river we could concentrate on the most dangerous of our enemies, the Danes.

I saw Einar Man Splitter. He was coming for me. I could not resist taunting him. "The witch watches and spins still. There is a knot for you Dane and Ragnar's Spirit wishes to drink Danish blood."

Doubt would be in his mind. I could not see his face for it was covered, as was mine by a facemask. He shouted, "Kill them!"

They raced at us. One of his younger warriors was more eager and faster than his jarl or perhaps Einar Man Splitter wished to increase his chances of survival. The young warrior had an open face helmet and as his spear struck my shield I rammed my own spear into his mouth. The spear head came out of the back of his head and his falling body pulled the spear from my hand. I drew Ragnar's spirit as Einar Man Splitter swung his Danish axe at my shield. I angled my shield and the axe struck the boss. It was a good blow for I felt it even behind the metal, wood and sheepskin. I think it was a blow which normally brought victory. He pulled back his arm for a second strike. That was the problem with an axe unless you did as Olaf and Rolf were doing and swinging them in a figure of eight before you, then you had but one strike. I rammed my sword over his shield towards his helmeted face. It would be a lucky strike if I killed him but the blow was hard enough to drive his head back and I punched with my shield at the same time. His hand was coming down with the axe. My boss caught his hand and hit it so hard that he dropped the axe. I saw a gap between shield and body and I lunged downwards. Ragnar's Spirit had a tip and the point went through the mail and his byrnie. It entered his body just above his waist. As blood spurted I twisted and pulled. Entrails and guts came with it as Einar Man Splitter fell. It was a mortal wound.

My Ulfheonar had killed their bravest and best. When Einar fell the remaining Danes fled. They raced, with the handful of Hibernians who had survived the attack towards the river. As they did so then Erik Short Toe, who had brought the drekar as close as he dared, had his archers send their arrows towards them. My men began banging their shields for the fyrd had stopped advancing and were making a shield wall.

Baldr shouted, "Jarl Dragonheart, the rest of their army comes and they have horsemen! They race towards Ylva!"

It was too soon to launch the attack by Ragnar for we needed the whole of their army across the river first. Ylva would be taken. I heard hooves and looked. Baldr had dropped the standard and was racing towards Ylva. I saw, in the distance, the standards of the mounted thegns. They were racing from the east. A group split off to head for Ylva. They would not fight from the back of horses. They would dismount but they would be able to kill the witch and then flank us. Their king had outwitted me. Already the housecarls were moving forward. We would have to endure another attack.

The Saxons who had crossed the river held their shields up as my archers and slingers kept up their attack. The Saxons now thought they knew my plan and were going to use overwhelming numbers to defeat me. I watched as Baldr galloped towards Ylva. It would be close. I saw then that, unlike the thegns, being a rider was in his blood. I saw a thegn dig his heels into his horse as he sought to reach Ylva. She took out her seax. She would not run. You could not out run a horse. Then Baldr did something quite remarkable. He swung away from Ylva and galloped towards the leading thegn. The other thegns were not as skilled as the leading thegn and were thirty paces behind him. None were as skilled as Baldr. The Saxon had eyes only for Ylva and he did not see Baldr's blade as it hacked into his side. As the thegn fell from his horse Baldr sheathed his sword and reached down to grab the reins of the Saxon horse. The other thegns were close behind. He stopped by Ylva and turned his horse in case he needed to defend her. He did not. Ylva grabbed the reins and pulled herself into the saddle. The thegns forgot their orders. Ten followed Baldr and Ylva as they led the horsemen towards the priory. Then I saw the hand of the Allfather. The ten thegns would be destroyed by Ragnar and his men. My plan had failed but the Allfather's would succeed.

"Double shields and walk backwards! We need to draw them away from the river so that Ragnar and our comrades can fall upon them!" It meant we formed a double line of shields with archers in a single rank behind us. It was not an easy manoeuvre. Haaken began a chant to help us march backwards.

> ***Ulfheonar, warriors strong***
> ***Ulfheonar, warriors brave***
> ***Ulfheonar, fierce as the wolf***
> ***Ulfheonar, hides in plain sight***
> ***Ulfheonar, Dragon Heart's wolves***
> ***Ulfheonar, serving the sword***
> ***Ulfheonar, Dragon Heart's wolves***
> ***Ulfheonar, serving the sword***
> ***Ulfheonar, warriors strong***
> ***Ulfheonar, warriors brave***
> ***Ulfheonar, fierce as the wolf***
> ***Ulfheonar, hides in plain sight***
> ***Ulfheonar, Dragon Heart's wolves***
> ***Ulfheonar, serving the sword***
> ***Ulfheonar, Dragon Heart's wolves***
> ***Ulfheonar, serving the sword***

I felt a shield in my back and turned. Sámr and Germund were behind me. Sámr held the discarded standard. "I will have to chastise Baldr! He should know never to discard the banner."

I laughed, "Perhaps we will forgive him this once."

The Saxons had seen our retreat and saw victory. They charged. The housecarls flooded across the river leaving just the King, his priests and his hearth weru on the south side of the river. He was a cautious king.

"Brace."

Most of my front rank had lost their spears and we had swords and axes. The ones who had been in the second and third rank, like Sámr and Germund still held theirs and two spears were thrust over my shoulders. As the thegns charged towards us I saw the first of my men emerge from the ruins. Ragnar and Gruffyd led them. They did not cheer. They wanted to achieve surprise. I watched Ketil lead his men towards the river. He was followed by Asbjorn. I heard a Saxon horn. It was recalling the housecarls. It was too little and too late. As the fyrd hit us I swung my sword in an arc. Haaken did the same. With two Danish axes sweeping to my left we had a wall of steel which unarmoured men could not face. My sword tore through the face of one Saxon and down into the shoulder of the next. As they fell Sámr's spear thrust to impale the next Saxon.

The thegns dismounted and shouted, "For God, Mercia and King Beorhtwulf!" They were trying to rally their men. They hurled themselves at the men on the left of our line. Ragnar and Gruffyd were leading three warbands to fall upon them and the rear of the fyrd.

It was time for us to be the anvil against the hammer that was Ragnar and his men. "Now! Push them towards our men! We have them!"

As our archers sent arrows into the men at the back of the Saxon horde we began to carve our way through them. There was a rhythm to this killing. I slashed down and then swept up and across. I punched with my shield. When I saw a body beneath my feet I stamped. I swung my sword as though it was not part of my body. It belonged to the shield wall. Sometimes I struck two men. They had small shields and no mail. Few had helmets and their swords and spears were made with poor metal.

When one Saxon had his spear broken by my shield his companion hit it with his sword. His blade bent and the boss of my shield spread his nose across his face. Germund finished him off.

There was a roar of 'Land of the Wolf'! Followed by a crack like thunder and a wail of pain. Ragnar and his warbands had hit the rear of their line. These were not housecarls. They were not oathsworn Danes. They were farmers, swine herders and shepherds. They were ordinary men who trained once a week with their thegn. Their thegns lay dead and they broke. They hurled shields to the ground for they were a weight and they ran. For many the only way to escape was towards the sand and the sea. Erik Short Toe and his men blocked the river and so many of them tried the deadly sands. Few made it but the shellfish who lived there prospered, in the years after, from the bounty of the battle.

The ones who could not escape either threw down their weapons and begged for mercy or a few, fought with brothers and fathers. They were butchered. Half of the fyrd who remained, some three hundred or so made it back to the river. There they joined the housecarls, the mercenaries and their king. As the last thegn was slain my men began banging their shields.

"Dragonheart!"

I had fought in the first battle since Miklagård and I felt no pain. I had returned. The Dragonheart would live a little while longer and his enemies would learn to fear him.

Epilogue

I did not take my entire army across the river. I took my warband with Ylva, Ragnar and Gruffyd. I also took the Saxon scout I had captured. I took off my helmet and sheathed my sword as I approached their shield wall. Baldr carried my standard. Sámr guarded the prisoner and walked ahead of me. Ylva, Ragnar and Gruffyd walked beside me. I saw the Danes clutching their amulets as Ylva approached. The twenty who had survived were petrified. I saw the Saxon priests holding up their crosses. As I looked at the enemy I saw that barely five thegns had survived.

I spoke in Saxon, "I would speak with King Beorhtwulf. I am Jarl Dragonheart and I would speak with the Saxon who dared to cross into my land and bring war to us."

To be fair to the King, he did not hide behind his men. He, his priests and his champion came forward. I wondered if he would challenge me. It had been known. The King took off his helmet, "What do you want barbarian?"

"First to return your prisoner. I promised him his life. Go." The Saxon could not believe his good fortune. He rushed to the safety of the housecarls' shields. "And now you will hand over these priests as hostages. When you have sent a thousand pieces of gold and two hundred head of cattle to me then they will be returned unharmed. You will also promise to never march north to my land again. I will have you swear it on one of your holy books! Your priests will be safe in my land. If you ask the man I just returned to you he will tell you that he was well treated."

"And if I refuse, what then?"

"If you could not defeat me with more than a thousand men what makes you think you can do so with less than five hundred? Will these Danes fight against my witch? Will your fyrd face my swords? It does not matter to me which choice you make. Either way I have won and you have lost."

I saw from his face that he would accede to my demands. He nodded and then spat out, "You cannot live forever, Viking! The Saxon's Bane will die one day!"

"But not this day!"

The priests were herded together and, holding their crosses and mumbling their prayers they were led away by Olaf Leather Neck and Rolf Horse Killer. The Saxons first collected and then burned their dead. My men collected the weapons, mail and treasure. Baldr gathered the horses. We found more than thirty. We had had more than just a victory. The horses were better than the ones we had. They were bigger. The Danes had carried their treasure with them as had the Hibernians. It was a great haul. Forty thegns had died and their mail was the equal of any. Men who had marched to war without mail were now armoured like a lord. Our dead were buried in a barrow by the priory. Ylva spoke to the spirits and planted bulbs along it so that we would know where our warriors lay. When that was done we watched the Saxons depart. They made a sorry sight. Their wagons were used to carry their wounded. They were all laden. As bodies were washed ashore the true magnitude of the Mercian defeat became apparent. King Beorhtwulf had learned a lesson. He never tried to attack us again.

We left the next day and my men were in high spirits. All had treasure and all had glory. Ylva made a charm for Baldr but promised him a golden horse when she reached our home. She also gave him his name, Baldr Saviour of Witches. I am not certain that he understood the significance of the name but it made him a member of the clan in body and, now, in spirit. **'Red Dragon'** took most of the goods we had gathered and the most severely wounded back to Úlfarrston. The rest of us began the long walk to Úlfarrston.

As we neared my land and saw Old Olaf Haaken One Eye said, "Jarl Dragonheart, when you were at the door of Valhalla why did you not enter?"

I had thought about this since we had left Miklagård. It was not the fact that my name had been called. I do not think that the Allfather wanted me yet. King Beorhtwulf had been a threat but I wondered if there was something more dangerous waiting. Was there another enemy? Time would tell but I knew that we were better prepared now. We had the luxury of horses and I turned in my saddle. I saw Baldr and Sámr flanking Ylva and behind them rode Gruffyd and Ragnar with Ulla War Cry and Mordaf ap Gruffyd. I had a purpose. More importantly, I had a legacy and my family would make certain that my land remained, the Land of the Wolf.

I turned to my oldest friend, "Simple, my work was not done. The Allfather knew that the Mercians were coming and had I not returned then what would have become of my clan and my family? I will know when it is time to leave this world. It is not yet!

The End

Norse Calendar

Gormánuður October 14th - November 13th
Ýlir November 14th - December 13th
Mörsugur December 14th - January 12th
Þorri - January 13th - February 11th
Gói - February 12th - March 13th
Einmánuður - March 14th - April 13th
Harpa April 14th - May 13th
Skerpla - May 14th - June 12th
Sólmánuður - June 13th - July 12th
Heyannir - July 13th - August 14th
Tvímánuður - August 15th - September 14th
Haustmánuður September 15th-October 13th

Glossary

Afen- River Avon
Afon Hafron- River Severn in Welsh
Àird Rosain – Ardrossan (On the Clyde Estuary)
Al-buhera -Albufeira, Portugal
Aledhorn- Althorn (Essex)
An Lysardh - Lizard Peninsula Cornwall
Balears- Balearic Islands
Balley Chashtal -Castleton (Isle of Man)
Bardas - Rebel Byzantine General
Beamfleote -Benfleet Essex
Bebbanburgh- Bamburgh Castle, Northumbria also known as Din Guardi in the ancient tongue
Beck- a stream
Beinn na bhFadhla- Benbecula in the Outer Hebrides
Belesduna – Basildon Essex
Belisima -River Ribble
Blót – a blood sacrifice made by a jarl
Blue Sea- The Mediterranean
Bogeuurde – Forest of Bowland
Bondi- Viking farmers who fight
Bourde- Bordeaux
Bjarnarøy –Great Bernera (Bear Island)
Breguntford – Brentford
Brixges Stane – Brixton (South London)
Bruggas- Bruges
Brycgstow- Bristol
Burntwood- Brentwood Essex
Byrnie- a mail or leather shirt reaching down to the knees
Caerlleon- Welsh for Chester
Caer Ufra -South Shields
Caestir - Chester (old English)
Cantwareburh -Canterbury
Càrdainn Ros -Cardross (Argyll)
Cas-gwent -Chepstow Monmouthshire

Casnewydd –Newport, Wales
Cephas- Greek for Simon Peter (St. Peter)
Chatacium -Catanzaro, Calabria
Chape- the tip of a scabbard
Charlemagne- Holy Roman Emperor at the end of the 8th and beginning of the 9th centuries
Celchyth - Chelsea
Cerro da Vila – Vilamoura, Portugal
Cherestanc- Garstang (Lancashire)
Cil-y-coed -Caldicot Monmouthshire
Colneceastre- Colchester
Corn Walum or Om Walum- Cornwall
Cymri- Welsh
Cymru- Wales
Cyninges-tūn – Coniston. It means the estate of the king (Cumbria)
Dùn Èideann –Edinburgh (Gaelic)
Din Guardi- Bamburgh castle
Drekar- a Dragon ship (a Viking warship) pl. drekar
Duboglassio –Douglas, Isle of Man
Dun Holme- Durham
Dún Lethglaise - Downpatrick (Northern Ireland)
Durdle- Durdle dor- the Jurassic coast in Dorset
Dwfr- Dover
Dyrøy –Jura (Inner Hebrides)
Dyflin- Old Norse for Dublin
Ēa Lōn - River Lune
Earhyth -Bexley (Kent)
Ein-mánuðr - middle of March to the middle of April
Eoforwic- Saxon for York
Falgrave- Scarborough (North Yorkshire)
Faro Bregancio- Corunna (Spain)
Ferneberga -Farnborough (Hampshire)
Fey- having second sight
Firkin- a barrel containing eight gallons (usually beer)
Fornibiyum-Formby (near Liverpool)
Fret-a sea mist
Frankia- France and part of Germany
Fyrd-the Saxon levy

Ganda- Ghent (Belgium)
Garth- Dragon Heart
Gaill- Irish for foreigners
Galdramenn- wizard
Gesith- A Saxon nobleman. After 850 AD, they were known as thegns
Glaesum –amber
Glannoventa -Ravenglass
Gleawecastre- Gloucester
Gói- the end of February to the middle of March
Gormánuður- October to November (Slaughter month- the beginning of winter)
Grendel- the monster slain by Beowulf
Grenewic- Greenwich
Gulle - Goole (Humberside)
Hagustaldes ham -Hexham
Hamwic -Southampton
Hæstingaceaster- Hastings
Haustmánuður - September 16th- October 16th (cutting of the corn)
Haughs- small hills in Norse (As in Tarn Hows)
Hearth weru- The bodyguard or oathsworn of a jarl
Heels- when a ship leans to one side under the pressure of the wind
Hel - Queen of Niflheim, the Norse underworld.
Here Wic- Harwich
Hersey- Isle of Arran
Hersir- a Viking landowner and minor noble. It ranks below a jarl
Hetaereiarch – Byzantine general
Hí- Iona (Gaelic)
Hjáp - Shap- Cumbria (Norse for stone circle)
Hoggs or Hogging- when the pressure of the wind causes the stern or the bow to droop
Hrams-a – Ramsey, Isle of Man
Hrofecester -Rochester (Kent)
Hundred- Saxon military organisation. (One hundred men from an area-led by a thegn or gesith)
Hwitebi - Norse for Whitby, North Yorkshire

Viking Shadow

Hywel ap Rhodri Molwynog- King of Gwynedd 814-825
Icaunis- British river god
Issicauna- Gaulish for the lower Seine
Itouna- River Eden Cumbria
Jarl- Norse earl or lord
Joro-goddess of the earth
kjerringa - Old Woman- the solid block in which the mast rested
Karrek Loos yn Koos -St Michael's Mount (Cornwall)
Kerkyra- Corfu
Knarr- a merchant ship or a coastal vessel
Kriti- Crete
Kyrtle-woven top
Lambehitha- Lambeth
Leathes Water- Thirlmere
Legacaestir- Anglo-Saxon for Chester
Ljoðhús- Lewis
Lochlannach – Irish for Northerners (Vikings)
Lothuwistoft- Lowestoft
Lough- Irish lake
Louis the Pious- King of the Franks and son of Charlemagne
Lundenburh- the walled burh built around the old Roman fort
Lundenwic - London
Maeldun- Maldon Essex
Maeresea- River Mersey
Mammceaster- Manchester
Manau/Mann – The Isle of Man(n) (Saxon)
Marcia Hispanic- Spanish Marches (the land around Barcelona)
Mast fish- two large racks on a ship designed to store the mast when not required
Melita- Malta
Midden- a place where they dumped human waste
Miklagård - Constantinople
Mörsugur - December 13th -January 12th (the fat sucker month!)
Musselmen- the followers of Islam

Njoror- God of the sea
Nithing- A man without honour (Saxon)
Odin - The "All Father" God of war, also associated with wisdom, poetry, and magic (The Ruler of the gods).
Olissipo- Lisbon
Orkneyjar-Orkney
Pecheham- Peckham
Pennryhd – Penrith Cumbria
Pennsans – Penzance (Cornwall)
Poor john- a dried and shrivelled fish (disparaging slang for a male member- Shakespeare)
Þorri -January 13th -February 12th- midwinter
Portesmūða -Portsmouth
Pillars of Hercules- Straits of Gibraltar
Prittleuuella- Prittwell in Essex. Southend was originally known as the South End of Prittwell
Pyrlweall -Thirwell, Cumbria
Qādis- Cadiz
Ran- Goddess of the sea
Roof rock- slate
Rinaz –The Rhine
Sabrina- Latin and Celtic for the River Severn. Also, the name of a female Celtic deity
Saami- the people who live in what is now Northern Norway/Sweden
Sabatton- Saturday in the Byzantine calendar
Samhain- a Celtic festival of the dead between 31st October and 1st November (Halloween)
St. Cybi- Holyhead
Scree- loose rocks in a glacial valley
Seax – short sword
Sennight- seven nights- a week
Sheerstrake- the uppermost strake in the hull
Sheet- a rope fastened to the lower corner of a sail
Shroud- a rope from the masthead to the hull amidships
Skeggox – an axe with a shorter beard on one side of the blade
Skreið- stockfish (any fish which is preserved)

Skutatos- Byzantine soldier armed with an oval shield, a spear, a sword and a short mail shirt
Seouenaca -Sevenoaks (Kent)
South Folk- Suffolk
Stad- Norse settlement
Stays- ropes running from the mast-head to the bow
Strake- the wood on the side of a drekar
Streanæshalc- Saxon for Whitby, North Yorkshire
Stybbanhype – Stepney (London)
Suthriganaworc - Southwark (London)
Syllingar Insula, Syllingar- Scilly Isles
Tarn- small lake (Norse)
Tella- River Béthune which empties near to Dieppe
Temese- River Thames
Theme- Provincial Army Corps
The Norns- The three sisters who weave webs of intrigue for men
Thing-Norse for a parliament or a debate (Tynwald)
Thor's day- Thursday
Threttanessa- a drekar with 13 oars on each side.
Thuni- Tunis
Tinea- Tyne
Tilaburg – Tilbury
Tintaieol- Tintagel (Cornwall)
Thrall- slave
Trenail- a round wooden peg used to secure strakes
Tynwald- the Parliament on the Isle of Man
Tvímánuður -Hay time-August 15th -September 15th
Úlfarrberg- Helvellyn
Úlfarrland- Cumbria
Úlfarr- Wolf Warrior
Úlfarrston- Ulverston
Ullr-Norse God of Hunting
Ulfheonar-an elite Norse warrior who wore a wolf skin over his armour
Vectis- The Isle of Wight
Veisafjǫrðr – Wexford (Ireland)
Volva- a witch or healing woman in Norse culture
Waeclinga Straet- Watling Street (A5)

Windlesore-Windsor
Waite- a Viking word for farm
Werham -Wareham (Dorset)
Western Sea- the Atlantic
Wintan-ceastre -Winchester
Withy- the mechanism connecting the steering board to the ship
Wihtwara- Isle of White
Woden's day- Wednesday
Wulfhere-Old English for Wolf Army
Wyddfa-Snowdon
Wykinglo- Wicklow (Ireland)
Wyrd- Fate
Wyrme- Norse for Dragon
Yard- a timber from which the sail is suspended
Ynys Enlli- Bardsey Island
Ynys Môn-Anglesey

Maps and drawings

Stad on the Eden - a typical Viking settlement

A wedge formation (each circle represents a warrior)

     0
    0 0
   0 0 0
  0 0 0 0
 0 0 0 0 0
0 0 0 0 0 0

A knarr (reproduced from the Hrolf series- same design)

Historical note

When writing about the raids I have tried to recreate those early days of the Viking raider. The Saxons had driven the native inhabitants to the extremes of Wales, Cornwall, and Scotland. The Irish were always too busy fighting amongst themselves. It must have come as a real shock to be attacked in their own settlements. By the time of King Alfred almost sixty years later they were better prepared. This was also about the time that Saxon England converted completely to Christianity. The last place to do so was the Isle of Wight. There is no reason to believe that the Vikings would have had any sympathy for their religion and would, in fact, have taken advantage of their ceremonies and rituals not to mention their riches.

Slavery was far more common in the ancient world. When the Normans finally made England their own they showed that they understood the power of words and propaganda by making the slaves into serfs. This was a brilliant strategy as it forced their former slaves to provide their own food whilst still working for their lords and masters for nothing. Manumission was possible as Garth showed in the first book in this series. Scanlan's training is also a sign that not all of the slaves suffered. It was a hard and cruel time- it was ruled by the strong. The word 'testify' comes from Anglo-Saxon. A man would clutch his testicles and swear that the evidence he was giving was the truth. If it was not, then he would lose his testicles. There was more truth in the Anglo-Saxon courts than there in modern ones! The Vikings did use trickery when besieging their enemies and would use any means possible. They did not have siege weapons and had to rely on guile and courage to prevail. The siege of Paris in 845 A.D. was one such example.

The blue stone they treasure is aquamarine or beryl. It is found in granite. The rocks around the Mawddach are largely granite and although I have no evidence of beryl being found there, I have used the idea of a small deposit being found to tie the story together.

There was a famous witch who lived on one of the islands of Scilly. According to Norse legend Olaf Tryggvasson, who became King Olaf 1 of Norway, visited her. She told him that if he converted to Christianity then he would become king of Norway.

The early ninth century saw Britain convert to Christianity and there were many monasteries which flourished. These were often mixed. These were not the huge stone edifices such as Whitby and Fountain's Abbey; these were wooden structures. As such their remains have disappeared, along with the bones of those early Christian priests. Hexham was a major monastery in the early Saxon period. I do not know it they had warriors to protect the priests but having given them a treasure to watch over I thought that some warriors might be useful too.

The Vikings had two seasons: summer and winter. As with many things a Viking lived simply and his world was black or white! There was no room for grey or any shades save the dead!

The coast lines were different in the eighth and ninth centuries. The land to the east of Lincoln was swamp. Indeed, there had been a port just a few miles from Lincoln in the Roman age. Now Lincoln is many miles from the sea but this was not so in the past. Similarly, many rivers have been straightened. We can thank the Victorians for that. The Tees had so many loops in it that it took as long to get from Yarm to the sea as it did to get down to London! Similarly, many place names and places have changed. Some had Saxon names which became Norse. Some had Old English names. Some even retained their Latin names. It was quite common for one place to be known by two names.

Windar's Mere is actually Ambleside. The Romans chose its location and Dragonheart is too clever a warrior to ignore its defensive potential.

The Vikings did not have a religion in the way that we do. There was no organisation. They had no priests or mullahs. They had beliefs. The gods and the spirits were there. You did not worship them. You asked them for help, perhaps, but you could equally curse them too.

The story of Gruffydd ap Cyngen and his murder is true. The story of the knife and King Coenwulf is pure fiction.

The Rus
The Rus were the Vikings who lived in Sweden and what is now the Baltic states. They sailed down the Volga and other

rivers to trade and raid in the Black Sea. They also ventured into the Mediterranean. '*The prosperous islands (the Balearics) were thoroughly sacked by the Swedish Viking King Björn Ironside and his brother Hastein during their Mediterranean raid of 859–862.*'

Witches and Weaving

Witches in the Viking world were different from our modern perception. There was no black and white. If an enemy faced you then she was evil. If she was on your side then she was good. It was all to do with belief. If a warrior believed that a witch had used a spell, a hex, then he was already defeated. Witches used weaving to weave their spells. This was not Macbeth's three witches. In theory, invisible fetters and bonds could be controlled from a loom, and if a lady loosened a knot in the woof, she could liberate the leg of her hero. But if she tied a knot, she could stop the enemy from moving. The men may have fought on the battlefield in sweat and blood, but in a spiritual way, their women took part. It is not by coincidence that archaeologists find weaving tools and weapons side by side.I used the following books for research:

> Vikings- Life and Legends -British Museum
> Saxon, Norman and Viking by Terence Wise (Osprey)
> The Vikings (Osprey) -Ian Heath
> Byzantine Armies 668-1118 (Osprey)-Ian Heath
> Romano-Byzantine Armies 4th-9th Century (Osprey) -David Nicholle
> The Walls of Constantinople AD 324-1453 (Osprey) - Stephen Turnbull
> Viking Longship (Osprey) - Keith Durham
> The Vikings in England Anglo-Danish Project
> Anglo Saxon Thegn AD 449-1066- Mark Harrison (Osprey)
> Viking Hersir- 793-1066 AD - Mark Harrison (Osprey)
> Hadrian's Wall- David Breeze (English Heritage)
> National Geographic- March 2017
> British Kings and Queens = Mike Ashley

Griff Hosker March 2018

Other books by Griff Hosker

If you enjoyed reading this book, then why not read another one by the author?

Ancient History

The Sword of Cartimandua Series
(Germania and Britannia 50 A.D. – 128 A.D.)
Ulpius Felix- Roman Warrior (prequel)
The Sword of Cartimandua
The Horse Warriors
Invasion Caledonia
Roman Retreat
Revolt of the Red Witch
Druid's Gold
Trajan's Hunters
The Last Frontier
Hero of Rome
Roman Hawk
Roman Treachery
Roman Wall
Roman Courage

The Wolf Warrior series
(Britain in the late 6th Century)
Saxon Dawn
Saxon Revenge
Saxon England
Saxon Blood
Saxon Slayer
Saxon Slaughter
Saxon Bane
Saxon Fall: Rise of the Warlord
Saxon Throne
Saxon Sword

Medieval History

The Dragon Heart Series
Viking Slave
Viking Warrior
Viking Jarl
Viking Kingdom
Viking Wolf
Viking War
Viking Sword
Viking Wrath
Viking Raid
Viking Legend
Viking Vengeance
Viking Dragon
Viking Treasure
Viking Enemy
Viking Witch
Viking Blood
Viking Weregeld
Viking Storm
Viking Warband
Viking Shadow
Viking Legacy
Viking Clan
Viking Bravery

The Norman Genesis Series
Hrolf the Viking
Horseman
The Battle for a Home
Revenge of the Franks
The Land of the Northmen
Ragnvald Hrolfsson
Brothers in Blood
Lord of Rouen
Drekar in the Seine
Duke of Normandy
The Duke and the King

Danelaw
(England and Denmark in the 11th Century)
Dragon Sword
Oathsword
Bloodsword
Danish Sword

New World Series
Blood on the Blade
Across the Seas
The Savage Wilderness
The Bear and the Wolf
Erik The Navigator
Erik's Clan

The Vengeance Trail

The Reconquista Chronicles
Castilian Knight
El Campeador
The Lord of Valencia

The Aelfraed Series
(Britain and Byzantium 1050 A.D. - 1085 A.D.)
Housecarl
Outlaw
Varangian

The Anarchy Series England 1120-1180
English Knight
Knight of the Empress
Northern Knight
Baron of the North
Earl
King Henry's Champion
The King is Dead
Warlord of the North

Enemy at the Gate
The Fallen Crown
Warlord's War
Kingmaker
Henry II
Crusader
The Welsh Marches
Irish War
Poisonous Plots
The Princes' Revolt
Earl Marshal
The Perfect Knight

Border Knight
1182-1300
Sword for Hire
Return of the Knight
Baron's War
Magna Carta
Welsh Wars
Henry III
The Bloody Border
Baron's Crusade
Sentinel of the North
War in the West
Debt of Honour
The Blood of the Warlord
The Fettered King

Sir John Hawkwood Series
France and Italy 1339- 1387
Crécy: The Age of the Archer
Man At Arms
The White Company
Leader of Men
Tuscan Warlord

Lord Edward's Archer
Lord Edward's Archer

Viking Shadow

King in Waiting
An Archer's Crusade
Targets of Treachery
The Great Cause
Wallace's War

Struggle for a Crown
1360- 1485
Blood on the Crown
To Murder a King
The Throne
King Henry IV
The Road to Agincourt
St Crispin's Day
The Battle for France
The Last Knight
Queen's Knight

Tales from the Sword I
(Short stories from the Medieval period)

Tudor Warrior series
England and Scotland in the late 14th and early 15th century
Tudor Warrior
Tudor Spy

Conquistador
England and America in the 16th Century
Conquistador
The English Adventurer

Modern History

The Napoleonic Horseman Series
Chasseur à Cheval
Napoleon's Guard
British Light Dragoon
Soldier Spy

1808: The Road to Coruña
Talavera
The Lines of Torres Vedras
Bloody Badajoz
The Road to France
Waterloo

The Lucky Jack American Civil War series
Rebel Raiders
Confederate Rangers
The Road to Gettysburg

Soldier of the Queen series
Soldier of the Queen
Redcoat's Rifle

The British Ace Series
1914
1915 Fokker Scourge
1916 Angels over the Somme
1917 Eagles Fall
1918 We will remember them
From Arctic Snow to Desert Sand
Wings over Persia

Combined Operations series
1940-1945
Commando
Raider
Behind Enemy Lines
Dieppe
Toehold in Europe
Sword Beach
Breakout
The Battle for Antwerp
King Tiger
Beyond the Rhine
Korea
Korean Winter

Tales from the Sword II
(Short stories from the Modern period)

Other Books
Great Granny's Ghost (Aimed at 9-14-year-old young people)

For more information on all of the books then please visit the author's website at www.griffhosker.com where there is a link to contact him or visit his Facebook page: GriffHosker at Sword Books

Printed in Great Britain
by Amazon